THE
DRAGON OF
TRELIAN

THE
DRAGON OF
TRELIAN

MICHELLE KNUDSEN

CANDLEWICK PRESS

Copyright © 2009 by Michelle Knudsen

First edition 2009

Library of Congress Cataloging-in-Publication Data

Knudsen, Michelle.

The dragon of Trelian / Michelle Knudsen. — 1st ed.

p.   cm.

Summary: A mage's apprentice, a princess, and a dragon combine their strength
and magic to bring down a traitor and restore peace to the kingdom of Trelian.

ISBN 978-0-7636-3455-1

[1. Fantasy. 2. Dragons — Fiction. 3. Princesses — Fiction. 4. Magic — Fiction.]   I. Title.

PZ7.K7835Dr 2009

[Fic] — dc22   2008025378

2 4 6 8 10 9 7 5 3 1

Printed in the United States of America

This book was typset in Adobe Jenson Pro.

Candlewick Press
99 Dover Street
Somerville, Massachusetts 02144

visit us at www.candlewick.com

For Matt,
with love and thanks

CHAPTER ONE

CALEN TRIED NOT TO LOOK DOWN. This was the best vantage point in the east wing of the castle — a thick window ledge that looked out over both the main gate and a good bit of the Queen's Road beyond. It was by no means the highest point in the castle, but it was still a good deal higher than Calen normally preferred to go. Climbing up to sit on the ledge had taken all his courage. He couldn't help imagining what it would be like to fall, screaming in terror and watching the shaped hedges rush up at him from below until he hit the ground and died a horrible and painful death.

He'd had to come, though. He wanted to catch that first glimpse of the procession as it approached, to witness the very beginning. It was like something from a story — a delegation from an enemy kingdom, bringing the prince of Kragnir to marry one of the princesses of Trelian and end a war that had been going on longer than most people today had been alive. Certainly it was the most exciting thing to happen in Calen's life in a long time. Maybe the most exciting thing to happen in his life *ever*, at least once he'd figured out that becoming a mage's apprentice was not going to be the whirlwind of glory and adventure he'd briefly imagined. And he was going to be here to see it, the arrival of the enemy prince and his family and whomever else princes generally traveled with, the first moments of an event that would be recorded in history books for future generations!

His heart was beating a little faster just thinking about it. Obviously it was the excitement, and not the glance he'd accidentally taken at the ground just now that was causing his insides to jump around that way. Calen took a deep breath, settled his back firmly against the edge of the window opening, and struggled to keep his eyes on the distant hills and his mind on anything other than the vast empty space to his immediate right.

There was plenty he could think about, but most of it was not especially pleasant. The procession was supposed to have arrived hours ago, and Calen was getting later by the second, but he wasn't leaving until he got to see something. He was bound to be in trouble — *more* trouble, he amended — once Serek discovered that he hadn't come straight back from the royal gardens with the silverweed. Calen had picked the silverweed first, of course — he wasn't that much of a fool — but he knew Serek had expected him to return at once, and that he hadn't done. Instead, he had circled around through the kitchen entrance, run down the Long Hall, then climbed the many, many stairs to the guest suites on the eighth floor. Heavy rust-colored curtains concealed the large window, and once he slipped behind them, he was invisible to anyone who might pass by. Undoubtedly one of the soon-to-be-arriving guests would be stationed here, and servants might stop in to check that the room was ready. If anyone did see him, he'd be caught — no one would believe he was up here on the mage's business, and he'd be forced to go back and face his punishment and miss everything.

Technically, he hadn't exactly disobeyed. Serek had only *implied* that Calen should return directly; he hadn't actually said it. Not that this distinction would hold much weight with Serek, but it was enough to soothe Calen's conscience. Besides, it wasn't like there was anything to rush back for. Calen thought back to the argument they'd had earlier. Well, *argument* wasn't really the right word. Mostly it had just been Serek making pointed comments about how lazy Calen was and glaring at him whenever he opened his mouth to defend himself. But he *wasn't* lazy. He just . . . didn't care. He didn't see the point in learning things if you were never going to do anything with them.

A flash of light caught his attention, and Calen leaned forward a tiny bit, squinting. Had that been the sun reflecting off armor? It was hard to tell at this distance. There was no way he was leaning any farther out the window, but maybe if he stretched his neck out slightly —

"I think that's the prince's escort," said a voice from directly behind him.

Calen jumped at the sudden sound and then screamed as he felt his balance desert him. He flailed uselessly at the air and had a moment to think, *This is it, I'm dead, I'm falling,* before he was jerked roughly back into the room and onto the floor beside the window. Heart pounding, and *not* from excitement this time, Calen looked up to see a girl about his own age standing above him.

"You dropped your flowers," she said, smiling innocently.

He gaped at her, then down at the silverweed scattered across the floor. Still breathless with fear, and now angry as well, Calen stood up. She had nearly killed him!

"You! You —" he began, unable to find suitable

words for what he was feeling. Swallowing, he paused to regroup.

"You —" he said again, this time pointing one shaky finger at her for emphasis.

"You're welcome," she said. "I suppose I saved your life just now. You almost fell, you know."

Calen stared at her incredulously. His eyes felt wide enough to fall right out of his head.

She looked back at him for a moment, then started laughing.

"Oh, your face —" she gasped, nearly doubled over with mirth. Calen, temporarily out of witty retorts, waited silently for her to regain control of herself.

"I'm sorry," she went on, finally. "I really am. I didn't mean to startle you like that, but after I pulled you back in, you were just so *funny*. . . ."

Calen glared at her. *Funny*, was he? He knelt and began gathering the fallen silverweed with violent swipes of his hands. She bent to help him.

"Leave it," he said, turning his back to her.

"Oh, please, don't be like that," she said, touching his shoulder. He shrugged her off without looking up.

After a moment she spoke again. "You're right — that was terrible of me. To laugh, I mean. I'm not very well behaved at times, as Nan Vera would no doubt agree." She held out the handful of silverweed she'd collected. "Please," she said again. "Let's start over. I really am sorry. I'm Meg. What's your name?"

Calen sighed. He hadn't *actually* died, he supposed. And it would be nice to finally get to know someone his own age. It had been more than half a year since he and Serek took up residence here, and in all that time nearly the only young people he'd seen had been the royal —

He looked up at her. "Meg?" he repeated stupidly. For the first time he noticed how she was dressed: her pale blue gown of obvious quality, the silver embroidery along the sleeves and bodice, the elaborate way her hair was twisted up behind her neck. And the delicate gold circlet resting above her forehead, glinting at him in shiny accusation.

"Meg — as in Meglynne? As in Her Royal Highness Princess Meglynne?"

Oh no.

Calen scrambled to his feet, then bowed, then changed his mind and dropped back onto his knees. "I'm sorry, Your Highness, I didn't —"

"Stop," she said. "Please, don't do that. It's just Meg. Now get up."

"But, Your Highness —"

She kicked him, hard.

"Ow!" He fell over onto the floor, rubbing his thigh. Princesses weren't supposed to kick you!

"If you call me 'Your Highness' again, I will throw you out that window, I swear it."

"But —" Calen pushed himself back up to his knees. This was confusing. Serek had made him learn all the appropriate titles of respect, and it was definitely not appropriate to call one of the king's daughters by her first name. Still, he almost believed she was serious about the window.

"Come on," she said. "Get *up*."

Calen just stared at her. Was it a test or something? What was he supposed to do? He couldn't seem to bring himself to move.

Finally, she rolled her eyes. "Oh, very well. I *command* you to get off your knees and stop acting like I'm going to chop your head off. Rise and obey, by order of King Tormon's third and least patient royal daughter."

Calen got up.

"Good," she said. "Now I command you to tell me your name."

"Calen."

"Good. Thank you. You're the mage's apprentice, aren't you? I mean, you must be, since you've got the . . ."

She waved a finger at the marks on his face, nodding. "All right, Calen, pleased to meet you. Now I command you to stop obeying me. What are you doing up here, anyway?"

Lying to a princess probably carried worse punishments than skipping out on work. "I came up to watch the procession," he admitted.

She smiled. "Good. Me, too. So let's get back out of sight before someone comes by and sends us both back to where we belong. They're probably close enough to see by now." And with that, she disappeared behind the heavy curtains.

Calen rubbed his thigh, which still hurt from where she'd kicked him. Part of him wanted to slowly back away while she wasn't looking. But if he left now, all the time he'd spent waiting and the trouble he'd get in when he returned would be for nothing. And he really didn't want to miss the procession. He'd been waiting to see it for weeks! He shook his head and squared his shoulders. No one, princess or not, was going to stop him from seeing history in the making. He ducked back behind the curtains to join her.

The approaching party was indeed now close enough to see, and Calen knew at once that it had been worth the wait. Princes, apparently, traveled with a great number of people, at least when they were riding into an enemy kingdom for a war-ending marriage. A dazzling jumble of colors and banners and horses and riders was pouring slowly over the rise and down along the Queen's Road. Mounted soldiers led the procession and created a formidable-looking border around everyone else. Bannermen held the flags of Kragnir aloft and musicians played instruments, which Calen realized he must have started hearing a few minutes ago without knowing it. As they reached the top of the rise, a pair of wagons carrying wicker cages paused and men jumped down to attend to them; in a moment, scores of colorful birds burst from the cages and spilled up into the sky like a living rainbow. Calen couldn't help grinning in admiration. If the prince had been hoping to make an impressive entrance, Calen thought he was succeeding.

Meg had boosted herself up to straddle the window ledge, one leg dangling insanely over nothing. Calen, not about to climb back up there, contented himself with standing beside her and resting his elbows on the ledge. She pointed.

"See the man on the tall black horse with the red trappings? That's Prince Ryant of Kragnir. He's the one who's going to marry my sister Maerlie. She thinks he's *quite* handsome, but of course she's only ever seen his portrait, and honestly, if I were painting a portrait of a prince, I'd probably make certain he looked handsome in it, too. They've never met in person, although they've been writing each other constantly since the betrothal. She thinks they might really be falling in *love*," she said, rolling her eyes again. "As though you can fall in love through letters!" But Calen thought Meg's face looked just a little wistful as she said it.

She turned her attention back to the scene below. "The three men directly in front of the prince are his personal guards. I met one of them before — Jorn. He's the one who brought Prince Ryant's offer of marriage. He has this scar that runs from one side of his forehead across his face and partway down his neck."

Interested, Calen squinted at the man he guessed was Jorn, trying to see the scar. "How did he get it?"

"No one knows, though there are stories enough. Everyone tells a different tale, but no one is brave enough to ask Jorn himself. Well, I would do it, but Nan Vera says it would be unforgivably rude, and I don't want to offend the prince's guard and embarrass my sister. I'm hoping Maerlie can find out the truth once she's married the prince. *He* must know."

Calen couldn't quite believe he was discussing scars

with one of the king's daughters. Were all princesses like this? Somehow he didn't think so.

"Your sister must be pretty brave," he said. "I mean, getting married to the enemy and everything."

Meg rolled her eyes again. She seemed to do that a lot. "Well, that's the whole point, isn't it? The marriage is supposed to bring the two kingdoms together so we can *stop* being enemies. Don't they teach you apprentices anything? Do you even know the story of why we were fighting in the first place?"

Calen shook his head. She was beginning to make him feel a little stupid.

"Oh, it's a good story," Meg told him. "Well, not good, exactly; actually it's rather terrible, but — well, here, I'll just tell you. Years and years and years ago — exactly one hundred as of next month, actually — Kragnir had a young queen named Lysetta. She had been a poor country girl, just like in a fairy tale, and all the people loved her. King Holister's first wife had died in childbirth, and he'd been so heartbroken that no one thought he would ever marry again, but they say Lysetta mended his heart and he came to love her more than anything. Soon after the marriage, Lysetta came to visit Trelian. That had been a tradition for as long as anyone could remember; every time Trelian or Kragnir had a new queen, she went to visit the other queen so that they could get to know each other and become friends. Our kingdoms were steadfast allies back then.

"The night of her arrival, there was a grand feast, and Lysetta was formally introduced to the Trelian royal family and all the visiting cousins and dignitaries and whoever else had come for the occasion. Everyone was charmed by the new queen, and the evening was considered a great success, even though Lysetta retired somewhat early. The next morning she failed to appear for breakfast, and when Trelian's queen — her name was Aliwen — went to her rooms to see if their guest was all right, she wasn't there.

"Where was she?" Calen asked, drawn in despite himself. Meg was a pretty good storyteller. This was a lot more interesting than the history lesson he'd been expecting.

"I'm getting there," she said. "Just listen. When Lysetta hadn't been found by midday, they began to search in earnest, for her escort was still at the castle and none of her attendants had any idea where she might have gone. They searched for two days and might never have found her, except that one of the kitchen boys reported hearing strange sounds in the cellar. When they went to look, they discovered a hidden passageway behind a wall, and at the end of a long dark tunnel they found Lysetta, imprisoned in an iron cell that no one had known even existed. She was dead, but there were no marks to indicate how she died, and they never discovered why or how she had ended up there."

Calen shuddered. He felt like a child at a ghost-telling, but he couldn't help it. He'd been down in that cellar countless times.

"When King Holister heard the news," Meg went on, "he went mad with grief. He blamed Trelian for his young wife's death and arrived at the castle gates with an army. My ancestors tried to convince him that they had nothing to do with what had happened, but he refused to believe them and demanded the head of Queen Aliwen in retribution."

"Her *head?*"

"Naturally, the Trelian king refused, and the Kragnir army attacked the castle. There was a fierce battle, and eventually Kragnir was defeated and returned home, but not without great loss of life on both sides. The war continued over the years, with violent assaults and assassination attempts and all kinds of ugly and horrible things."

Calen was fascinated, the procession below temporarily

forgotten. "But then — how did the marriage offer come about? If we've been fighting with them all this time . . ."

"My father and King Ryllin — that's Prince Ryant's father — had wanted to find a way to end the feud between our families. They had met each other as boys, completely accidentally, when Trelian and Kragnir had both sent envoys to the coastal nations in the south without realizing that the other kingdom was doing so, and there was a terrible storm and they all ended up at the same inn — that's a really good story, too, actually. But the short version is that after that chance meeting they kept in touch, secretly, and wanted to find a way to stop all the fighting, but when they tried to make it happen, neither of their fathers would allow it. Now that the old kings aren't around anymore to say no, and King Ryllin and my father both have children of marriageable age, they decided to try again. And the hundred-year anniversary makes it seem all the more significant and important. There are some who still don't trust Kragnir and are against the wedding, but my parents both believe in Ryllin and the promise of peace."

"And do you?" Calen asked.

"Of course," Meg said quickly. "Certainly I want the chance to meet this Prince Ryant for myself, but my parents wouldn't let Maerlie marry someone they didn't trust.

And no one can deny that now would be a very good time to renew the old friendship between our kingdoms."

Calen knew what she meant by that, at least. Each time Serek sent him to the market for supplies, the traders — those who still came — always seemed to have new stories of thieves and bandits on the roads. And sometimes, worse things, although surely *those* stories weren't true. Supplies were stolen, or never sent at all, and there were even rumors that some traders who ventured into the vast Hunterheart Forest, which bordered the castle grounds and stretched over much of the distance between Trelian and Kragnir, disappeared and were never heard from again.

They watched as more riders came into view, Meg pointing out those whose names she knew and sharing bits of stories she'd heard about them. Calen had never met anyone quite like Meg before. She was nicer than she'd seemed at first, he thought. Maybe she couldn't help being bossy; she was a princess, after all. And she sure did talk a lot. He wasn't used to it, but at the same time it was a welcome change from his usual nonconversations with Serek. Even if he was mostly just listening. It was nice to actually have someone to listen *to*.

When the prince and his guard reached the main gate, Meg jumped down from the window.

"I have to go — I'm sure Father will be angry I missed

his discussion on how to behave at dinner, but if I'm not back in time to greet our guests at the table, I'll really be in trouble."

Thinking of trouble reminded Calen of his own situation. Serek would not be pleased he had been gone this long.

Meg started to push through the curtains and then turned back. She looked at him for a long moment. Finally she asked, "Can you get away tomorrow afternoon?"

"I think so. Why?"

She smiled mysteriously. "Meet me by the small gate at first bell. I'll share a secret with you."

MOST OF THE CASTLE HALLS WERE lined with tapestries and paintings. Some showed glorious battles, or what Calen guessed were important friends and ancestors of the royal family, but others were complete stories in themselves, with entire lives depicted scene by scene. Calen usually stopped to admire them when he passed, but right now he hardly saw them at all. He turned down a dimly lit corridor that led to the mage's quarters. No point lingering in the hallway worrying; he'd find out soon enough how much trouble he was in and would just try to say as little as possible about where he'd been and what he'd been doing. He'd leave Meg out of it entirely. Serek probably wouldn't believe that he'd been talking with the princess anyway — Calen still hardly believed it himself! — and if Serek did believe it, Calen was afraid he'd decide it was improper for his apprentice to be interacting with royalty outside of duty's requirements and forbid him to see her again. Meg might be a bit pushy and condescending, and perhaps slightly intimidating, and, okay, yes, she had nearly killed him, but she was also the first person he'd had a real conversation with in a long time. And she seemed to find him interesting enough to want to talk to him again tomorrow. To share a secret! He didn't want Serek to take that away. It would be nice to make a friend.

In the six years he'd been apprenticed to Serek, they'd spent time in several different households, among families of varying ranks and stations, and Serek had never seemed interested in getting to know anyone closely or, gods forbid, actually making *friends* anywhere. He kept to himself, focused on his craft, and seemed disdainful of other mages they'd encountered who mixed personal relationships with work situations.

Which was all very well for him, but Calen had no desire to live the rest of his life with no one but Serek and his ill-tempered gyrcat for companionship. Life before Serek hadn't exactly been perfect, but at least in between the work there had been moments with other people — feastdays and shared errands with the other inn workers, friendly patrons and occasional kind words from the cooks or the stable master, gifts from the innkeeper's wife once a year at Turning Day. But Serek seemed to go out of his way to avoid other people. Even Calen's company sometimes appeared to be more than he could bear.

Which was something the great mage really should have thought about before dragging Calen away from the only life he'd ever known to be his stupid apprentice.

That day, the day Serek had carted him off to be initiated, Calen had thought he was leaving his mundane and unimportant existence far behind. He'd looked back at Arster's inn as the other boys stood outside, watching him ride away in the wagon. He'd felt different from them, special. Destined for a new and exciting future. He'd imagined all the grand spells he would cast, working wonders, fighting enemies, defending his patrons . . . and when Serek began teaching him those early lessons, he'd loved the way it felt to cast, to channel the magical energy toward a purpose, shaping it to accomplish whatever he held in his mind. But soon enough it became clear that most of the time there *was* no purpose. It was nearly all just books and learning and memorizing things to recite back to Serek. What was the point in becoming a mage if you never really got a chance to use magic?

Serek spent nearly all his time with his nose buried in books and papers, coming up for air only long enough to assign Calen some pointless task that was supposed to be furthering his magical education but seemed more likely just a way to keep him busy and protect Serek's beloved solitude. And lately it had gotten even worse. Ever since

Serek had been appointed King's Mage, he'd been more distant than ever, sending Calen off on errands rather than letting him help with anything or letting him know what was going on. At least at their last post he'd been able to work in the gardens, so he'd felt that he was doing *something* . . . but here they had a whole army of royal gardeners for that, and it had been made quite clear that they didn't want the mage's apprentice hanging about or, gods forbid, actually doing anything useful.

With a sigh, Calen opened the narrow door at the end of the corridor and stepped inside.

Serek was at his desk, running one hand distract-edly through his short black hair and apparently trying to read the contents of several books at once. Four or five huge volumes lay before him, pages held open with small but heavy stones and, in one instance, the grinning skull of Serek's late mentor, Rorgson. Calen closed the door with a little more force than necessary. Serek glanced up at him.

"There you are. Took you long enough. Get lost on the way back from the garden, did you?" He shook his head, bending back over his books. "No, I don't want to hear it. Put the silverweed by the window and fetch me the Erylun book from the library."

Calen closed his mouth and did as he was told.

Something was obviously wrong — Serek never let him off that easy — but he wasn't about to question his good fortune.

The library was a large room down a short hallway from Serek's workshop. Fredrin, Serek's predecessor as King's Mage, had acquired a huge collection of books during his tenure at the castle, which Serek had been overjoyed to discover. He had actually *smiled.* Serek had a sizable collection of his own, as no doubt all mages did, but Fredrin's library was truly something extraordinary. There were many books on the shelves that looked interesting, like the one on Crostian death rites or the various texts regarding secret ancient languages, but Serek had forbidden him to touch anything in the library without permission, and then of course refused to grant him permission to look at any of the more appealing titles.

The Erylun book was near the top shelf, which required the use of one of the rolling ladders to reach. Serek consulted this book all the time but refused to reshelve it in a more convenient location that would violate the existing system of organization. Calen reflected bitterly on this as he dragged the enormous thing from its place and began to back his way down the ladder. Why should Serek care where it was shelved? He was never the one who had to get it down.

Calen lugged the book to the workshop and then waited, arms aching, while Serek cleared a space for it on his desk. The Erylun was a compendium of knowledge and research on all sorts of topics, gathered from learned individuals across various lands and times and organized by Mage Erylun, who had been, apparently, quite the learned individual himself. Serek allowed Calen to use the book on occasion for research related to his lessons, and the array of information was astonishing. Huge as it was, Calen suspected that the book held far more text than could physically fit on its actual number of pages. Serek refused to confirm or deny this, which meant there was almost certainly some sort of sorcery involved.

Serek began paging through the book, muttering anxiously to himself. Knowing better than to interrupt, Calen started toward the chair on the far side of the desk — might as well sit down while he waited, since there was no telling how long it would be until Serek decided to acknowledge him again.

Luckily, he heard the low growling in time and stopped a few steps away.

Squinting, Calen was just able to make out Lyrimon's ample shape against the surface of the chair. The gyrcat wasn't really invisible, just . . . *very* hard to see. He was able to blend in with just about anything, and it wasn't only that he could change his color. He became less substan-tial, somehow, as if he weren't quite as real as whatever was behind or under him. So any observer would see the chair, not the cat, until it was too late. Well, almost any observer. Serek could always seem to tell exactly where Lyrimon was. Calen had been surprised by the creature more times than he cared to remember. Lyrimon tended to react nastily to being sat or stepped upon. One espe-cially unpleasant encounter had required more than a few bandages. Serek had refused to heal him magically, citing a need for Calen to "learn to respect the personal space of others."

Calen backed away from the chair and resigned him-self to leaning against a wall instead.

After a while, Serek looked up.

"What have I taught you about divination?" he asked.

"That it's difficult, dangerous, not always reliable, and that I'll learn more about it when and if you feel I'm old enough to handle it," Calen said. "Why?"

Serek's lips twitched slightly into what might have been a smirk. "I suppose I've just decided you're old enough. Come here."

As Calen approached the desk, Serek reached into a drawer and brought out a small wooden box. He opened it and withdrew a thick deck of illustrated cards held together with a knotted piece of silk.

"Do you know what these are?"

"Spirit cards," Calen breathed, leaning closer. He'd never seen an actual set of them before. "They're used to see the future, and the pictures are from some old wizard who drew them in his sleep or something. And they all represent things that are going to happen, if you know how to read them right."

Serek looked at him, raising an eyebrow.

"I—I happened to see a description in the Erylun book while I was working on potions last month," Calen said quickly. "I didn't even know you had a deck."

Serek looked at him a moment longer, then shook his head and began shuffling the cards. "Yes. Well, that's basically correct. The 'old wizard' you're referring to is Syrill, whose name you would know if you were as far along with your potions work as you've led me to believe, since he developed many of the elementary potion spells in your assignment."

Calen winced, but after a brief, meaningful pause, Serek went on. "He drew the illustrations while in a deep trance state, and all modern decks are based on his drawings. The pictures don't represent specific incidents or events, just general suggestions—they're intended to be interpreted by the reader, based on their position with regard to the other cards, among other things."

Serek stopped shuffling and handed the cards to Calen.

"Every so often, I use these to get a sense of things to come. Lately I've been trying to see the shape of near-future events for Trelian. Now, as I've said, spirit cards — or any form of divination — can be unreliable, because so much rests in the interpretation of the reader. It takes years of regular practice to learn how to read the cards, and even then, it's possible to misread what the cards are saying. Sometimes, though rarely, experience can even work against you and lead you to distort the meanings. So we're going to try a little experiment. You're going to read the cards and tell me what you see."

Calen blinked, astonished. "But I don't —"

Serek held up a hand to stop him. "I know you don't know how to read them. That's exactly the point. I need a fresh perspective, an interpretation unclouded by prior knowledge or experience. It might not work, but we're going to try it."

Calen nodded, anxious but excited. Serek usually made him study something *forever* before he finally got a chance to try it, and the long hours of reading and discussing often exhausted his attention and led his mind to wander, making him a much poorer student than he knew he could be. And since focus was at the heart of every act of sorcery, it was always difficult to convince Serek that he was ready, even if he couldn't remember the names and dates and other facts that never seemed nearly as important as the method and practice itself.

Still, jumping right in like this made Calen nervous. How could he do it right if he didn't know what he was doing?

"All right," Serek said. "Hold the cards in your hands, and focus your mind on the kingdom. Nothing specific, just the kingdom itself."

Calen cleared his mind. This part, at least, he knew how to do. Almost every act of magic Serek had ever taught him began this way. Once he felt completely empty of random thoughts, he filled the space he'd created in his mind with the idea of Trelian.

"Good," said Serek. His voice was soft, unintrusive; Calen was able to hear him without interrupting his focus. "Now shuffle the cards and invite the question of Trelian's future. Allow yourself to be open to what the future may bring."

Calen complied. After a moment, Serek took the cards back from him and began to lay some of them out, faceup, one by one. He placed the first three in an arc across the desktop, then the next three in another arc with one single card below them in the center. The next three formed another arc beneath this, and a final, eleventh card went facedown below that.

"All right," Serek continued. He rose and had Calen sit in his chair. "Maintain your focus, and try to direct it at each card in turn, starting on the top left. For all of them except the two single ones, you need to consider the cards both individually and within each group of three. The single cards should be interpreted on their own. I'll talk you through it as you go. You must be receptive and allow the meaning of the cards to come to you. Ready?" He waited for Calen's hesitant nod, then continued. "Now, start with the first group and tell me what you see."

Calen looked at the first card. It showed water, flowing in what seemed to be a swiftly moving river. It made Calen think of motion, of being swept along in the current. Holding that idea in his mind, he looked to the next card. This one was divided across the center and showed two images, one right-side up and one upside down from his perspective. Both were nearly identical pictures of a young woman looking into a mirror, but the mirror on the top half, which was right-side up, was dim and murky, while the mirror on the lower half was clear and bright. The dark mirror made him feel uneasy.

The third card showed a small girl clutching a rag doll against her chest. Calen frowned. He was sure the card must mean something about children, or pretending, but the girl seemed so serious —

"Don't force it," Serek said softly. "Don't try to figure anything out. Just accept the meaning that comes to you."

Calen took a breath. "Okay," he said. "The water means change, or lots of changes, happening soon or maybe already happening now. The dark mirror means the changes are difficult to see, not anything obvious. Hidden. And the girl —" Calen frowned again, then shook his head and continued. "She means importance. Something, or maybe many things, that are important, that really matter. I know that's probably not right, but that's what she makes me think of."

"That's fine," said Serek, still speaking in that low, soothing voice. "Keep going. Move on to the next group."

The next card showed a tiny ship deep in a raging storm. Dark clouds blotted out the sky, and it seemed that any moment the ship would be lost under the violent waves. The meaning there seemed pretty obvious — danger. Calen held on to that and went on.

The picture on the next card was also rather dark and also seemed to give up its meaning easily. It showed a woman weeping into her hands. Somehow the picture suggested that she had just fallen to her knees, that the force of her grief was such that she could no longer stand. Looking at it, feeling the intense sorrow it contained, Calen almost wanted to cry himself.

The third card in the group showed a far cheerier and lighthearted image — two laughing boys winning a three-legged race, their arms raised in joy and victory as they broke through the ribbon marking the finish line. It should have meant happiness, or success, and in a way, it did . . . but the card was upside down, and the victory it showed felt wrong, and threatening. It was someone else's victory, someone whose success meant exactly the opposite for Trelian.

"These are all about bad things," Calen said. "Danger, and sorrow, and the victory of someone or something who should never be victorious." He looked up at Serek, concentration faltering. "What does it mean? Is this the future? Is something terrible going to happen?"

Serek nodded toward the cards. "Keep your focus, Calen. Don't stop to ask questions. Not of me, and not of yourself." His voice was still soft, but there was a slight edge to it now, like a warning. Calen swallowed and closed his eyes, trying to regain his clarity of mind. Questions were for later. All he needed to do was receive the information from the cards. And he *was* receiving information — he could feel it. There was something happening, a connection between the cards and his mind. This was different from following some recipe from a spellbook; this felt . . . real. It was like the way he used to feel, in the beginning, before — he gave his head a little shake. Not now. *Focus*, he reminded himself sternly. After a moment he felt calm again and opened his eyes to continue.

The next card was the one standing alone below the second arc, and it was death, plain and simple. It showed a grinning skull, white against a black background. Calen almost lost his focus again at this, but managed to keep his mind under control. Somehow the one skull seemed to suggest many, and Calen saw a vast landscape of death and destruction, bleak and terrible in its scope. He tried to force himself to remain objective, but he felt on the verge of trembling as he looked up at Serek. "This is death," he said quietly. "Death for many, close to home."

Serek looked back at him calmly. "All right," he said. "Keep going."

Right, Calen thought. *Right. Keep going.* His heart was beating too fast, and suddenly it felt difficult to breathe; his fear and worry at what he saw was threatening to take over, and that, of course, was not going to help anything. For the first time, Calen could see the advantage in the

30

way Serek kept himself like steel, like stone, seemingly always cold and unfeeling and impenetrable. Reading the cards required exactly that kind of emotional distance, and without it he was never going to maintain the necessary concentration. Calen looked back at the cards and tried to make himself cold and hard and strong.

The next three cards formed the lowest arc. The first image was a blacksmith forging a heavy chain. What seemed important was the joining of the links of metal, the combined strength of all of them together. The chain felt solid and good, something to be believed in and trusted. And treasured.

The next card showed a figure entering a dark tunnel. There was a distant light at the end of the tunnel, but Calen could sense that there were also many dark passages that never came out to the light at all. There was no way to tell whether the figure itself was aware of this, but it was clearly entering the tunnel all the same.

The final card of the arc showed beams of light streaming through an open window into a dark room. The room itself felt close and dangerous, except where the light touched it. A heavy curtain obscured part of the window, and a hand was reaching toward it. Calen felt that it was desperately important for the hand to pull the curtain the rest of the way open, but there was no way to tell its intent in the image — it was just as likely that the hand was about to draw the curtain completely across the window, shutting out the light once and for all.

"The chain is about joining forces, or of separate things coming together to make something new and stronger," he told Serek. "The tunnel is a journey, but I can't tell whether the important thing is the light at the end or the journey itself. And the window —" He paused, considering the image. "No. The light, the light is what's important. It means truth, I think."

Serek nodded, and Calen turned over the final card. It showed a silver coin, spinning on its edge. He waited, expecting more of the meaning to come to him, but finally looked back up at Serek.

"I can't tell what the coin means," he said. "Only that it's about to fall, heads or tails, and either side would mean something drastically different."

Serek stood silently for a moment, apparently thinking all of this over, and Calen waited, strangely exhausted. And also strangely exhilarated. When he looked at the cards now, they seemed only static images. But during the reading it had been different — they'd been like living things, flush with meaning and power. They'd been . . . almost talking to him. It had been frightening in parts, true — but he wanted to experience that feeling again.

"Well, Calen," Serek said, finally. His voice had lost its soft cadence and was back to its normal brusqueness. "There's no doubt you've got a talent for this. I saw some of the same things in my earlier readings, but not nearly so completely. Once we're done with potions, we'll come back to divination in your studies, beginning at the beginning this time, of course, and start to explore your ability more thoroughly. Well done."

Calen tried hard not to stare. He did feel he had done well, but Serek hardly ever admitted that anything his apprentice did met, let alone exceeded, his expectations. Calen felt the beginnings of a smile touch his lips. *Well done*, he thought. Then he realized that Serek had scooped up a few books and started for the door.

Calen twisted around the chair. "But — where are you going? Aren't you going to tell me what all this means?"

Serek seemed surprised by the question. "No," he said. "I'm not. If you're so thirsty for knowledge, get back to work on your potions assignment. I should be back by late evening, and you can show me your progress then."

"*What?*" Calen heard his tone edging toward what he knew Serek would consider disrespectful, but he couldn't help it. "After everything I saw, you're going to walk out and not give me any idea what it means or what's going to happen? You just said I saw more in the cards than you did, and now you're not even going to —"

Serek turned slowly back around, and Calen knew he had gone too far.

"Listen, *Apprentice*," Serek snarled. "You would do well to remember who is the master here and who is nothing but a willful boy who yearns to rise above his station but lacks the discipline, drive, and quite possibly the intelligence to ever do so. The meanings of the cards are for me to discuss with King Tormon and Queen Merilyn and are none of your concern. Yes, you might have a talent for divination. Yes, you managed to read the cards this afternoon. But that doesn't mean you have anything close to the wisdom or maturity to translate those meanings into a useful context, and I am not going to waste my time explaining things to you that you don't need to know. Certainly not when the kingdom would be far better served by my quick progress to the royal chambers so that men and women of knowledge and power can make the necessary decisions to avert impending disaster."

After a final contemptuous glare, Serek stalked out and slammed the door behind him.

Calen stared sullenly after him. "*That* seemed uncalled for," he muttered. After seeing all those cards about danger and death, it didn't seem unreasonable for him to want to know what it all meant, did it? Stupid mages and their arrogant tempers. For a moment Serek had actually seemed pleased with him, but Calen should have known that would never last. He sighed angrily and pushed back from the desk. He lacked discipline and drive, did he? And *intelligence*? Fine. He'd do his stupid potions assignment. He'd do it right now, and let Serek try to find one thing wrong with it, just one —

Calen's thoughts broke off as his eyes fell across the Erylun book, still sitting open on the desk.

Sitting open, in fact, to a chapter on spirit cards.

Calen sank slowly back into the chair and smiled. Perhaps it was time for a little independent study. Perhaps Serek would discover that his apprentice had a little drive after all.

CHAPTER THREE

STUPID, STUPID, STUPID, STUPID, STUPID!

Meg kicked open the wooden door at the top of the stairs, slamming it back against the wall, not thinking until too late that someone might be on the other side. But that was exactly like her, wasn't it? Not thinking until too late. Or just not thinking at all.

The doubt had blossomed within her almost as soon as she had turned her back on Calen and started down the hall, growing in intensity and quickly becoming self-directed fury as her stupid words echoed in her incredulous mind. "I'll share a secret with you," she repeated angrily under her breath in the singsong voice she usually reserved for mocking her sisters. "I just met you. You're basically a total stranger. Let me tell you the one thing I shouldn't be telling anyone, especially not the mage's apprentice, who could tell the mage, who could and would tell my parents without a second thought."

She was an intelligent girl, wasn't she? She always did well at her lessons, held her own at dinner-table discussions of policy and trade, and routinely trounced Maerlie *and* their father at games of turn-stones. She outwitted Nan Vera on a daily basis, as well as an assortment of castle guardsmen assigned to keep an eye on her. She was smart, she knew she was. Why, then, was she being such a gods-cursed idiot?

Even now, Meg could feel her secret pulling at her, demanding her attention, pulsing and clutching at her like a physical thing. *No,* she thought. *Not like.* It *was* a physical thing. She had to stop pretending otherwise. In the beginning, perhaps, it had only been something she thought about a lot, but there was no denying that it was getting worse. It was there, in her head, in her body, all the time. Real. And she didn't know what to do.

Maybe that's why she had said what she did. She just had to tell someone. She couldn't tell her parents. She couldn't tell Maerlie, which was hard to acknowledge, because she could always tell Maerlie everything . . . but this was too big, too frightening, and Maerlie would feel obligated to tell their parents. Oh, she wouldn't want to — she'd hate it, she'd feel terrible — but she'd do what she thought was right. Meg didn't want to put her sister in that position. Besides, this was supposed to be a happy time for Maer — she was getting married, to a man she actually might like, who was young and handsome and seemed to genuinely care for her — and Meg didn't want to ruin all of that.

And of course she couldn't tell her other sisters. Maurel was too young, Mattie was just a baby, and Morgan . . . Morgan was back to help with the wedding preparations, but she wasn't anyone Meg could talk to about things. Meg had been only eight when Morgan was sent away to be married, and although they'd been close enough before, when Morgan came back to visit she was — different. Changed into a grown-up woman with no interest in children's games or children's worries. And so it had always been Maerlie who Meg went to with hurts and joys and questions. And secrets. Until now.

Meg pounded her fist along the stone wall on the last flight of steps, just hard enough to hurt, letting the scratchy pain of contact override the other, less manageable, pain. Nan Vera would scold her for scraping her princessy skin, but no doubt she'd have some salve or cream to apply and make her presentable by dinnertime. One more door, kicked open without thought, and Meg emerged into the noise and bustle of the main hall.

Stewards and serving girls ran about on their errands, trying to make sure everything was in order for the guests. One maid with her arms full of bedding glanced at Meg in passing and actually squeaked in alarm before ducking her head and hurrying on her way. Sighing, Meg made an effort to soften her expression. She'd need to pull herself together before she got back to the royal suites, in any case, unless she wanted to explain what was wrong. Which she did not. Or at least, could not. And of course that was the worst thing of all, really. The secret itself was troubling enough, but to have to *keep* it secret, to have to be afraid and alone and pretend that everything was perfectly fine . . .

No, she thought, her inner voice a tiny whisper deep inside. The *very* worst thing was that despite how frightened she was about what was happening and how it made her feel, how strange and different and wrong and scared, sometimes . . . sometimes she liked it.

Sometimes she *loved* it.

Meg strode a little more quickly through the hall. That didn't bear thinking about — not now. There wasn't anything she could do about that. Not without figuring some things out, and she thought she had figured out everything she was going to on her own. She needed help. So she would tell Calen.

She smiled suddenly at the memory of his expression when he'd realized who she was. Maybe that was why she'd spontaneously decided to trust him. He seemed completely without guile, his face unable to disguise anything. *Probably not the best person to tell a secret to, in that case,* she pointed out to herself. She knew it was ridiculous to simply decide that she could trust him. But somehow it didn't feel ridiculous. It felt . . . right.

Squaring her shoulders, Meg started up the south staircase.

"And as I have decreed, so let it be accomplished," she said aloud, repeating the words she'd heard her parents say countless times at hearings and petitioner days.

"Let what be accomplished?"

Maurel bounced up beside her on the stairs. Meg reached over and yanked on the end of one of her sister's slightly uncoiled braids. "My royal decree that all little sisters should wear bells around their necks so people can always hear them coming."

"*You're* the one who's always disappearing," said Maurel. "I think you should wear the bell. Where were you?"

"Oh, you know, the usual . . . having tea with fairies in the garden, shrinking down to mouse size and riding about among the flowers."

"You never tell me." Pouting, Maurel stomped several steps in silence before relenting. She could never stay angry for more than a few seconds. Meg envied her that sometimes. "Besides, fairies are stupid. If you're going to make up stories, it should be pirates and sea monsters or something else good."

"I'll remember that for next time. And where were *you*, dear sister? You realize we're both late, don't you?"

"I'm not late," said Maurel. "I was on an assignment. Nan Vera sent me to look for Mattie's bear. You're the only one who's late. Everyone's waiting for you."

Meg grimaced. "Wonderful." She climbed a little faster. "Did you find the bear?"

"Yes," Maurel answered proudly, holding the poor tattered thing aloft. "And also the sock she lost last week *and* Maerlie's missing hair ribbon. Cook's cat had the ribbon. It's a little chewed."

Meg solemnly examined the ribbon as Maurel displayed it for her. It seemed a *lot* chewed, in her opinion, but she kept that to herself. "I'm sure Maerlie will still be glad to have it back," she said. "You're pretty good at finding things, all right."

"Yes, I am. And now I've found you, too!"

Meg laughed. "Yes, you have. Now let's hurry so you can get the praise you deserve and so I don't make Mother and Father any angrier than they already are."

They ran the rest of the way, Meg only having to pull in her stride a little to let Maurel keep up. Breathless and laughing, they arrived at the sitting room of the royal

41

suites. Father had been speaking, but he stopped as they staggered in. Everyone turned to look.

"Welcome, Meg," said Father sardonically. "So nice of you to finally join us."

"I found her," Maurel announced. "Also I found Mattie's bear and her sock. And your hair ribbon, Maerlie!" She bounded over to distribute the assortment of items. Grateful for the distraction, Meg slipped onto a couch beside Morgan, who gave her a neutral nod. Maerlie, meanwhile, flashed her a half-hidden smirk from across the room.

"Don't encourage her, please," Mother said, catching the exchange. "Really, Meg. Is it so difficult for you to be where you're expected *when* you're expected? This is not the first time we've had to wait for you."

"Especially lately," added Nan Vera unhelpfully.

With a monumental effort of will, Meg managed not to glare at Nan Vera and instead tried to look appropriately chastened. "I'm sorry, Mother. Sorry, Father. Sorry, everyone. Please, don't let me interrupt. Father, I believe you were speaking?"

The look her father gave her said plainly that he knew she was trying to avoid giving an explanation for her lateness. She could almost see him teetering on the brink; would he scold her? Demand to know where she had been? Or shake his head and give her one of those grins that used to come so easily to his face when she was small? He was a different person when he smiled. But Meg supposed that most of the business of being a king didn't call for smiling as much as it did solemnity. Especially — to echo a certain annoying nursemaid — lately.

She was almost sorry when Maerlie came to her aid. It would have been interesting to see which way he would have gone.

"Father was just about to tell us exactly how and when you're all going to meet my handsome future husband and his family," Maerlie said brightly, blinking up at him in exaggerated innocence. That did evoke the rueful head shake and the grin, but of course now it was for Maerlie, not for her. Their mother rolled her eyes goodnaturedly, Nan Vera frowned at the opportunity for discipline wasted, and the moment of danger was past. No need to make up excuses or feel guilty about lying to her family.

"Yes, well. Now that we're all finally assembled," he said, indicating Meg and then, with another smile, Mattie's bear, "we can go to meet them at once. We did of course offer to postpone dinner until they had more time to rest up from their travels, but King Ryllin and Queen Carlinda did not wish to put off meeting the rest of the family any longer, and so we will proceed as planned. I know I do not need to remind everyone to be pleasant and agreeable or to remain present for the entire evening" — this last with a meaningful glance at both Meg and Maurel — "and — yes, except for you, of course, Nan Vera, when it's time for Mattie to be put down — and to do everything possible to represent our family in the best possible manner to our future new relations. Maerlie, on the way, please inform your tardy sister about the seating arrangements and other matters we've already discussed."

At that, everyone rose. Meg gave her mother one more quiet apology and received a forgiving hand-squeeze in return. Then the queen walked off with Morgan at her side, speaking of whatever it was such a pair of grown-up women might discuss at times like these. Meg carefully approached Nan Vera and swooped in to give Mattie a quick kiss on the forehead before ducking aside to the relative safety of Maerlie's protective company. Now that Maerlie was getting married, Nan Vera seemed to think she was suddenly off-limits for scolding. Meg hoped that wasn't going to mean an extra helping for herself from now on.

"You didn't miss anything, really," Maerlie said, lacing her arm through Meg's and whisking her along into the hallway. "After we spend a few minutes with Ryant and his family, we'll all proceed to the Great Hall for dinner, which will include a bunch of ambassadors and royal cousins and other interesting and not-so-interesting individuals. We won't be sitting together; they're mixing us about to ensure that all the guests end up with someone of royal blood to talk to so no one gets offended. So there won't be an opportunity until much later for you to report in on what you think of this man I'm about to run off with. Don't think that lets you off the hook, though. I expect full details of your thoughts and reactions."

"You'll have it," Meg said, laughing. "Have you ever known me to keep my opinion to myself, requested or not?"

"Good point. I needn't have worried. Now, if you'll excuse me, I must become the proper princess and future daughter-in-law."

Meg smiled as Maerlie straightened up and visibly assumed her formal persona before entering the candlelit room adjoining the dining hall. But really it wasn't as silly as Maerlie pretended. Soon she'd forget that the proper princess was just a role, and that's who she'd become, for real, forever. And then it would be Maerlie giving her neutral nods instead of mischievous, half-hidden grins.

"I'm nervous," Maurel whispered, coming up beside her. Meg pulled herself out of her melancholy thoughts and gave her sister a quick hug. "Don't worry," she said. "They'll love you. How could they not?"

About to pass through the door, they suddenly found themselves yanked aside by Nan Vera. "Wait, wait, wait!" the woman whispered frantically, first handing the baby to Meg while she pinned Maurel's braids swiftly back into place and then shifting the baby to Maurel and rubbing, not quite gently, a creamy salve into Meg's scraped hand.

"Thank you," Meg said quietly, suddenly touched by Nan Vera's care about such things.

Nan Vera only nodded impatiently and ushered the girls into the room before her.

The next hour or so was something of a whirlwind — a blur of new faces and names and smiles and bows and curtsies and lots of those careful, expressionless nods that so many adults seemed so fond of. Meg had been prepared to suffer through a somewhat boring evening of royal posturing, punctuated by moments of happiness for Maer and sadness for herself accompanied by a continuous effort to not think about her secret no matter how much it clamored for her attention. But despite her ambivalence about the impending wedding and her dread of all that it threatened to change, Meg found herself swept up in the excitement of the whole thing. Secrets aside, sadness aside, there was something irresistibly enthralling about the cascade of new people. Especially, she had to admit, certain new people.

Especially, in fact, one in particular.

King Ryllin and Queen Carlinda had brought a number of distinguished members of their household along with them to Trelian, and all of them had been seated at the enormous table together. The head and foot of the table were left empty, to represent equality between the two kingdoms, and everyone was seated along the two long sides. Maerlie and Prince Ryant, along with both sets of royal parents, were seated in a group at one end, but as her sister had foretold, everyone else from both households had been mingled together, so that instead of her usual place between her next oldest and next youngest sister, Meg found herself surrounded by new and *very* interesting dinner companions.

On her left was none other than Serek, which was especially fascinating for two reasons. First, after having just met Calen that afternoon, it was impossible not to take a greater interest in his master, this mysterious new mage who had been rather elusive ever since his arrival at the castle. No one had been able to get much of a sense of him, other than that he seemed very serious and not much inclined to socializing. The second and even more compelling reason, however, was that Serek had quietly intercepted her parents upon their entry to the hall, which surely must mean something significant — that there was something he had to tell them that could not wait. Unfortunately, by the time Meg had edged close enough to hear anything, her father was thanking the mage and asking him to meet them later that evening for further discussion. Serek bowed his head and walked away, and the king and queen hastily recomposed their features into happy, proud parental expressions. But for a moment, they had seemed anything but happy. What had Serek said to them?

After a formal welcome, in which both kings and queens spoke briefly and eloquently of their joy at the impending marriage and hopes for renewed peace between their kingdoms, everyone was led to their seats by a flurry of nervous-looking pages. Serek gave Meg a silent nod of greeting as he sat down beside her, and such was her surprise at suddenly being this close to him, it was all she could do to smile and nod politely in return. Sadly, he didn't seem interested in making conversation, which made it difficult to keep finding excuses to turn toward him and study him, as she wanted to.

Luckily, that wasn't true of Meg's other table companions. On her right was Richton, another of Prince Ryant's
personal guard. She had expected him to be something
like Jorn, quiet and mysterious and brusque, but in fact
Richton seemed to enjoy talking almost as much as
Serek seemed to avoid it. He had all sorts of fascinating tales of travel and danger and adventure, and he told
them with such humor and skill that he had enraptured
that entire section of the table by the time the soup was
served.

The only thing able to distract Meg from Richton's
stories was the young man sitting directly across from
her. Wilem was the son of Sen Eva Lichtendor, the
senior advisor to the throne of Kragnir. He was also a
trusted companion of Prince Ryant, which made him
a potentially invaluable source of all kinds of interesting information. He was *also* incredibly — almost
unbearably — handsome . . . even better-looking, in Meg's
opinion, than the prince (who had actually turned out to
be as nice-looking in real life as in his portrait). This had
the unfortunate side effect of making it rather difficult
for Meg to think clearly or come up with appropriately
charming and intelligent things to say to him.

Richton was just finishing a particularly exciting
account of how he and Jorn had nearly been killed during

49

a pirate attack when Meg heard Maurel speak up from her place on Richton's right.

"Was that how Jorn got that big scar? From the pirates?"

Meg winced and was about to apologize on her sister's behalf, but Richton spoke first.

"I am sorry, young princess, but that's not my tale to tell," he said, not unkindly. "If you want to know about Jorn's scar, you're going to have to ask him yourself. Shall I call him over for you?" He rose partway out of his chair.

"No!" Maurel cried immediately. Her eyes had grown enormous in her small face.

Richton laughed softly and sat back down. "I'm only teasing, little one," he said, patting her hand gently. "It would take a braver man than me to interrupt Jorn during a meal."

Everyone laughed at this, and Maurel gave a tentative smile, perhaps not sure of the joke but realizing all the same that Richton was only playing. Meg smiled, too. Richton seemed a happy and good-natured man, and that seemed to indicate good things about Prince Ryant as well. Meg very much wanted to believe that the prince was as perfect as he seemed. Marrying for love was seldom an option in a ruling family, and although Meg knew and accepted this fact in theory, the idea that

Maerlie might find actual love within an arranged marriage . . . well, that would be wonderful. Wonderful for Maerlie, and wonderful in that it meant maybe such a thing would be possible for Meg as well.

Meg cradled this thought in her mind as she stole another glance at Wilem, across the table. The son of a royal advisor was not the most likely match for a princess. But they couldn't *all* marry princes, probably, and she was going to have to marry *someone* eventually, once she was older and well . . . ready. And Wilem was so striking, and tall, and strong-looking, and well spoken, and polite, and he chewed with his mouth closed — she'd been checking — and when he smiled, one side of his mouth curved up higher than the other in a way that made her feel sort of sweetly nervous and silly. And then there were his eyes, his beautiful dark eyes, which she suddenly realized were looking right back at her across the table. . . .

Meg blinked and quickly looked away. *Stupid, stupid,* she thought angrily, reaching for her heavily watered wine to stall until she could think of some reasonable explanation for why she had been staring at him. Her brain refused to cooperate. She risked looking back up and found him still watching her, though not with annoyance or contempt as she had feared. Instead he gave her one of those smiles, which did nothing to help quiet the mad fluttering of her heart within her chest, and held her gaze a moment more before turning to respond to something his mother, seated to his right, had asked him.

Freed from her momentary paralysis, Meg looked away and found Maerlie smirking at her from the far end of the table. Meg shrugged helplessly, and Maerlie shook her head, laughing.

For the rest of the meal, Meg did her best to avoid looking at Wilem as much as possible. This was made easier by two things. One, that Maurel was keeping Wilem occupied with endless boring questions about what it was like living in Kragnir, which Wilem was too polite to do anything other than answer, and two, that Sen Eva, Wilem's mother, had actually managed to draw Serek into a conversation, and nearly all of Meg's attention was focused on this rare and informative event.

"It was fortunate that Trelian was able to secure your services so quickly after Mage Fredrin's passing, Mage Serek," Sen Eva said as a serving boy replaced her plate with the next course. "Although I'm sure your previous patrons were sorry to lose you."

"The Magistratum is careful not to reassign a mage without a replacement at hand," Serek answered. "I believe Mage Arlena arrived within hours of my departure, in fact."

"Of course." Sen Eva inclined her head slightly. "I suppose after more than three hundred years, the Magistratum has things well in hand." She flashed a radiant smile at him, the kind of smile that usually made one feel compelled to smile back. Serek pursed his lips; Meg wondered if that passed for a smile as far as he was concerned.

"I don't have a great deal of experience in these matters," Sen Eva went on. "Our mage at Kragnir has been at his post for as long as I can remember, and we have not had many dealings with the Magistratum in recent years. Is it difficult, moving around as often as you have?"

"Difficult, madam?"

"Well, adjusting to a new place, new people . . ."

"A mage's life is dedicated to his work, wherever he is posted. I am, of course, honored to have been appointed King's Mage, but I serve King Tormon and Queen Merilyn best by focusing on the work, not the environment."

Meg was impressed by Sen Eva's ability to persevere with such poise in the face of Serek's determined bluntness. Most people probably would have given up, but Sen Eva smiled warmly at him again. "I'm sure this dedication is indeed what led to your appointment, Mage Serek." She paused, then went on, "May I ask — is an appointment such as this one, an honor like this — is it recorded in your marks? Forgive me, but I've never understood the full scope of what a mage's marks include."

That was an interesting question. Meg had wondered about the same thing herself. Calen's face was barely marked, just a few lines and small shapes under his left eye, but Serek had delicate black lines spiraling across both sides of his face, with tiny symbols and dots of color worked into the design at various points.

Serek shook his head. "No." For the first time, Meg thought she detected the barest touch of emotion in his voice. "No, the marks are given for years of study, fields of expertise, and accomplishments of that nature, Sen Eva. A mage may serve many masters in his lifetime, but it is the work and the study of magic that defines his life and purpose. Those are the things that set him apart from others, and the reason why no mage may go unmarked — what he is capable of, not where he performs his duties." He gestured at her with his knife. "If political appointments were important enough to be writ in flesh, madam, surely one as accomplished as you would bear some marks herself."

"I — I see, yes. Thank you, Mage Serek. I had not

fully understood. I can see why you feel so strongly about this. I hope I have not offended you with my questions."

Serek suddenly seemed to realize he was pointing his knife at her. He lowered it and offered the hint of a smile, perhaps in apology. "It is a serious matter, Advisor. And one that all mages feel passionately about. But not one that non-mages are usually called upon to understand. I took no offense."

He near-smiled again, and Sen Eva smiled back with far more conviction. Maybe she was hoping her example would inspire Serek to do it right next time; apparently no one had ever told him that a smile was supposed to include your eyes as well. But Serek's eyes never seemed to change, no matter what the rest of his face was doing. They were blue, and bright, but there was no warmth in them that Meg could see. Sometimes you could get a good sense of people through their eyes — Calen's eyes, for example, had been like open windows showing the slightest change in what he was thinking or feeling, constantly flashing in anger or widening in amazement — but Serek's eyes gave nothing away. It was as if he were hidden behind a wall, able to see out but revealing nothing of his own thoughts or emotions.

Sen Eva turned away from the table to signal for

more wine, and Serek suddenly and deliberately turned to stare back at Meg. She felt herself flush. *Caught again,* she thought ruefully, but this time she didn't look away. This was too good a chance to miss.

"How are you settling in at the castle, Mage Serek?" she asked politely. It wasn't the most dazzling of questions, to be sure, but it was the first acceptable thing that came to her mind. She could hardly ask the sorts of things she really wanted to know. "I hope it's beginning to feel like home."

"Thank you for your concern, Your Highness," he answered formally. "My quarters are quite comfortable and adequate for my needs."

Well, *that* was certainly revealing. Before he could turn away, she quickly spoke again. "I'm glad to hear it. Mage Fredrin seemed to like his quarters very much, and I know my parents hoped you would be as happy with them as he was." He nodded, clearly doing his best to avoid prolonging the conversation. A question, she had to ask a question. She cast around desperately for something to ask. "How, um, how do they compare to your former residence? Where was that, again?"

Clumsy, but it did the job. "My last station was in Eldwinn, Your Highness. I had the pleasure of serving the governor of that province. One of your royal cousins,

I believe. My residence in Eldwinn was also quite comfortable, though certainly not so grand as this castle."

"Ah, yes. I hear Eldwinn is lovely, though I have not yet had the opportunity to visit there myself." They sat for a moment, looking at each other. He just wasn't going to give up anything willingly, was he? Finally she added, "And was Calen with you at Eldwinn as well?"

Serek raised his eyebrows at this, and she knew immediately that Calen hadn't mentioned their meeting this afternoon. Well, of course not. She was being stupid again. He'd been sneaking around just as she had. Certainly he wouldn't have told his master about it.

"I was not aware you had met my young apprentice, Your Highness." *Now* he seemed interested. Meg cursed inwardly. The last thing she wanted was to get Calen in trouble! "I hope he hasn't been making a nuisance of himself."

"Not at all," she said, trying to think. "In fact, I met him only once, by chance, while he was on an errand." That was true, technically. "He seemed very nice. I mean, polite. Not that we spent much time talking. He was eager to continue on his errand. Not that he said that directly, of course, but I could tell. He wasn't rude or anything." This was terrible. "I mean, we just exchanged a few words. He seemed very nice."

Meg turned away and feigned a deep interest in the remains of her meal. She could feel Serek's cold eyes staring at her, but he said no more. After a minute she heard Sen Eva ask him a question about his experience with medicinal herbs and, with great relief, felt his focus leave her.

Had she managed to accomplish anything this evening other than embarrassing herself? She hoped Wilem hadn't overheard any of that conversational disaster. She glanced up at him and found him looking at her again. Her face flooded with heat. Again. *How red is my face by now? I wonder.* But this time she didn't look away from him. If she was going to stare at people, she might as well be strong about it. With a mighty effort, she forced herself to smile. He smiled back.

Gods, but he had a nice smile.

At the end of dinner, Maerlie rose and invited everyone out to the royal gardens. It was a warm night, and the gardens were wonderful for walking off the effects of a heavy meal or just enjoying the night air. A few of the young men, who perhaps had had a bit too much wine with dinner, decided to attempt the enormous hedge maze, leading many of the others to speculate that a search party would need to be organized before the night was ended.

Most of the remaining guests took to the stone benches nestled among the slender, elegant trees of the main garden or walked around admiring the manicured hedges trimmed in the shapes of various animals.

Meg was looking for Maerlie, to find out what sort of interesting things had happened at her end of the table, when she felt a light touch on her arm. She turned to find Wilem at her side.

"Wh — hello," she said stupidly, grateful that she was standing far enough away from the lanterns that he probably couldn't quite see her blushing this time. "I mean, good evening, Wilem. I'm surprised to see you on your own — I thought you'd be eager to rejoin the prince."

"While I enjoy Prince Ryant's company enormously, I do get to speak with him often, and there are some here tonight whose company I have not yet been able to enjoy nearly enough." His voice was low and confident, and Meg felt her pulse racing at the sound of it. She knew she was being silly, but she just couldn't help it. She couldn't. Wilem was unbelievably charming, and handsome, and he had that *smile*, and here he was, talking to *her*, and not Morgan or Maerlie or the prince or his mother or any of the other important people he could be talking to.

He offered his arm, and she took it, feeling more than a little as though she were dreaming. They began strolling slowly along one of the tree-lined garden paths. For a while neither of them spoke, and the only sound, other than the muted conversations of other guests, was the night breeze rustling through the leaves. Meg looked down, enjoying the sight of their feet walking in step, side by side. For all her earlier staring, she suddenly wasn't sure what to do with her eyes. She fought the urge to look up at Wilem. Somehow she felt sure he'd be looking right back at her, and without the table between them, the idea of his face so close to hers made her so nervous and excited it was almost frightening.

"So," he said finally, "Princess Meglynne. What would you be doing at this moment had I not lured you away to walk with me?"

It was so hard to think; half of Meg's mind was still shouting *He's talking to me! He's talking to me!* in giddy delirium. Meg willed her brain to silence and tried desperately to emulate Maerlie's calm princess demeanor. "Nothing else quite so pleasant, I imagine," she said finally. "Wandering the garden, making polite conversation, watching after Maurel to keep her out of trouble . . ."

"Does she require a great deal of watching?"

"Oh yes," Meg said, laughing. "Please don't misunderstand — she's very sweet-natured, and rarely actually *intends* mischief. Yet somehow even with two or three older sisters keeping an eye on her, not to mention Nan Vera ever close at hand, she almost always manages to get into trouble. Very shortly we will probably hear shouts of alarm and run back to discover that she has set the gardens ablaze or lost the prince in the hedge maze or released four hundred minks among the guest suites."

Wilem glanced sideways at her. "Are those actual examples of her past exploits?"

Meg shrugged. "Well, only the minks."

"Four *hundred*?"

"A visiting merchant brought them to display before my mother. When Maurel discovered they were to be killed for their coats, she stole the key to their cages and released them into the castle. It took weeks to catch the last of them. The merchant was *not* pleased. Nor were the guests who found angry, frightened minks roaming the halls at night. Or hiding under the bedclothes."

Wilem shook his head, chuckling.

"I'm not so sure you should be laughing," Meg said, smiling herself. "There's always a chance they missed one, you know. You *are* staying in the guest quarters, aren't you?"

"I see I shall have to be on my guard. I had no idea Trelian was such a dangerous place."

Meg sobered at that. "Unfortunately, that seems all

too true of late. At least as far as the roads go. When the prince's party hadn't arrived by midafternoon, we all began to worry that something had happened."

"It would take more than bandits and thieves to threaten a royal escort."

"From what we've been hearing, there *are* more than bandits and thieves. Especially in the Hunterheart. Some of the stories have been quite frightening, and I'm sure there are worse that I've not been allowed to hear. You didn't — you didn't encounter anything unusual during your travels? Anything — unnatural?"

"Unnatural?" Wilem smiled gently. "I think you may have been listening to a few too many of those stories. It's true that the roads are no longer safe for the lone traveler, or even small groups, and that roaming bands of thieves and other criminals have been attacking people in the Hunterheart. But although their *actions* may be described as unnatural, the bandits themselves are as natural as you or me. Any stories you hear of monsters in the forest are just that — stories."

Meg didn't say anything. Perhaps worried that he'd offended her, Wilem didn't pursue the topic further. They walked in silence for a while, but Meg's mind was anything but quiet. Was this a comfortable silence? Or an awkward silence? How did one tell these things? Should she say something? She should say something. But she couldn't think of anything to say.

"How do you get along with your sisters?" Wilem asked, saving her from her stupid floundering. "Is it difficult, to be part of such a large family?"

"Are we such a large family? I didn't think five children was so many, really. But either way, it's all I've known. I don't think it's difficult. On the contrary, when anything happens, when I need to talk, or if I'm sad, there's always someone there for me. Maerlie is the one I talk to most often, but Maurel is always good at lifting my spirits, and of course the baby is such a sweet little thing . . . I feel so lucky to have them." *Am I babbling? I'm babbling.* "And you," she asked, "do you have any siblings?"

"No," he said, looking away suddenly. "Not anymore." He paused. "I had a brother, Tymas, but he and my father were killed when I was very young."

Meg was shocked. "Oh, Wilem. I'm so sorry. I — I never would have asked —"

He shook his head. "It's all right. You couldn't have known."

"I'm so sorry," she said again. She couldn't think of what else to say. She'd always thought that children without siblings must be lonely sometimes, but to have a brother, then have him taken away. . . . She couldn't imagine losing one of her sisters. It would tear her apart.

Wilem stopped walking and turned to face her, touching her hand. She looked up at him, startled.

"Please, don't be sad, Meglynne. It was a long time ago. And it's my own fault the conversation led to such a . . . difficult . . . topic." One corner of his mouth turned up slightly. "I was trying too hard to think of something to say, I suppose. You know, you got so quiet, and I feared you were becoming bored with my company."

Meg gave a snort of laughter before she could stop herself. "You feared *I* was getting bored! Me, with my endless babbling about nothing. . . ." She trailed off, embarrassed.

"You underestimate your own charms, I think," he said quietly after a moment.

Meg's heart was pounding so hard, she was sure he must hear it. She should say something, it was her turn to speak, but he was looking at her, looking down with those beautiful, sad, dark eyes, and she couldn't find any words. They stood that way for several seconds, or maybe it was hours — Meg stopped trying to think of what to do or say and just looked at him. Could it be that under his beautiful polished exterior he was just as awkward and nervous as she was? She thought about Maerlie's "proper princess" role and the roles Meg herself sometimes played depending on where she was or who she was talking to. Was there another Wilem underneath, more real and frightened and imperfect and all the more appealing for all those things?

He smiled at her again, sending new, ridiculous shivers running through her and driving the last of her thoughts out of her head. Meg let herself get lost in that smile. It was a nice kind of lost. She didn't think about anything else for a long time.

CHAPTER FOUR

THE SMALL GATE WAS THE FARTHEST and least ornate of the entrances to the castle's outer ward. Presumably it was called the small gate because it was intended for the "smallfolk"; it was generally used by servants and couriers, as well as apprentices on errands. The gate itself was actually fairly large, in Calen's opinion. Most of the nobility ignored it, if they even knew it existed. The fact that Meg wanted to meet *here* made him all the more curious about what her secret could be.

As he neared the gate, Calen scanned the crowd for the princess. She didn't seem to have arrived yet, so he walked over to lean against a section of the outer wall. It gave him a good view of the main road from the castle proper, so he'd be sure to see her when she approached. In the meantime, he amused himself by watching other people. While it was true he hadn't gotten to know anyone closely, there were plenty of people he knew by sight, some well enough to pass a few words with now and then. Some folk were always happy to share news and spread gossip, and Calen liked to hear tales of the world outside his own dreary existence.

So far the only familiar face he saw was Lammy, the kitchen boy. Lammy was about seven and not the most reliable source of information, especially since he liked to make things up. He was hauling a huge sack of what appeared to be turnips, and not being all that careful with his burden, either. As Calen watched, two of the pale vegetables tumbled out onto the ground, and the sack showed definite signs of having been dragged through the dirt for at least part of its journey. Calen shook his head and jogged over to rescue the fallen turnips.

"Need some help with that, Lammy?" he asked, handing the turnips over to the boy.

"*No*," Lammy said testily, grabbing them and stuffing them back into the sack. "I *got* it. I could carry this a hundred miles if I wanted to. A *thousand*, probably." He paused, considering. "Unless you want to make it fly for me?" He looked up at Calen hopefully. "Not because I can't carry it, 'cause I *can*, but I never seen flying turnips before, and so that would be good. Also Cook would probably shout when she saw them and drop her spoon." He seemed to find this last idea especially appealing.

Calen smiled down at him. "Sorry, Lammy. Mage Serek hasn't taught me anything about levitation yet." At

Lammy's blank stare he clarified: "That means making things fly. I could turn them into toads for you, though, if you wanted. Then they could hop to the kitchen on their own." He lifted a hand theatrically, pointing at the turnips and raising his eyebrows at the boy.

Lammy scowled and thrust the sack higher up against his shoulder. "That's dumb. What's Cook gonna do with toads? Can't make turnip soup from toads!" He started walking again, muttering about toads as he went.

Calen laughed and headed back toward the wall. He couldn't really have turned them into toads, of course. Serek still denied that such transformations were even possible, although Calen was pretty sure Serek just didn't want to teach him about it. He frowned. Probably didn't think he had the *discipline* or *intelligence* to handle it. Well, that didn't matter anymore. Calen had decided to take more of his education into his own hands. You could learn a great deal from a book, he'd discovered. The pages he'd read in the Erylun had been far more informative than anything Serek had deigned to tell him, although he still hadn't found any clear instructions about interpreting the spirit card reading he'd done yesterday. There were apparently hundreds of different ways to deal and read the cards, and Calen hadn't seen anything that seemed to relate to the specific pattern Serek had laid out. Also, Mage Erylun assumed a certain level of knowl-edge and experience in his readers, and so didn't explain a lot of things in detail that Calen guessed most full mages would already know. But that didn't matter, either. With time, and lots more reading, he'd eventually be able to understand. And he wouldn't need Serek's help to do it.

Calen looked around with growing impatience. Where was Meg? It was all very well for her to tell him not to treat her like the princess she was, but she couldn't at the same time expect him to wait around all day so she could show up at her leisure. Unless — His heart went small and tight within his chest. Had she only been hav-ing fun with him yesterday? She *was* a princess, after all; she certainly didn't need to befriend some lowly appren-tice in order to have someone to share secrets with. Suddenly he felt very stupid. Of course, that had to be it. She had probably laughed about it all evening with her sisters, mocking the silly, lonely boy who actually thought a princess wanted to be his friend.

He pushed away from the wall, his face hot with embarrassment, but couldn't help looking around once more. As he turned back toward the castle, he noticed a scruffy-looking girl eyeing him with an amused smile. Calen glared back at her. What did *she* think was so funny?

Oh.

Oh!

He walked over to her, struggling not to grin like an idiot. "How long have you been here?"

"Just a short while," Meg said. "I was wondering how long it would take you to recognize me."

"I almost didn't. You look really — different." She was wearing a tunic and faded breeches, similar to the clothing of most boys and many girls whose responsibilities had them running long errands or working outside the castle. Hers were certainly dirty enough to look authentic; perhaps she had borrowed them from a real errand girl. Her boots were splattered with dried mud, and her hair was loose over her shoulders and looked rather tangly. It was hard to believe this was the same girl he had seen yesterday.

"Well, good. It certainly wouldn't be much of a disguise if I looked the same, would it? Now, come on." She started briskly for the gate, and he hurried to catch up.

"Why do you need a disguise?"

She gave him a disgusted look. "You seemed smarter than this yesterday. For one thing, princesses do not go wandering outside the castle grounds by themselves. My parents would never permit it, and the guards know it.

Maurel tries it often enough, so they're always on the lookout for her, but they believe we older girls have more sense." She flashed him a wry smile, and he had to smile back. Even after his doubts a few minutes before, her comment about his intelligence lacked the same bite as Serek's more pointed remark. And besides, he hadn't been stupid. She was here, just like she said she'd be.

They were almost at the gate. Meg shook her head, causing some of her hair to fall around her face. Her hands were thrust into her pockets, and she walked with a slumped posture that was completely unlike the normal way she carried herself. The transformation was amazing — no one would ever imagine she was really a princess. Calen forced himself to stop staring, lest he draw unwanted attention to her, and looked up at the nearest guard instead. The guard was one he recognized — Lared, he thought his name was — and Calen waved as he walked past. Lared nodded back at him and then turned his eyes to the next in line. Meg walked through beside him without incident.

"For another thing," she went on once they were safely past the gate, "this is a secret, remember? Even if I were allowed outside as myself, people might wonder where I was going, and why, and arousing curiosity about something is generally not the best way to keep it secret. Mellie, the dirty errand girl, however, can go virtually anywhere without attracting anyone's interest."

"Mellie?"

She shrugged and pushed her hair back behind her ears. "I had to have a name ready, just in case anyone asks."

"Yes, but *Mellie?*"

"You be quiet, or I'll make up a name for you, too."

Calen held up his hands. "All right, you win. No more teasing about the name. So where are we headed, Mellie? Are you going to tell me this secret or not?"

She looked back over her shoulder toward the gate. "Once we're out of view of the guards, we're going to leave the road and head for those trees at the bottom of the hill."

"And then?"

"And then you'll find out what the secret is."

"Can't you tell me now?"

She shook her head, smiling. "Sorry. You'll just have to learn to be patient, I'm afraid."

The road from the gate took a sharp turn toward the south, heading to where it would eventually branch into two roads, one going on to meet up with the Queen's Road and one continuing toward the market grounds.

Once they passed the turn, Meg took a final glance around and then pulled Calen off onto the grassy field beside the road.

"Walk casually," she said, "as if we're just wandering over to the trees to rest in the shade."

They stepped slowly through the field. Tiny flowers — peablossoms — grew among the tall grass, sprinkling the green with bright flecks of pink and yellow and violet. Calen stretched his arms up and closed his eyes for a moment to focus on the feel of the warm breeze against his face. It was nice to be out in the sun. One of the worst parts of being a mage, he often thought, must be having to spend so much time cooped up in a dark study. As an apprentice, at least he got to travel to the market once a week and run occasional errands outside the castle, but most of the business of magic itself seemed to require darkness and dust and shadows. He couldn't even remember the last time he'd seen Serek outside in the daytime. No wonder the man was always in such a foul mood.

Suddenly Calen pitched forward. He managed to get his feet back under him just in time to avoid falling on his face, and twisted around to look for whatever had tripped him. After a second he saw it. Stupid rock.

Meg was smirking at him again. "You might want to

try walking with your eyes open," she suggested innocently. "Sometimes that can help."

Calen just looked at her until she turned away, laughing. He shook his head. She certainly did seem to find him amusing. But somehow it didn't bother him so much today.

They had come to the outer line of trees. The grassy field gave way to forest floor. Calen tried to keep an eye on his feet, not wanting to give any rocks or bulging tree roots a chance to trip him. Meg seemed a lot quieter than she'd been yesterday. Maybe she was just thinking about her secret. He hoped that was it, and not that she was getting bored with him already.

"How was the big dinner last night?" he asked her.

"Hmm? Oh, it was wonderful," she said. "Prince Ryant seems almost as perfect as Maerlie's made him out to be, and I think everyone had a good time."

"Did you talk to anyone interesting? Like that guard with the scar?"

"Jorn? No, I didn't get to talk to him. But I sat next to one of the other guards, Richton. I think you'd like him — he told great stories. He had all of us caught up in tales most of the evening. And I met the son of King Ryllin's chief advisor. His name is Wilem." She stopped and looked as if she were deciding what to say next. Then

74

she suddenly looked startled and grabbed his arm. "Oh, and I can't believe I almost forgot — I also sat next to Serek!"

"What? He was there?"

She nodded. "He sat next to me after having a mysterious private word with my parents, which unfortunately I wasn't close enough to overhear. I didn't even realize he'd be at the feast until I saw him come in."

"Me neither," Calen said. "I mean, I knew he went off to talk to your parents, but not that he'd be staying for the dinner."

"Do you know why he wanted to talk to them? They didn't say a word to us about it."

"Yes," Calen began, then stopped, suddenly feeling like an idiot again. He'd been so preoccupied with his anger at Serek's dismissal of his abilities that somehow he hadn't given further thought to what his reading of the cards had already suggested. Even with Serek's refusal to explain anything to him, it was obvious that bad things were involved. Bad things that were going to be happening to Trelian. And of course Meg would want to know that. He should have thought to tell her right away. Except — he didn't know what to tell her, exactly. That terrible yet vague dangers were on their way — look out?

Something in his face must have reflected his

thoughts. Meg stopped walking, her eyes wide and concerned.

"Well, what? What is it, Calen?"

He shook his head. "I don't really know."

She poked a finger at him angrily. "Don't do that," she said. "You do too know, and you're going to tell me." She poked him again, harder. "Right now."

Calen rubbed his chest. Did she always have to be so violent? "No, you don't understand. I want to tell you, it's just that it's — it's complicated."

Meg folded her arms across her chest and stood there, staring at him. He sighed. Then he explained about the cards, and the reading, and how Serek refused to tell him anything more about it.

"So even I can see it's about something bad," he said finally. "But I just don't know what." He thought back to the card with the grinning skull, and shuddered.

They started walking again. "Well, I can't pretend I'm not concerned," Meg said after a minute, "but I think it's too soon to get too upset over this. For one thing, you don't know for certain what the cards meant." She looked up at him apologetically. "I mean, you are just starting with divination — you said it yourself."

He shrugged. "Well, yeah, that's true."

"For another, it sounds like some of the bad images

you saw were balanced out by more positive ones, so maybe the overall meaning isn't necessarily a dire one. That's possible, isn't it?"

Calen looked over at her, impressed. For someone who didn't know anything about magic, she was doing some pretty clear thinking on the subject.

"Yeah," he said again. "I guess that could be true also."

"Don't mistake me — I fully intend to find out what's going on. I'm just saying we shouldn't automatically assume the worst. The world is a big, wide place, with all kinds of wonderful things in it. One of which, I should point out, you are about to see."

Suddenly they were standing before the entrance to a cave. It looked extraordinarily dark and mysterious in there — just the sort of place that cried out to be explored by a brave adventurer. Calen found himself impressed again. He wouldn't have thought a princess would be the sort of girl who went crawling into dark caves in the woods.

Of course, he wasn't usually the sort of boy who went crawling into dark caves in the woods, himself. But Meg didn't need to know that.

"In here?" he asked, ducking his head to step inside.

"Calen, wait!" She grabbed his arm and pulled him

back from the entrance. His surprise at being suddenly yanked backward combined with his seemingly infallible ability to find rocks with his feet conspired to spill him gracelessly onto the hard ground. He raised his head to stare at Meg, who blushed.

"Sorry." She reached out a hand to help him up. "But I need to go in first. I've never brought anyone here before, and it might be dangerous for you to go in without me."

Calen raised his eyebrows at this.

"Don't take it personally," she said. "Trust me — you'll understand in a minute."

With that, she turned back toward the entrance. But then she stopped again, one hand touching the rough stone wall, the other motionless at her side.

"Meg? What's wrong?"

It took her a moment to turn back around. Her face had changed; suddenly she seemed lost and unsure, not at all the brash and confident girl she'd been just a few seconds earlier.

"Meg?"

She stood there looking at him, thinking gods knew what. Then she shook her head. "Nothing. Nothing's wrong." She hesitated, then went on. "It's just strange. I can't tell my parents, my sisters, not even Maerlie . . . But

I do think I can tell you. I know we only met yesterday, and it's crazy that I'm so sure I can trust you, but" — she shrugged — "I do."

Meg turned back to the cave entrance. Calen didn't say anything; he didn't want to accidentally say the wrong thing and make her hesitate again.

Before she went in, though, she spun back around to face him one more time. He blinked; her face and her pointy finger were inches away from his nose. "Of course, if you prove me wrong, I'll have to hurt you. Just, you know, keep that in mind." Then she grinned and ducked inside.

Calen swallowed nervously, then went in after her. The cave wound back into a tunnel. In an awkward crouch, he stepped forward carefully, keeping one hand against the cave wall for balance. Up ahead, he could just make out Meg's shape in the dwindling light from the entrance. She turned back to whisper softly, "Careful — it bends to the right here." Then she disappeared.

Advancing slowly, Calen followed the tunnel around the sharp turn. The light from the entrance was cut off completely now, and he couldn't see at all. Calen didn't normally consider himself the timid sort — well, except maybe where heights were concerned, but that was only common sense — but this was like being blind. He stepped forward again, and again, one hand stretched out before him, certain each time that his foot would encounter nothing but empty space and he'd go plunging to his death. How had Meg ever found this place? He was fairly certain he wouldn't have had the courage to venture in this far alone.

Suddenly there was a sound from the darkness ahead, making him jump.

"Meg?" he called out. Surely that sound had just been her. No reason to assume it was anything evil and scary. If some horrible cave creature was lurking in here, Meg would probably have already encountered it. She'd clearly been here before. But then again — she *had* been concerned about his safety when they entered. So maybe there was something to be afraid of after all. These were not helpful thoughts. "Meg?" he called again. His voice sounded very small. *Probably just some effect of the cave ceiling,* he told himself reassuringly.

"Here, Calen." He felt her hand brush his fingertips, and he took hold of it gratefully. She pulled him forward around another bend, to where a slight glow began to illuminate the tunnel walls. He could make out her face now in the darkness. Her eyes were shining with excitement.

"Ready?"

Calen nodded, though at the moment he wasn't sure he *was* ready. What kind of crazy secret was this, anyway? She could have warned him about the dark tunnel at least. His heart was still beating a bit too fast as she led him around another corner into a softly glowing chamber.

"There he is," Meg whispered, squeezing his hand.

Calen felt his jaw drop. He froze in the entrance, staring.

It was a dragon.

Curled up against the rock wall, it lay as if sleeping, with its pointed tail resting over its forelegs. As the first moment of shocked recognition passed — *a dragon, it's a dragon* — Calen realized that it was probably still very young; from the little he knew about them, full-grown dragons were supposed to be enormous, and this one seemed barely bigger than some of the king's warhorses. Its scales were a rich dark green, deepening to nearly black at tail and wing tips, and its slender head was crowned with sharp spikes that continued partway down its long neck. He supposed it was beautiful, in a frightening, serpentine way, but most of all, in that small confined space, it was terrifying, and Calen couldn't imagine how they'd be able to make it back out the tunnel entrance before it caught them and killed them. Or simply burned them to a crisp from where it lay, assuming it was old enough to make fire.

Before he could even begin to think of what to say, Meg released his hand and began walking toward the creature. It opened great yellow eyes and calmly watched her approach. Calen stared in horror, certain he was about to see her torn apart with claws and teeth before his eyes.

Instead, the dragon rolled over onto its back and let her scratch its scaly belly.

Calen was aware of his jaw falling even farther toward the ground and quickly closed his mouth before Meg could notice and make fun of him.

She looked over at him and smiled. "Come on," she said. "I think it's all right."

"You *think* it's all right?" he asked under his breath. All the same, he found himself walking toward them. He still couldn't quite believe it. He had certainly never expected to see a dragon close-up in his lifetime; they tended to avoid populated areas, and as a mage in service, he would most likely always live in or near large towns or cities. Yet here he was, not only looking at a dragon but apparently about to touch it, assuming it didn't decide to kill him before he got the chance.

The dragon, meanwhile, had returned to its previous position. It watched him with those unblinking yellow eyes. Meg stroked it and whispered to it softly.

When he was only a few steps away, Meg stopped him. "Now slowly hold out your hands," she said. "And wait."

Calen did so. For a moment nothing happened. He and the dragon looked silently at each other. Was he supposed to look at its eyes? Or would that be seen as some kind of challenge? He hoped it was all right, because he couldn't seem to look away. The dragon was mesmerizing, as still as if it were carved in stone, except that it was clearly very, very much alive.

Slowly, it started to move. It uncurled itself and slid toward him, sharp claws scraping against the rock floor. Calen remained frozen as the thing circled him, twining snakelike around his legs and inhaling with great snorts of breath. It was amazingly supple; it twisted bonelessly to surround him with its long body as it finally brought its head up to face his own. The yellow eyes stared into his with a strange alien intelligence for several slow seconds. Calen could just see Meg back against the wall, watching silently. Then the dragon began moving again, twisting around and bringing its scaly neck up to rub against the undersides of his outstretched hands. Calen released the breath he had been holding and thought he heard Meg do the same. He ran his hands along the creature's neck, feeling the smooth scales move under his skin. It was amazing — he was stroking a dragon. He'd bet Mage Serek had never done anything like this.

Finally the dragon slid back over to where Meg was now sitting. It curled up around her and appeared to go back to sleep. Calen shook his head in wonder and went to sit beside her.

"His name is Jakl," she said. "Or at least, that's what I've been calling him."

"How —?" Calen didn't even know how to finish the question. His mind was still reeling. A dragon!

Meg rested a hand on Jakl's neck and looked down at him fondly. "I found him about five months ago. I have no idea where he came from — crawled down from the mountains, I imagine, but he was so little, and there was no sign of his mother or any other dragons. Nan Vera had taken all of us out for a walk in the woods, and as usual, we had all wandered off in different directions." She paused to glance up at Calen, grinning. "She really hates when we do that. I was walking near a creek, not really thinking about where I was going, and suddenly I heard this terrible hissing. I looked up and there he was, perched on the edge of a rock near the water. He was tiny, then, about the size of a big dog, but still, with his wings spread and his mouth open like that — it was terrifying. I didn't know then that he didn't have any fire yet, either."

"What did you do?"

"Well, at first I didn't do anything. I was too scared. That was probably a good thing, I think. If I had tried to run right then, or cry out, I'm not sure what he would have done. So I just stood there, frozen, and I tried to radiate goodwill. That must sound pretty stupid, but it's all I could think of. They're supposed to be able to sense things; at least, I thought I remembered that from stories, and so I thought, let him just sense that I'm not going to hurt him. . . ."

"No, that's not stupid at all," Calen said. "I mean, I don't really know about dragons, but Serek *has* taught me about dealing with aggressive creatures in the wild, and you're supposed to try to communicate physically, let them know you're not a threat. You probably did exactly the right thing."

She shrugged. "Well, it seemed to work. After a few minutes he came over, sort of like he did to you just now. Stared at me, like he was trying to see who I was. Then he relaxed and rubbed his head against my leg. Just like a cat! I swear, I expected him to start purring. Anyway, just then I heard Nan Vera calling for us, and I knew I couldn't let her see him — she'd tell my parents, and I didn't know what they would do. I'm sure they wouldn't just leave a dragon to grow up within sight of the castle, though. So I told him to wait, that I'd be back. I know he couldn't really understand me, but he didn't follow when I backed away, so either he somehow picked up some of my meaning or he was just too cautious to go toward the other voices. After that I started sneaking out every couple of days to visit him, and eventually I found the cave and brought him here."

She cocked her head, frowning. "He's growing so fast, though. Pretty soon he'll get too big for the tunnel. I don't know what I'll do with him then."

"Aren't you worried at all about what will happen when he's fully grown? I mean, about him attacking the castle or carrying off serving girls or something?"

Meg shook her head. "No. I know I should be, but I'm not. I feel — connected to him, somehow. Maybe it's all the time we've spent together or that he was separated from his mother so young, but somehow I know he's not going to hurt me. And I don't mean just physically. I mean, I know he's not going to threaten the castle or do anything that would cause me pain." She tapped her heart, then looked at Calen, clearly wanting him to understand. "I know it in here. I can feel it. Is that crazy?"

Calen looked down at the dragon, sleeping with his head snuggled tight against Meg's body. What she was saying did sound a little crazy, really, and yet — there was clearly *something* going on here. He looked back at her. Her eyes were still on him, more open than he'd seen them before, questioning, wanting his — approval? Understanding?

"I don't know, Meg," he said slowly. "It seems possible, but at the same time, it's a big risk to place that much trust in a feeling."

"But it's more than a feeling. I can't really explain." She paused, seeming to steel herself before she went on. When she spoke again, it was in a rush, as though she didn't want to give herself time to think. "We're connected, Calen. I mean truly connected. I can feel him, all the time. He . . . pulls at me. As if he wants something, but I don't know what it is. It's like there's a part of him that lives inside me now. It gets stronger when I get closer, but even when I'm farther away, he's with me. I can't make it go away. And sometimes . . ." She looked down at her hands, which she was wringing nervously. "Sometimes I don't want it to go away. It makes me feel . . . strong. Powerful. Like I can do anything. But even when it feels good, it's scary. I'm different. I'm *changing*. I — I don't know what to do."

She fell silent. Calen tried to think of what to say. The bold, brash princess was gone again; during those last few sentences, Meg had sounded frightened and alone. *She's asking for my help*, he realized. Maybe that shouldn't have been so startling, but it was. Had anyone ever asked for his help before? Ever? He didn't think so. There had never been anyone to ask him. People had always been *telling* him to do things — the innkeeper and his wife, cooks and masters of hearths and stables, Mage Serek, in abundance — but no one ever *asked* him. For anything. He felt something small and bright and warm flare into existence deep inside him — the same sort of feeling that magic used to inspire in him, before it became clear that Serek had been wrong about him, that he didn't have whatever natural ability the mage had thought he'd sensed all those years ago that day at the inn. His spark, he thought. Serek had used that word, and Calen had assumed he'd meant it metaphorically. But that's really what it was. He could feel it. He hadn't realized how much he'd missed it until he suddenly had it back again.

"Calen, please," Meg whispered into the silence. "Say something. You're the only person who knows. I can't tell anyone else. If my family knew, they'd take him away. I couldn't stand that."

She looked up at him, hopeful and scared. Calen watched her watching him, both of them trying to read the other.

"I'll help you, Meg," he said. She smiled, and Calen thought he had never seen a sweeter sight. "Of course I'll help you. I don't know anything about dragons, really, but I'll learn. Mage Fredrin's old library —"

Her worry returned in an instant. "But you can't ask Serek! If he found out about Jakl . . ."

Calen smiled grimly. "I won't ask him. I know how to find some things out on my own."

If Meg heard any of the bitterness in his words, she gave no sign. "You really think there might be something in Fredrin's books?"

"Have you ever seen that library? I'm pretty sure *everything* is in one of Fredrin's books somewhere. It's just a question of figuring out where to look." That would be the hard part. He could start with the Erylun — there must be *something* about dragons in there, and maybe that would lead to other references. . . .

Meg placed a hand on his arm. "Thank you, Calen."

He smiled back at her, a real smile this time. *She's my friend*, he thought suddenly. *I have a friend. Why would Serek try so hard to avoid this?*

They stayed for a good part of the afternoon, talking about everything and nothing in the way that Calen supposed friends did. Meg asked him questions about his life before Serek, and seemed shocked to learn that he didn't have any family of his own. When she told him stories about her sisters and parents and that Nan Vera person who always seemed to be around, Calen tried to imagine what it must be like to be part of such a large and complex arrangement of people. Sometimes it just sounded exhausting, but he thought that other times it must be kind of nice.

Jakl nudged at Meg for attention periodically, but otherwise seemed content just to have her nearby. Calen kept stealing glances at the dragon, still trying to accept what he was seeing. A *dragon*, by the gods! If someone had told him yesterday that today he'd be sitting in a secret cave with a princess and a dragon, he never would have believed it. And here it was, really happening.

Eventually they got up to leave, saying good-bye to Jakl — Meg with another belly rub, Calen with a more reserved pat on the neck. Those yellow eyes still made him more than a little nervous.

As they made their way back through the tunnel, Calen spoke into the quiet blackness. "Thank you for bringing me here, Meg," he said. "I'm honored that you shared your secret with me."

He couldn't see her face, but somehow he knew she was smiling again. "You're welcome," she said softly. "And thank you, too."

CHAPTER FIVE

THEY PARTED ON THE ROAD, OUT of sight of the gate. Calen went back toward the castle, and Meg waited, not wanting anyone to notice the two of them too long together. She was probably being overly cautious, but all it would take was one person asking awkward questions and she would be in big trouble. She and Calen both, now. She hadn't done him any favors, taking him to see Jakl like that. She still couldn't really believe that she'd done it.

She also couldn't really imagine how this situation could ever turn out well. Did she honestly expect to be able to hide Jakl forever? Someday, the truth was going to come out. And then — what? There was no way Mother and Father would ever just allow her to raise a dragon. Dragons had been systematically driven away from the castle environs for years and years for a reason, after all. They were dangerous! They flew around and breathed fire and were big enough to eat cows and horses and people and anything else they chose. Any guard or soldier who saw a dragon would attempt to kill it on sight. No one would be able to understand how attached she'd become — even now, she could feel Jakl's warm, comforting presence back in the cave, like a small and distant sun.

The thought of losing that was awful. And there was no doubt that if the wrong people found out, they'd try to take him away from her.

Lately, though, she'd begun to realize that Jakl might not . . . *allow* that to happen. Which gave her another good reason to keep him a secret. She knew he wouldn't just go off and attack the castle, or her family, but if anyone tried to come between them . . .

Squinting into the distance, she decided enough time had passed since Calen had gone ahead through the gate. She began walking, slipping into her Mellie persona as she went — head down, shoulders slumped, focused on nothing but getting back to her mistress, errands complete. The gate guard barely glanced at her as she went back through. *How nice it must be,* she thought wistfully, *to have such freedom! To be beneath notice, free to come and go as you please.*

Once past the gate, she took off running across the ward. Gods, she loved to run. Loved the feel of her legs pumping, stretching out, propelling her forward, her loose hair flying behind her. Running down the long, dark hallways of the castle just wasn't the same, especially not while wearing a dress and balancing a golden circlet on her head. Nan Vera invariably caught her at it and made her stop, anyway. *Princesses walk, Meglynne!* Ugh.

She took a roundabout way back to her rooms, checking the hallway to make sure it was empty and then slipping quickly and quietly past her sisters' doors and down to her own. She opened the door and darted inside, closing it behind her. Safe at last.

Then she turned around and saw Maerlie and Morgan sitting side by side like disapproving bookends in the deep, rose-colored chairs Mother had had made for all the girls' rooms several years ago. Her sisters were staring at her expectantly, arms crossed and eyebrows raised.

Meg froze, torn between trying to explain her way out of this and turning and running right back out the door. What were they *doing* here?

Several seconds of unpleasant silence passed. Finally, Morgan leaned forward in her chair.

"Hello, sister," she said calmly. "Did you have a good afternoon?"

Meg swallowed. "Yes, thank you," she said. "And you?"

"Yes, lovely, thanks. Maerlie and I met with the seamstress about our dresses for the wedding, and then we had a pleasant lunch with Mother and Queen Carlinda."

"How nice," said Meg, still standing with her back pressed against the door. "Queen Carlinda seems very kind. Do you find her so?"

"Yes, quite," Morgan answered. "You really must take some time to chat with her soon."

Meg nodded politely and stole a glance at Maerlie. She was sitting back in her chair with an amused smile on her face. When she caught Meg looking, she gave a quick shake of her head: *Sorry, you're on your own.*

"Maerlie," said Morgan, after watching their silent exchange, "why don't you tell our dear sister who came calling for her this afternoon?"

"Oh, do you mean that handsome young man with the prince's party? What *was* his name? Winston? Wilhelm?"

"Wilem?" Meg blurted, stepping away from the door. "Wilem came calling for me?"

Both sisters turned slowly back to look at her with predatory smiles.

"Yes, Wilem, *that* was his name. Quite the charmer, wasn't he, Morgan?"

"He certainly was," Morgan said. "He seemed so disappointed to find you not at home, Meg."

95

Meg looked back and forth between them. "What —
what did you tell him? Where did you say I'd gone?"

Morgan's eyes went round and innocent. "Well, that
was quite a quandary, since we had no idea *where* you
were. We had to come up with something, of course,
so we told him you were out riding with your favorite
suitor — what name did we give him, Maerlie?"

"Micah."

"Yes, right, we said you were out with dear Micah and
that we didn't expect you back anytime soon, because out
of all the eager young men pursuing you, this one was
especially handsome and intelligent —"

"And muscular," Maerlie put in.

"Right, and *muscular*, and so we were certain you'd
want to spend as much time as possible in his company. . . ."

Meg stared, unable to think of anything to say. Surely
they were only teasing; surely they would never —

When both of them burst into helpless peals of
laughter, she had her answer. Maerlie was practically crying, she was laughing so hard. Meg felt her face go red
with mingled anger and embarrassment.

"That wasn't funny," she said softly.

"Oh, Meg," Maerlie said, wiping at her eyes. "You had
it coming, for the position you put us in today."

"Then — did he really come calling for me? Or was that a joke, too?"

"Yes, he really came calling," said Morgan. "But we told him you were off seeing to some wedding details for Maerlie and that we didn't know when you'd be back. Of course, it was harder to convince Mother —"

"*Mother* was looking for me, too?" This was awful.

"You were gone for hours, Meg!" said Maerlie. "Did you think no one would notice?"

Morgan shook her head. "If Maerlie hadn't argued so passionately on your behalf, I would have told Mother the truth. But instead we told her we'd had an argument and that you went out to take a walk and cool off."

"So we've covered for you with everyone else," Maerlie said, "but I'm afraid you're going to have to tell us where you really were. And to save you some time, I'll say straight out that we will not believe you were merely out for a walk somewhere. Not dressed like that, you weren't."

Meg stood silently, head down, trying to think. What could she say that they'd believe? Maybe it was all right to mention Calen, but that still wouldn't explain her clothing. . . .

At a loss, she looked up to find them staring at her again. Morgan looked angry. Maerlie looked hurt.

"You've always been able to tell us the truth before,

Meg," Maerlie said quietly. "It's obvious you're standing there trying to make something up. Why won't you just tell us? Do you really trust us so little?"

"Don't, Maerlie. Don't say it like that. I do trust you." She hoped Morgan wouldn't notice that her last sentence wasn't exactly directed at both of them.

"But?" asked Morgan.

Meg bit her lip. "But I can't tell you this. I'm sorry."

Morgan and Maerlie looked at each other. Something passed wordlessly between them, and Morgan rose. She touched Meg's hand on the way to the door, and left.

"Can you tell me, Meg?" Maerlie asked once she was gone. "Just me? You know I won't say anything if you don't want me to. Not even to Morgan, although you must know you're hurting her with this secrecy." *Hurting me, too*, Meg could hear her saying beneath the words.

Meg walked over and sank into the chair Morgan had left empty. She closed her eyes to shut out Maerlie's unhappy face and rested her head back against the rich, soft fabric. She wanted to tell. She wanted to throw herself down on the floor with her head in Maerlie's lap and confess everything, to feel her sister's strong hands stroking her hair and hear her calm, wise words making sense of it all. She had always gone to Maerlie with every problem, every pain, every bit of news she'd been bursting to tell, every fear and worry. But this time she knew she couldn't. She held Jakl's life in her hands. She had already risked one friend's life today — that was true, no matter how many times she told herself Jakl would never have hurt Calen — and the instincts that had guided her then, that had convinced her that bringing Calen to the cave was the right thing, those instincts were screaming at her now to be strong, keep silent. *Don't let her in.*

"Gods, what *is* it, Meg?" Maerlie whispered. "Why can't you trust me?"

I can't. I'm sorry. Meg opened her eyes. She suddenly felt very tired. "Please stop. Just stop asking. I can't tell you."

"Meg, please —"

"Can't you please just leave it alone? Why do you need to know so badly?"

Maerlie seemed taken aback. "Because . . . because we're worried about you. *I'm* worried about you. You disappear without a word to anyone, and not for the first time, I might add, and then you show up in those clothes —"

"Why do you have to worry?" Meg leaned over the arm of the chair. "Why must you assume it's something to worry about?"

"Meg —"

"Why can't *you* trust *me*, Maerlie? Why can't you trust me to have this to myself, to take care of it by myself?"

Maerlie didn't say anything. She sat back in the chair and watched Meg's face unhappily.

"All right," she said finally. "I'll stop asking. I do trust you, Meg. And I love you." She folded her hands in her lap and paused, then went on. "But please be careful. Secrets . . . secrets can be dangerous. If you keep them too long, too close, they get bigger. They breed. They come between people, push them apart. And I don't want anything to come between us, Meg. Ever."

But it has, Meg realized sadly. *It's come between us already.* She reached over toward her sister, and Maerlie grasped her hand. "I'll be careful, I promise," Meg said.

Maerlie nodded, releasing Meg's hand, and with visible effort set aside all the other things she clearly still wanted to say. Meg loved her intensely in that moment.

"Well," Maerlie said, a weak but genuine smile tugging at her expression, "I hope you'll at least agree to tell me about Wilem. There must be something to tell — you should see what your face looks like when you hear his name. You go all red and dreamy."

Meg could feel herself blushing even now. It made Maerlie laugh, though — a real laugh — and that made it all right.

"He *is* very handsome, isn't he?" Meg asked. She could see him clearly in her mind, the way he had looked last night in the garden, somehow managing to smile and look serious at the same time.

"So you do fancy him, then," Maerlie said. "I saw the two of you walking together after dinner, and I had to wonder."

"I've never met anyone like him before," Meg admitted. "He makes it hard to think. Did anyone ever make you feel like that? Before your darling prince, I mean."

Maerlie chuckled. "Well, almost — do you remember Cousin Frystan?"

"Oh, no!"

"Yes, I'm afraid so. I don't know what I was thinking. In my defense, this was before he grew the unfortunate beard. It was right after he did so well at the trials, and I was temporarily smitten. All the other girls were so jealous, and he danced with me for every dance at the feast . . . it was absolutely magical, until he tried to kiss me."

"He tried to kiss you?"

"Well, I guess he did kiss me. For a second, I kind of wanted him to, but then . . . ugh. I had to wash my face afterward. He was so — *slobbery*." She shuddered theatrically. Meg laughed.

"But let's not dwell on such unpleasant memories. Tell me more about Wilem! I want to hear everything. Start from the beginning."

"Well, there was no kissing, I'll just say that straight away. Not *yet*, anyway," Meg said, winking rakishly. Oh, the thought of Wilem kissing her . . . it was almost too exciting to even imagine. Almost.

At her sister's continued prodding, Meg drifted delightfully back to the previous night, reliving each moment of their conversation and relaying it faithfully to Maerlie, who was the best audience imaginable. Her heart felt heavy and light at the same time, remembering, the effect of Wilem's face and charm — and gods, that smile — temporarily overshadowing even Jakl's faint warm presence. For a while she was free of thoughts of Calen and spirit cards and dragons and caves and secrets, entirely consumed by the memory of Wilem's beautiful face, his sweet, sad eyes looking deep into her own.

CHAPTER SIX

THE STUDY WAS DIM AND SILENT, but Calen wasn't fooled. He stood in the doorway, squinting nervously into the confines of the room. Lyrimon was in there somewhere. Calen could feel the gyrcat's fiery little eyes staring at him — the familiar malicious weight of them was unmistakable. Calen was not in the mood to be mauled by nearly invisible claws, but he needed to get through the study to reach the library. If he could just figure out where the little beast was hiding, he could probably stay far enough away to be safe. Lyrimon never attacked him openly; even Serek would draw the line at that. He merely waited for Calen to unknowingly wander too close, or sit down on him, or something, and used that as an excuse to lash out in "self-defense."

"I don't have time for this," Calen muttered. He took a step into the room, wincing in anticipation, but nothing happened. He could still feel Lyrimon's glaring eyes upon him, though. He took another step, waited, took another. The hall leading to the library still seemed very far away.

"What exactly are you doing?" Serek's deep voice spoke suddenly from the doorway behind him.

Calen jumped with surprise, but at least managed to stay on his feet this time. Why did everyone insist on sneaking up on him like that? He turned around. Serek was leaning against the door frame, a small pile of books and papers tucked under one arm.

"I am looking for that stupid — uh, for Lyrimon," Calen said. "I know he's in here. I can feel him watching me."

One corner of Serek's mouth turned up slightly. "Oh, he's watching you, all right." He jerked his chin toward the window. Calen whipped his head around to look. Lyrimon was sunning himself idly on the stone wall that ran through the yard. He *was* watching, though. Even from this distance, Calen could see the evil glint in the gyrcat's eyes.

"How do you *do* that?" Calen asked plaintively.

"Do what?"

"*Find* him like that. You always know where he is. You can see him even when he's practically invisible. Why won't you teach me how to do it?"

"Now, what fun would that be?" Serek strode forward into the room and dropped his pile carefully onto his desk.

Calen sighed. Serek was infuriating, but at least he didn't seem angry anymore. The library would have to wait, now, obviously. Lyrimon had probably done him a service by slowing him down; he wouldn't have wanted to try to explain what he was doing in the library if Serek had caught him nosing around in there.

Serek had perched on the edge of his desk and was now favoring Calen with a most disturbingly penetrative stare. Calen shifted but said nothing. Serek was hard to read, and this look could mean anything. Or nothing. He had learned early on that it was usually best to wait at times like these. He just wished he had a wall to lean against or something. He felt horribly exposed and vulnerable, standing in the middle of the room as he was.

"We have some things to discuss, I think," Serek said finally.

"Oh?" Calen asked. He kept waiting.

Serek narrowed his eyes. Then, to Calen's shock, he laughed — a short, harsh bark, but undeniably genuine. "I don't know what it is you're trying so hard to hide from me," he said, "but let me put you at your ease: I don't care. I imagine it has something to do with your friend the princess" — he chuckled — "which your face has just confirmed. But that's not what I want to talk about."

Calen struggled to control his features. How did

Serek know about Meg? And on the heels of that, an even more alarming thought — what else did he know? Serek's face gave away nothing. As usual.

"What — what do you want to talk about?" Calen asked.

"An excellent question. Come over here and sit down." Serek indicated the chair on the far side of his desk. Calen walked around to the chair and sat. Serek continued to stare at him. Calen stared back defiantly. Or at least suspiciously. What was the man *looking* at?

"Do you feel it?" Serek asked finally. "The change?"

What change? Calen almost asked. But he thought he knew. He nodded instead.

Serek eyed him silently for another few seconds, then went on. "I must admit that in recent years I began to fear I had made a mistake about you. Oh, you showed moderate ability, but nothing out of the ordinary, *nothing* like what I'd sensed — or thought I'd sensed — in the beginning, and you lacked the focus and drive required for any kind of serious advancement. I had resigned myself to the probability that you would remain a mediocre student and grow into a mediocre mage, and eventually go off to serve in a minor household somewhere. Nothing to be ashamed of, I suppose, but certainly nothing to be especially proud of, either. I confess that I . . .

106

relaxed somewhat with regard to your training, believing any additional effort would likely be wasted and preferring to focus my energy on my own studies instead.

"In the last day or so, however, I've been forced to reconsider yet again. Something began to seem different about you, and you showed that surprising skill with divination . . . and now, as of this moment, the spark is there — I can sense it strongly, as I haven't since the very beginning. It's as though it's been hidden, or in slumber, and only now has reawakened." He shook his head distractedly. "I don't entirely understand it. I would swear to you that yesterday morning it wasn't there at all."

Calen stared, unsure whether to feel insulted or hopeful or angry or something else entirely. His jaw worked soundlessly, waiting for his brain to supply some sort of intelligent response. Finally he managed, "But —"

Serek silenced him with a glare. "Don't interrupt. I'm not finished. Spark or no spark, I'm not going to waste my time. You've never demonstrated that you can apply yourself consistently and fully to your studies. Perhaps this is my own fault, in part, since I've stopped expecting or requiring the necessary level of dedication from you. But that ends now.

"You have a choice to make. You will swear to me that you will fully commit yourself to the path before

you, working to the absolute best of your ability, pushing yourself to learn and excel and master every challenge I set before you from this moment forward. Or you
will acknowledge that you are not willing to commit the
amount of energy and dedication required, and we will
set about finding you another apprenticeship more suitable to your personality and temperament. You would
always bear the marks you already have, of course, and
there would be safeguards put in place to prevent you
from continuing to practice magic. You would not be the
first apprentice to leave the order; it's rare, but it does
happen. The mage's life is not for everyone."

Serek pulled out his chair and sat down, facing Calen
across the desk. His voice was low and serious, his gaze
level and direct. "The choice is yours, Calen. I will not
bear you any resentment if you choose to leave, but if you
choose to stay, I will not accept anything less than your
full dedication. Think, now, and decide whether you truly
wish to follow this path."

Calen tried to recapture his whirling thoughts, tried
to ignore Serek's heavy gaze and direct his mind where
he wanted it to go. This was crazy. Since the day Serek
had pulled him from the kitchens six years ago, he had
never anticipated any other future than that which lay
before him as a mage's apprentice. A second choice was

not something usually granted. His hand strayed up to trace the small initiate's tattoo under his left eye, given when Serek brought him before the Magistratum to recite the vows of training. He had never bothered to consider whether he *wanted* to be a mage or not; he was a mage's apprentice, and that was that.

He tried to consider it now. *Was* this truly the life he wanted for himself? A mage's life was not an easy life, by any means. A mage in service could have any number of masters during the course of his years, and he would be expected to serve each one faithfully and fully, using his abilities without hesitation in whatever manner required, barring certain forbidden practices no mage would willingly engage in.

There could be a whole new life waiting for him, a future not bound by the walls of a dark study or years of secret tradition or the solitary practice of the difficult mage's arts. No more memorizing useless information, cataloging trivial names and dates and formulas. No more running off on pointless errands or tiptoeing around trying to avoid Lyrimon. No more living with Serek's constant disapproval. Maybe he really wasn't meant for the mage's path; if so, there was no shame in owning up to that fact.

For a second, it was tempting. The dark walls of the

room, the weight of Serek's eyes (and Lyrimon's, *still*, curse him), and the endless years of study that lay before him — all of it seemed to press down relentlessly until the thought of breaking free was infinitely appealing.

But then he thought of the way it felt when he successfully mastered a spell — the way he had felt when reading the spirit cards, the energy flowing through him, the clarity of mind, the rush of power and purpose. He thought of the Erylun book, its countless pages filled with the mysteries of the universe. He thought of all the other books in the library, all the other books that must exist in the world, everything there must be to learn and see and explore and find out — he didn't want to walk away from that, he realized. He wanted to know, wanted to understand. He wanted to learn to control the power he'd had only fleeting glimpses of, wanted to find out what else he could do, how far he could go.

He thought of Meg, and Jakl, and his promise to help her. And he knew he didn't want to walk away from that, either.

He looked up at Serek, meeting that level gaze squarely across the desk. He could feel his spark brightening, even now, feel it burning within him, waiting for him to help it grow into a blazing fire of knowledge and power.

"I'm staying," Calen said quietly.

"Good," said Serek. "Then let's begin."

"Right now?" Calen asked, surprised. Serek merely looked at him, and Calen nodded. "I'm ready."

Serek rose from the desk and began to pace slowly around the room. Calen waited. Rorgson's yellowing skull was back in its usual place at the edge of the desk. It grinned at him silently.

"When I said I had relaxed with regard to your training," Serek said after a minute, "I did not mean to imply that I had neglected it entirely. Everything you've learned so far has been part of the essential grouping of basic skills necessary to any sort of more advanced practice. These must be mastered before one can even attempt anything more serious. So, right now we need to discover which of these you have indeed mastered and which you have not."

Serek stopped pacing and leaned against the far wall. "Candles," he said. "Now."

Calen closed his eyes and emptied his mind. Lighting candles was one of the first acts of magic an apprentice learned; not only was it relatively easy, and a good stepping stone to more difficult magics, but it was also highly practical. Quickly he visualized the candles he wanted to light — two fat, solid cylinders of wax on the desktop, the iron candelabra on the table across the room, the ring of candles set into the simple chandelier hanging from the ceiling. A gentle push, a flicker of mental energy, and he felt them all burst into tiny flames at once. Opening his eyes, he was rewarded by the soft glow emanating from each source of light.

"Good," said Serek. "Now the fireplace."

Same principle, just bigger. Calen reached into himself to draw upon a slightly greater amount of energy. He extended one hand toward the fireplace; not necessary, really, but it helped him to focus. He sent the gathered energy, barely visible as a faint, golden flow of light, out through his fingers across the room and into the small pile of kindling. At the whoosh of the flames, he looked back to Serek expectantly.

"Doors."

Calen smiled; he liked this one. Objects could fairly easily be manipulated to move in ways they were used to moving. He reached out with his mind to the three doors off the study — the main door; the side door, which led to Calen's own small room; the back door, which led out to the yard — and pulled them all shut with one satisfying slam. The candles flickered wildly, then recovered.

"Good," Serek said again. "Now —"

But just then the door to the main hall burst open again, and one of the king's household guards staggered through, panting. "Sorry," he managed between breaths. "Sorry Mage Serek, to — to interrupt —"

"Gods, man, what is it?"

The guard swallowed and seemed to get a better hold on himself. "There's been an accident, an attack — a man wounded. Your skills are required."

Serek was striding toward the door before the guard had finished speaking. "Calen," he said over his shoulder, indicating that Calen should come, too. Serek grabbed a pouch of medicinal herbs and powders hanging on a cord near the door, then took off down the hall on the heels of the guard, who had broken into an unsteady run. Calen leaped from the chair and ran after them. The pleasant warmth of the magic energy from his exercises was driven out by a chill of dread. What had happened? He knew he'd find out soon enough, but he couldn't help imagining various possible scenarios as he ran, unseeing, past the tapestry-lined walls.

The guard led them out toward the main castle gate, where a small crowd was clustered around a figure lying on the grass. The guard who'd fetched them pushed some of the gathered people aside to clear their way. *New uniforms?* Calen thought distractedly as they approached the wounded man. The style was that of the Trelian Royal Guard, but the color was wrong, too dark, sort of a blackish red —

Then he realized it was blood.

He stumbled to a stop as Serek and the house guard dropped to their knees on either side of the fallen man. He appeared to be unconscious. Someone had wrapped thick strips of cloth around his torso, but the blood had soaked through both cloth and what remained of his tunic. Serek swore, tearing open his pouch of medicines.

"We could not stop the bleeding," the house guard said quietly.

"Unwrap the bandages," Serek commanded as he pulled assorted items from the pouch. "I need to see the wound."

The guard paled but began to gently unwrap the sodden cloth. Several people standing nearby turned away. Calen stared, horrified, as the layers of covering came off to reveal an enormous gash across the man's chest. The edges of the wound were dark and angry-looking, and blood continued to well up from within, refusing to congeal.

"What happened?"

The other guards looked at each other uncertainly. "We don't really know," one said, finally. "We were returning from patrol when they set upon us. Bandits, we thought at first, although we'd never expected them this close to the castle. But then something came at us out of the woods. Something . . ." He shook his head. "Some *thing*. I don't even know how to describe it. It was huge, and — wrong." He looked at the other men again, as if for support. "It was no natural creature, sir. None that any of us had ever seen. We think the bandits themselves actually drove it off; at least, it fell back when they did, but not before it took a swipe at Roeg. It seemed only a shallow wound . . . but there was so much blood, and when we reached the gate, he suddenly went white and fell to the ground —"

Serek waved his hand impatiently, silencing the man. "Calen."

Calen swallowed and walked over to kneel beside Serek. This close, he could feel a terrible heat radiating from the fallen guard. He could also see spidery thin red lines in the man's skin, branching out from the wound.

"What's wrong with him?" Calen whispered.

"Don't ask questions," Serek snapped. He handed

several vials to Calen and tossed the pouch with the rest of its contents to the grass. "Find the bloodleaf and terric powder and set the rest aside." Serek closed his eyes and placed his hands a few inches above the man's chest.

The house guard peered uneasily at his comrade. "Can you save him, sir?"

Serek's mouth tightened irritably. "Don't you ask questions, either," he said without opening his eyes.

The guard opened his mouth again — perhaps just to apologize, unless he was a particularly stupid man — but at a warning glance from Calen he shut it without speaking and sat back on his heels. Calen nodded. Once Serek made it clear that he didn't want to be interrupted, it was very, *very* unwise to say anything else. That danger averted, Calen hurriedly turned his attention to the vials. The bloodleaf was easy to recognize. The large red-tipped leaves were wrapped tightly around one another inside the glass container. The terric powder was a bit harder — it looked a lot like snowdust, and confusing the two would be extraordinarily bad, although he couldn't remember exactly why. Thank the gods Serek hadn't asked him to identify anything too difficult or, even worse, suggest which medicines to use. Memorizing reagents and their uses and effects was one of those things Calen had always considered a waste of time. Why memorize something you could just look up in a book or chart whenever you needed to? Clearly he'd never really thought it through before. The man on the ground — Roeg, the other guard had called him — didn't exactly have time to wait for Serek to page through reference material in his study.

Calen found the terric and held the two vials out to Serek, who was muttering to himself as he moved his hands slowly through the air above his patient. The mage was gathering information, trying to determine the nature of the injury — Calen could just see the faint white tendrils of energy flowing between Serek's hands and the wound. The man groaned and tossed his head, although he still didn't seem to be awake. Serek opened his eyes and frowned. Looking up, he picked out two of the other royal guards who were standing around watching. "You and you. Come here and hold him down." Glancing at the house guard, he added, "You, too. What we're about to do is going to be painful, and it's essential that he remain still."

He noticed Calen holding out the vials. "When I tell you, start sprinkling the terric into the wound. There's a poison at work, and if we don't stop it, nothing I do will save this man." Calen nodded, tucked the bloodleaf

vial between his knees, and then carefully opened the terric powder. He could smell its acrid odor and tried desperately to remember if this was one of those powders
that was dangerous to inhale. Probably Serek would have
warned him, but if it was something he was already supposed to have learned . . . Calen breathed discreetly yet
forcefully out through his nose and held the vial as far
away as he could.

The guards Serek had selected — one appeared to be
the patrol unit's captain — were all in place, one holding
the man's legs and the other two each gripping an arm
and shoulder. They nodded at Serek to confirm that they
were ready. Serek held out his hands again over Roeg's
chest. Serek didn't speak, but Calen felt the hair on his
arms and neck standing up in response to the sudden
flow of energy. He'd seen Serek heal minor ailments
before, but this felt different, not like healing energy at
all. Calen let his eyes unfocus, a trick he'd discovered
long ago that would sometimes let him better "see" a
spell at work. Different kinds of spells involved different
kinds of magic energy — sometimes he could just feel
the difference, as a person might note a difference in the
weight of the air before a storm — but he'd found that
color was usually the best clue to puzzling out something
Serek was doing. This wasn't something Serek had ever

taught him — on the contrary, Serek had never even mentioned the significance of colors relating to magic, probably because he didn't want Calen using the colors as a shortcut. Why teach your apprentice a shortcut when you could make him waste hours studying the long way around?

The man groaned again and tried to move, but the other guards held him fast. Another came forward to grip his head as it tried to turn. *Red,* Calen thought suddenly, as images of energy began to take shape at the edge of his vision. Why would it be red? Healing energy was green, or golden . . .

"Now, Calen," said Serek. Calen jerked himself back to the task at hand. He tipped the vial and began sprinkling the thick powder onto the exposed wound. As the first particle touched Roeg, he began to scream. The guards held him tight, but it was clear that he was trying to arch his back and pull away from the pain. Calen glanced at Serek, wondering if he should stop, but Serek remained focused on his own efforts. Well, he'd warned them it was going to hurt. Calen swallowed and kept pouring. The man's screams became even more intense. The other men looked at each other nervously. Calen didn't blame them. He felt sickened by it himself. The guard seemed to be in such agony.

Only Serek seemed unaffected, and Calen couldn't help but admire his focus. *Like stone*, he thought again.

The man's voice was beginning to go hoarse. One of the guards spoke hesitantly. "Please, Mage Serek. Can't you stop now? The pain, it's killing him."

Serek didn't respond. Calen doubted he had even heard. Apparently the guard had the same thought, because he swallowed and tried again. "Please —"

"Be quiet!" Calen hissed. He understood the guard's concern, but distracting Serek certainly wasn't the answer. They had asked for his help, and now they had to accept it, whether they understood what he was doing or not. The guard glared angrily at Calen but did not speak again.

Finally Serek looked up and told Calen to stop pouring. Calen tipped the vial up immediately, with relief. The man's screams tapered off to exhausted whimpers.

"Now," said Serek, "take three leaves and lay them across the wound, covering as much as possible."

Calen winced as the first leaf touched the man's flesh, but there was no reaction from the guard. Either the bloodleaf didn't hurt or Roeg had passed out completely again.

"Will he be all right?" the house guard asked.

Serek looked down at the leaf-covered gash. Roeg seemed to be breathing easier, but the edges of the wound peeking out from behind the leaves still looked swollen and unhealthy to Calen's eyes. "I don't know," Serek said finally.

The captain sighed heavily. "I've got to make my report to the king."

Serek nodded and rose to his feet. "I'm coming with you."

The captain gave orders for the wounded man to be carried to the infirmary, then he and Serek started toward the castle. As the guards set about their work, Calen gathered up Serek's supplies and returned them carefully to the pouch. He knew better than to try to follow or ask any questions. Serek would tell him more later, or he wouldn't. In the meantime, he might as well use this opportunity to get back to the library and start his dragon research. It was strange — only a day ago, he knew he would have been sullen and furious at being left behind yet again. But today everything was different. Suddenly he felt invested in his own future in a way he'd never experienced before. He had a purpose — two, actually. He was going to prove to Serek and himself that he could master whatever challenges Serek set before him and become the powerful, successful apprentice he knew he could be.

And he was going to find out everything he could about dragons for Meg.

Yesterday he had been alone, and not particularly happy with his lot.

Today he had a friend and a secret. And a spark.

CHAPTER SEVEN

MEG SAT AT HER DRESSING TABLE and began to brush the tangles from her hair. Now that her errand-girl clothes were safely bunched into a ball and stuffed in the back of her wardrobe, her face was clean, and she was dressed more appropriately (in the pale blue gown with rose satin trim that Morgan had given her for her last birthday), she supposed she looked a little more like herself again. Even if sometimes lately it was hard to remember which version of herself was the real one.

Maerlie came up behind her and took the brush, gently working it through the hard-to-reach parts in the back. Meg watched her in the mirror. At seventeen, with her dark hair caught up in an elegant knot below the thin gold circlet all the girls wore, Maerlie was beginning to look every inch the respectable future queen. She was a woman now, Meg realized — no longer the playful girl who would wrestle her sisters on the floor or hide giggling behind the bed as Nan Vera came to collect them for tea. She hadn't lost her warmth or her mischievous smile, but somehow it was clear that she had put certain childhood games and activities behind her. *Will that happen to me, too?* Meg wondered gloomily. She didn't want to grow up into someone else. She didn't want Maerlie to, either.

A sharp tug on her hair interrupted her melancholy thoughts.

"Ow!"

Maerlie smirked but didn't look up to meet her eye in the mirror. She took up another section of Meg's hair and pulled it tight, twisting it together with the first section.

"Maer, that hurts!"

"Oh, quiet. Do you want to look ravishing at dinner or not?"

"Not. Stop pulling."

"Not even for your precious Wilem?"

"Very funny. You know he's not . . ." She trailed off, watching her sister's smirk stretch out into a grin. "He is? He's coming to dinner tonight? But I thought, I mean, he wasn't . . ." Meg closed her mouth in disgust. Did she have to turn into a babbling idiot at the mere mention of his name? Groaning, she pressed her hands to her face, which she could feel flushing with heat even now. "What's happening to me, Maer? I never used to get all moon-eyed over a pretty face. Remember that ambassador from Black Island who came up a year or two ago? He had those two sons with him, and they were by far the handsomest boys I've ever seen. Finer-looking than Wilem, even. And they didn't have this kind of effect on me."

Maerlie paused in her hairdressing. "I think that was closer to three years ago, Meg. At least. And that probably makes all the difference. When the Black Island boys were here, you were only eleven. They saw you as a child, and that's probably how you saw yourself. But you're a young woman now. More of an age to notice young men, and to be noticed — fourteen's not too young for a betrothal, you know. Wilem sees you as a young woman, maybe even a potential match."

Meg tried to ignore the way her heart lurched at that. Maerlie looked at her in the mirror. "I thought you liked the way he made you feel."

Meg considered. "I did. I do. Mostly. I mean, he chose *me* to walk with after dinner, and it was so . . . I felt . . . but he also makes me feel — not myself. I get all tongue-tied and stupid. That's not who I want to be."

"Well, I imagine most of that's only nervousness, and in time you'd be able to relax around him and be more yourself. For now maybe you should just try to enjoy it."

She smirked again as she went back to work on Meg's hair. "Who knows? Father might eventually marry you off to some ugly old nobleman, and then you'll be pining away for the days when a man made you feel tongue-tied and stupid."

She meant it as a joke, although they both knew something like that was a definite possibility.

They didn't speak for a time. Maerlie finished Meg's hair and stood back to admire her work. Meg had to admit it looked lovely. She was never able to style her own hair like that.

Maerlie stood beside her in the mirror for a moment, then abruptly leaned down and hugged her. "Don't worry so much about everything," she said softly, pressing her cheek against Meg's face. "Soon enough we'll all be grown up and find ourselves with more responsibility than we ever wanted."

Meg hugged her sister back tightly. "I know," she whispered. Maerlie's words suddenly made her think of what Calen had told her about the spirit cards. That was something else she could share, she decided. *Should* share. They both had a right to know what was going on, after all. Maybe together she and Maerlie could get their parents to talk to them about it. Before she could open her mouth to speak, however, there was a tap at the door.

They both turned at the sound. Then Meg noticed that her sister's grin was back. She looked at the older girl, a sinking feeling in the pit of her stomach.

Maerlie's grin widened even farther at her look. "Oh, didn't I tell you?" she said innocently. "Wilem asked if he could escort you to dinner this evening. That must be him now."

The early part of the evening meal had the quality of a half-remembered dream; Meg vaguely recalled engaging in polite conversation with various members of the small dining party and seemed to remember the fish tasting spicy and delicious. In addition to Wilem, her parents had invited Sen Eva and Sen Salyn R'ambe, another advisor to the Kragnir throne, and the talk had been lively and informative. At least, she thought it had been. Most of the details were fuzzy. Wilem had seemed interested only in her, and the force of his unwavering attention had been like a spear of white-hot light, pinning her across the table from him and throwing everyone and everything else into dim shadow by comparison.

Until she'd heard about the attack on the royal guard that afternoon. That dire news had eclipsed even Wilem's shining presence. To think that their soldiers could be set upon so close to home! Maerlie apologized quietly when she realized Meg hadn't known what had happened, but Meg couldn't be entirely sorry that her sister hadn't told her; it had been so nice to just talk about boys and kissing and lighter things, once the secret-keeping discussion was over. Still, it was not good for a princess to be uninformed about something so important, she supposed. Everyone else in the castle already knew all about it, since that poor man had collapsed right at the gates and gossip flew faster than falcons around here. Unfortunately, gossip also showed little regard for separating facts from fancy. What everyone "knew" was contradictory and confusing in its variety. Meg wanted real answers, but no one seemed to have anything other than guesses.

"Could it have been a dragon?" Morgan asked.

Meg's heart stopped in her chest, but King Tormon only shook his head. "A dragon would more likely use flame than claws, and even so, the men would have recognized a dragon. All of them swear this was no creature any of them had ever seen."

"But perhaps —"

Their father held up his hands. "Please, Morgan. This speculation serves no one. I do not want rumors of dragons to be added to those already in circulation."

Sen Eva spoke from across the table. "You speak

of rumors, King Tormon; is it possible your men were simply influenced by the tales being spread by merchants and traders? We've all heard of the fantastic stories going around. Surely your soldiers have heard them as well."

"If I didn't personally know the men involved, if they hadn't been able to supply such disturbing detail, I might be tempted to agree with you," said the king. "But these are experienced fighting men, trained to recognize known dangers and evaluate unknown ones. They all agreed this creature was something foreign. Enormous, black as night, with pointed horns of uneven length, and of course, the poison ... Well, I cannot pretend I am not concerned. But that doesn't mean we're speaking of ghosts and monsters out of tales, either. I have soldiers out in numbers, searching the area where the attack occurred. I have no doubt that we will discover what manner of creature roams about and prevent it from causing further harm. At the very least, my men will not be taken by surprise again." He turned his attention back to his meal, a subtle signal that he wished to end the discussion.

Meg's mother smoothly turned the conversation to other topics, asking Sen Eva and Sen Salyn more questions of Kragnir life and local customs, and soon the table was humming again with many smaller exchanges between table companions. Wilem smiled reassuringly at Meg, and she could not help but smile back. She tried to follow her parents' example and put the matter of the attack aside for now. There was little that could be done at the moment other than to pray for the wounded man and hope that the soldiers were successful in their search. At least they had quickly dismissed the idea that it had been a dragon. Of course she knew it hadn't been *her* dragon, but the last thing she needed right now was some kind of fevered dragon hunt. She didn't think anyone would happen upon Jakl's cave by accident, but she didn't really want to put that to the test. Besides, she was sure he left the cave sometimes. That thought gave her a moment of panic — what if Jakl encountered that creature? Meg took a sip of wine while she recomposed her expression and tried to make herself relax. *He's a dragon, you idiot. He can take care of himself.* Still, she reached out toward him, trying to sense his presence more strongly. This far away, he was just faint warmth; she'd have to go and visit him again tomorrow, just to make sure he was all right.

After dinner, Meg found herself escorted once more along the garden path, her arm delightfully linked through Wilem's. The night was cool and lovely, and many of the increasing number of castle guests were also out enjoying the gardens. Poor Nan Vera was trying to keep up with Maurel, who was skipping joyfully ahead into the hedge maze.

Wilem had cast his charming spell upon her again at the meal, tying her tongue and brain into senseless knots, and only now did the cool air seem to be restoring her to some sense of equilibrium. She struggled to take advantage of it. *Come now, Meg,* she told herself sternly. *Think of something intelligent to say before he falls asleep from boredom.* "I was sorry to have missed you this afternoon, Wilem. My sisters told me you had come to call."

"I was sorry to have missed you as well. I understand the demands of a wedding, however. The men seem to have it easier, but I've been assisting Prince Ryant with such preparations as have been necessary."

"Will you be standing with him, at the ceremony?" Mother had begun planning the arrangement for the bride's court as soon as Jorn had delivered the offer of betrothal, but the groom's court was planned by the groom's family.

Wilem nodded. "As the prince has no brothers, I am honored to say that he has chosen me to be his second."

Meg couldn't help wondering if Wilem could ever say the word *brother* without thinking of his own. That wasn't the sort of thing she could actually ask him, of

131

course. She gave his arm a little squeeze, though, just in case. He looked down at her and gave her another of his sweet, sad smiles.

"Are you —" he began, then stopped, looking out suddenly beyond her, into the night.

"What is it?" she asked, but then she heard it, too. Cries of alarm, distant, but growing closer. Everyone in the garden seemed to be aware of it now; some began walking in the direction of the commotion, heads craning, others stood in place, talking in low voices and looking worried.

Meg stepped forward to follow those walking toward the shouts, but Wilem's arm was still linked with hers, and he hadn't moved. She looked back at him. "Wilem, will you come with me? I want to find out what's happening," she said.

"No, Princess. You should stay here. It could be dangerous."

She fixed him with one of the steely glares that had such satisfying effect on Calen. "Well, yes, Wilem. People are shouting. I'm sure it is dangerous. That's why I want to know what's going on. Are you coming with me or not?"

"Meglynne —"

Suddenly a horrible, piercing scream tore through

the night around them. Wilem's face went white; Meg felt the blood draining from her own as well. Her hand gripped Wilem's arm like a vise.

"What is that?" she whispered.

He could only shake his head silently. Around them, the other people in the garden began running for the castle doors just as several castle guards came running out. They saw Meg and approached quickly.

"Your Highness, please accompany us indoors at once," the lead guard said briskly. Meg nodded reluctantly. Normally she would have resisted being whisked away like a helpless child, but that scream had completely unnerved her.

The guard looked to Wilem. "You, as well, sir, if you please." Wilem looked torn but seemed to decide that it was best to honor the guard's request. He took Meg's arm again, and together they hurried toward the castle. The guards followed immediately behind.

There was another scream, closer this time. It seemed to vibrate in the air around them. Meg glanced back over her shoulder and gasped, stumbling to a stop. An enormous dark shape was visible past the trees that lined the royal gardens.

"What is that?" Meg whispered again. Her question came out sounding more like a whimper, and she struggled to pull herself together. She was not going to collapse in terror like some ridiculous coward.

The lead guard swallowed and forced his eyes back to Meg. "Please, Your Highness."

Before she could move, something burst out of the entrance to the hedge maze behind them. The guards, obviously jumpy by now, whipped their swords around to face this new threat. Meg almost laughed when she realized it was only Nan Vera, until she saw the woman's face. Nan Vera staggered forward, waving the swords away as if they were flies. "Your sister," she cried, "she's still in the maze — I can't find her. . . ."

"Maurel!" Meg cried. Her own fear forgotten, she lunged toward the maze, only to have Wilem pull her back.

"Meglynne, no!" he said. Two of the guards ran off through the maze entrance. "The guards will find her. You need to go inside."

Meg shared an agonized glance with Nan Vera. Then she pulled loose from Wilem's grip and launched herself at the entrance. Someone swore behind her and she knew they'd be following, but she dashed ahead, hoping to lose them in the first few turns of the maze. The guards would never find Maurel in here; they wouldn't even know how to look for her. She could hear them faintly, calling

Maurel's name. *Fools*. Maurel would only think she was in trouble and work all the harder at remaining hidden.

After several turns, Meg forced herself to stop. There were no sounds of pursuit directly behind her; now she had to focus on finding her sister. She looked around, frowning. Once she had known the maze almost as well as Maurel did now, but that had been a long time ago. With a start, she realized that she wasn't even entirely sure which turns she had taken so far. Meg fought the urge to panic. It didn't matter. Maurel would know the way out. She just had to find her.

She started walking again, quickly, her feet nearly silent on the soft path of dirt and hedge needles. The tall hedges blocked most of the sound from outside the maze. It was like a separate world, self-contained and indifferent to what went on beyond its borders. Lanterns hung from poles at long intervals, creating pools of light in the otherwise dark passages. Meg looked up. The moon was large in the sky tonight, nearly full, but even so its light seemed unable to penetrate deep into the maze. The moon was the symbol of the Hunter god, the dark consort of the bright Goddess, who ruled the day. Most people preferred to make their prayers to her, since the Hunter was more inclined to justice than to mercy. Still, Meg thought she would take whatever help she could.

Besides, I'm not asking for mercy. She closed her eyes and sent a quick, silent prayer up to the moon. *Tonight, I'm a hunter, too. Please, if you can, help guide my steps so I can bring my sister safely home.*

When the passage came to a fork, Meg hesitated only a second, then turned to the right. She dug a line in the ground with her foot, so she'd know which way she'd chosen if she circled back this way. She continued to walk quickly, searching for signs of her sister and straining to hear the sound of footsteps other than her own. Any time she had a choice of path, she chose without thinking, stopping only to make her mark upon the ground.

Suddenly another of those terrible screams tore through the darkness, close enough that the shock and force of it made her stumble into the hedge wall beside her. She sank to the ground, barely aware of the needles that scratched her arms and face, for the moment unable to move or even think coherently. Her mind couldn't seem to focus on anything other than the one repeating thought that it was close, it was very close now; that thing, whatever it was, was very close and possibly getting closer and closer and closer and closer —

Meg dug her fingernails into her arm, using the pain to break herself out of her spiraling panic. She couldn't remember ever feeling this afraid before in her life. Something about that sound was so . . . *wrong*. What kind of creature made a sound like that?

The silence that followed the last echoes of the scream was oppressive. The small sounds of her feet against the path as she forced herself to stand again seemed to ring out like the bells of noontime. *It can't hear you*, Meg told herself angrily. But how did she know? Maybe it could. But she couldn't cower in the dirt forever, regardless. She had to find Maurel. She made herself step forward. When nothing darted out of the darkness to kill her, she took another step. She kept going until she came to a T in the maze. Left or right? The task of choosing suddenly seemed beyond her. She looked down the left-hand passage, at another featureless green walkway. There was nothing to indicate that this path was better than any other. Sighing, she turned to the right. And there, at the far end of a lengthy green-walled passage, she saw a flash of red.

Afraid to call out, she nevertheless found her mobility again and raced down the long tunnel, arriving just in time to see another flash of color vanish around another corner up ahead. It had to be Maurel; no one else selected clothing of quite that startling a shade, and certainly no one else would be dashing through the maze right now other than the guards, whose uniforms were uniformly blue and gold and gray.

Meg lunged around the next turn and then the next, whereupon she emerged into a long straightaway that clearly did not contain her sister. She spun around, saw the narrow, backward-angled passage she had missed; and continued running. This wasn't going to work, she realized; Maurel could easily outrun her and had the additional advantage of knowing where she was going. Meg lurched to a stop and struggled to quiet her gasping breath so she could listen. Several quick footsteps and then silence — Maurel must have stopped when Meg's own footsteps ceased. There was no help for it; she was going to have to call out while her sister was still in earshot.

"Maurel!" More than a whisper, less than a shout. "Maurel, please! It's Meg!"

"Meg!" Another quick series of running steps and then Maurel appeared, coming from the direction Meg had already been. She ran up and bounced to a stop, not the slightest bit out of breath. "Why didn't you say it was you? I thought —" She stopped and stepped closer, lowering her voice even further. "I thought you were the monster. Did you hear it? Did you hear it screaming?"

Meg dropped to one knee and pulled her sister into a quick, relieved hug, then pushed her away again in irritation. "Of course I heard it. That's why I came in here after you, you idiot. They were trying to take us all inside to safety, but Nan Vera said you ran away from her and she couldn't find you."

"Oh," said Maurel. She half gasped in sudden understanding. "Is that why the guards are in here, too?"

"Yes, of course." She took Maurel's hand firmly in her own and stood up. "Now they're probably wandering around lost, thanks to you." Meg chose not to mention the additional guards who must have followed when she ran into the maze herself. She looked up and down the passage doubtfully. "I think I might be lost, myself. What were you thinking?"

Maurel starting walking, pulling Meg along. "You're not lost. I'll show you," she said. She looked up at Meg, not seeming to even need to glance ahead to know which way to turn. "And I didn't mean to run away from Nan Vera," she said. "Well, at first I did, but that was just for fun. I was right behind her practically the whole time. But then we heard the monster, and I was so scared . . ." She looked away, all lightheartedness gone. "I jumped right into the hedges. I guess I thought maybe if I hid in there, it couldn't find me. By the time I felt okay to come out, Nan Vera was gone. I didn't even hear her calling me."

She had stopped walking, still looking down and away. Meg reached over and touched her face, tracing one of the scratches the hedges must have made. "It's all right to be scared, Maurel," she said. "The sound of that thing screaming was the scariest thing I've ever heard. I'll tell you a secret, if you promise not to tell anyone."

Maurel looked up, hopeful. Her eyes were blurry with unshed tears. Meg whispered, "I was so scared, I fell down. Right into the hedges and down onto the ground. I bet I've got scratches just like yours. Maybe even worse."

Sniffling, Maurel examined Meg's face. She nodded soberly. "You ripped your dress, too. And it's dirty." She looked down at her own dress, which was in a similar state. "Mother's going to be mad at us."

Meg smiled. "I think Mother is just going to be glad to see us safely home. Now, come on. You said you knew how to get out of this crazy place."

Maurel smiled back and quickened her pace, pulling harder on Meg's arm. "The entrance is just around here," she said, her normal bounciness back in her voice as well as her step. "Do you think the guards came back out already? I'd feel a little bad if they're still walking around in there. They probably should have taken a copy of the map."

Meg stared at her sister. "There's a map? To the hedge maze?"

"Sure," said Maurel, surprised. "Didn't you know? It's in the library. I'll show you." They turned the corner and there was the entrance, wide and welcoming and right where Maurel had said it would be. She chattered on, literally bouncing now, punctuating her words with little jumps along the path. "Of course, it's more fun to find your own way, but still it's probably good that —" She glanced up, her eyes growing huge and frightened as she froze, staring. Meg looked up to follow her sister's gaze.

The monster was in the courtyard.

It was very large. It had four squat legs, thick with dark knotted muscle, but most of its bulk was its massive body hulking just inside the row of delicate thistle trees that lined the outer edge of the royal garden. The moon's light seemed to slide right off it, leaving it cloaked in shadow and darkness, but what little detail Meg could see was far more than enough. Two thick horns, one larger than the other, stretched out and upward from either side of its wide head, each ending with an evil-looking hooked point. That head, thank the gods, was facing slightly away from them, but not so much that Meg couldn't see the way its narrow eyes seemed to glow with a sickly red light. It moved with an eerie silence; nothing that enormous — and certainly nothing that could scream the way it did — should be able to move so quietly, but it didn't make a sound as it slunk slowly among the trees. It twisted its head from side to side as though looking for something. *Looking for dinner?* Meg couldn't help wondering. The thought made her want to cry and throw up at the same time.

Meg managed to pull her eyes away for a second to look longingly at the straight, inviting path that led from the maze entrance to the inner courtyard steps. Several guards stood grimly at the top of those steps. Too far away to help in time if the monster should turn and see them. It was much closer to the hedge maze than the castle.

As she watched, one of the guards turned slightly and noticed her. His eyes grew wide with surprise and then darted quickly toward the monster, as if to be sure she knew it was there. As if she could have missed it! She nearly rolled her eyes at him in exasperation. The guard — it was the same one who had spoken to her earlier, to convince her to go inside — stared at her helplessly. They both knew there was nothing he or the others could do.

Moving slowly and oh so silently, Meg pulled Maurel back against her and reached around with her free hand to cover her sister's mouth. Maurel probably would have screamed by now if she were going to, but Meg did not care to take a chance at this particular moment in time. It hadn't heard them talking as they approached, but that didn't mean it wouldn't hear them now without the hedge walls to muffle any sound they made. Meg swallowed and then, pulling her sister along with her, backed deeper into the maze until they reached a point beyond the monster's line of sight.

Meg desperately wanted to run, but there was nowhere to go; the maze had only the one exit. She looked down at her sister; Maurel was staring up at her, terrified. *Expecting me to know what to do,* Meg realized. *And I have no idea.*

Maurel was trembling. Meg sank to the ground and hugged her sister tight against her. And tried to think. There were only two choices, really. Wait here, hoping the monster didn't see or smell or otherwise sense them and that eventually it would just go away, or be driven away, or be killed by a great horde of deadly royal soldiers and chopped into tiny, harmless pieces. Or try to leave the maze and get inside the castle without it seeing them.

She couldn't really imagine trying to sneak out past that thing. She looked up at the hedge wall across from them. Too thick to push through; Maurel had managed to squeeze herself into the hedges before, but even she couldn't get all the way in and then out the other side. Toward the middle the ancient branches were just too wide and strong. Maybe if they'd had a knife or something, but of course, they didn't.

Another dreadful scream tore through the night, far worse than any of the others — it was so *close*! Meg and her sister both clamped their hands tight against their ears. The force of the sound was like a sword thrust deep inside Meg's head; it hurt, it *hurt*, and it wasn't until the dire echoes finally began to fade away that she realized both of them were screaming along with it. Maurel seemed to realize it at the same time. They snapped their mouths shut and stared, horrified, first at each other and then up over the edge of the hedges closest to the entrance as the now-ominous silence stretched out for several long, terrifying seconds. And then the monster's hideous head swung slowly into view. Staring down at them with its impossible glowing red eyes.

For a moment none of them moved. Then Meg saw the creature's chest expand with an intake of air and she had just enough time to shout, "Cover your ears!" to Maurel and slap her hands back over her own before another gut-wrenching wave of sound crashed over them. It was slightly better having been prepared, but not by much — especially since the latest scream was accompanied by a blast of the monster's unspeakably foul breath. Meg didn't want to imagine what it might have been eating. Staring up at its immense presence, she had a short, stupid moment of relief as she thought, *Well, at least it's too big to fit through the maze entrance.* And then it smashed directly through the outer hedge wall, and suddenly Meg was staring at several long, red-tipped talons attached to one of the monster's misshapen five-toed feet, which was now close enough for her to reach out and touch if she wanted to.

Maurel was moaning softly beside her. The monster was moving slowly, either because it saw no need to hurry or because that's just how it moved. Meg prayed it was the latter. She groped for her sister's hand, found it, held it tight, and whispered fiercely, "Get ready, Maurel. We have to run. We have to run right now." Maurel's moans didn't change, but Meg just had to hope she had heard. Or at least that she'd be able to drag her sister along with her. She lunged to her feet, yanking Maurel up and launching them both past the creature's front leg. Its head jerked back in surprise and then snapped forward — not slowly now, she noted with sick dismay — but Meg ran on, directly toward it, pulling Maurel beside her and then pushing her onward, ducking under the barely existent neck and out the other side before the creature could twist its head around. The hedges were now an impediment as it tried to turn to follow them. They ran out through the maze entrance and flew along the blessedly clear, wide path. And nearly collided with the palace guard who, it appeared, had been ready to attempt a rescue after all. Just a little too late.

Meg heard the hedges tearing behind them. She kept running, past the startled soldiers, pulling Maurel on relentlessly, up the inner courtyard steps and into the castle. She wasn't once tempted to stop and look back.

CHAPTER EIGHT

CALEN SAT ON THE OLD HALF-WALL near the small gate, swinging his feet against the stones and watching for a familiar face. He hadn't seen Meg in several days; security had been tight, to say the least, since the appearance of the monstrous creature in the royal garden, and she had been unable to find a suitable pretext for slipping away unsupervised. At least, that's what her note had indicated, though Calen wouldn't have been surprised if she just hadn't *wanted* to go anywhere on her own. From the tales he'd heard from servants and some of the soldiers, she and her little sister had nearly been killed. Calen found himself looking over his shoulder half the time after just *hearing* the story — he wouldn't blame Meg if she was frightened of leaving the castle after actually having lived it.

He had managed to miss the entire thing, for which he was profoundly grateful. Serek had been long in conference with the king and queen, and then stayed by the side of the wounded soldier late into the night, studying the continued effects of the poison and trying to ease the man's pain as much as possible. That had left Calen free to begin his dragon research undisturbed — except by Lyrimon, who, after twice startling Calen so badly that he nearly fell off the ladder, found himself forcibly evicted from the library with the door slammed in his furry, annoying little face. Calen's arms still showed the scars of that encounter, but it had been worth it.

He squinted up at the sun. Where was Meg? He pulled her note out of his sleeve and checked it again, to make sure he hadn't misremembered the time. The note had come by way of Lammy, who demanded a coin for his trouble, and had been signed by "Mellie" in a rough script that Calen suspected bore little resemblance to the princess's normal handwriting. He had been relieved to receive it. Not just because he wanted to see his friend again, but because he needed to tell her what he had discovered in his research regarding Jakl.

Soon.

Finally, he saw her dirt-smudged face appear among the passing servants and other castle folk. He jumped down from the half-wall and walked over to meet her.

"I'm sorry to be late," she said. "Maerlie made me repeat every promise I made to her a hundred times before she'd let me go."

"You told her where you were going?" he asked, surprised.

"No," she said, falling into step beside him as they headed for the gate. "We have — an understanding. I told her I had something very important I needed to do and swore that I would be very careful and not place myself in any danger." She flashed a grin at him. "And that I wouldn't be alone."

"Oh, so I'm your bodyguard now, is that it?"

"That's right. So don't let anything kill me, or you'll have Maerlie to answer to."

"She can't be nearly as difficult to deal with as you are," he said. "All your pushing and punching and the like."

"Huh. That's what you think." She looked up at him again, smiling. "I'm so glad you've left behind all that 'Your Highness' nonsense. Sometimes it gets so tiring."

Calen laughed. "Sure. Everyone bowing and doing everything you say all the time. Must be awful."

She shook her head at him. "You'd be surprised. Outside of my immediate family, no one ever sees me as a person. Just a princess. Royal daughter number three."

They stopped talking as they passed by the guard at the gate — not someone Calen knew by name today. Calen was glad for the chance to adjust his thoughts. He

149

felt a little stupid. Again. It had never occurred to him that Meg might have wanted a friend as badly as he had.

"So — how are you?" Calen asked after a moment. "I mean, are you all right? You know, since the, um, thing. And everything."

Meg nodded. "Yes. I think so." She took a big breath and let it out slowly. "It was terrible. That creature. I thought it was going to kill both of us. And those screams . . ." She glanced at him. "Well, you must have heard them."

He shook his head. She stared.

"How is that possible? Were you off the castle grounds?"

"No. In Serek's library. I think it must be magically enhanced to block out sound. Once I closed the door, it was absolutely silent in there the whole evening. I didn't even know anything had happened until the next morning."

"Well, that's probably fortunate. The sounds were . . . just horrible. I can't begin to describe it." She took another breath. "In any case, we were lucky, and it didn't touch us. We both got back inside, and then the soldiers killed it."

"Is it true that you ran right between its legs?"

Her mouth couldn't seem to decide whether to smile or smirk. "Not really. More like under its neck."

Calen could only shake his head again. "Gods, Meg. I think you're the bravest person I've ever known." Not that that was such a big sampling, but still.

She laughed. "Hardly. I was so scared I could barely think."

"But to run right toward it —"

"There was no other choice. It would have torn us apart if we had stayed where we were."

Calen felt his face go a little green. Meg must have noticed, because she quickly moved on. "Anyhow, it's done now, and the creature is dead, so there's nothing else to worry about. I'm just glad I could finally get away today. Poor Jakl must think I've forgotten him entirely!"

"I'm glad, too. I have some things to tell you."

She looked at him, studying his expression. "Tell me."

Now it was his turn to take a deep breath. They had reached the meadow and were getting close to the edge of the forest. Calen fought the urge to turn his face up to the warm sun and kept an eye out for ill-natured rocks instead. He took a quick moment to organize his thoughts.

He had not been disappointed with the wealth of information available in Mage Fredrin's library — his biggest obstacle so far, other than getting to and from the library without being caught, had been choosing which references to pursue. The Erylun had a wonderful summary of information on dragons, and it had taken him several visits just to finish scanning through it. Most of it was fascinating but not immediately useful: common sizes and colors, various mages' historic confrontations with specific dragons, uses of dragon scales in spellcasting, and so on. Apparently dragons were highly resistant to magic, or mage magic at least, which was probably good to know. There had been some information about growth rates, which indicated that Meg was going to have to find another place for Jakl very soon, probably before another month went by. And then he had finally found an entry on something called linking.

"All right," he began. "The good news is that you were not imagining things regarding your connection with Jakl. You really are sensing his feelings. And he should be beginning to sense yours, if he's not already doing so."

She nodded, her eyes guarded. "What's the bad news?"

"It's not — it's not *bad* news, exactly. Just, um —"

"Calen."

"Right. Okay. This connection that you have, it's called linking. Dragons usually link with other dragons, if they link at all — many don't — but sometimes they can be led to link with humans instead. Hundreds of years ago, there were people who regularly stole baby dragons from their nests and attempted to link with them. Actually, I think this might be the source of some of the legends we have today — I found a whole book of those, mostly nursery stories, and you probably heard some of them yourself when you were little — those tales of people enslaved by dragons, like that one about the woodcutter's son who goes off and . . ." He noticed Meg's impatient stare, which seemed to be deepening toward more of a glower, and skipped ahead. "Well, anyway, those people who stole the babies, depending on how successful they were, either they raised the dragons into a sort of symbiotic partnership or, uh, the dragons killed them."

"Oh."

"But you're definitely past the stage where Jakl would have killed you if he were going to. So don't worry about that."

She looked at him in exasperation. "So *what's the bad news?*"

"Well, so you're linked with Jakl, right? Somehow you managed to do whatever needed to be done to forge the connection without, um, getting killed, and so now the link will continue to get stronger over time. You won't be able to sense what he's thinking, exactly — dragon's brains don't work like ours that way — but if the link gets strong enough, you'll be able to sense what he's feeling so clearly that it will *almost* be like you can hear his thoughts."

He glanced at her and went on, quickly. "The bad news, if you want to call it that, is that dragons, if they link, link for life. It can't be undone. You and Jakl will stay connected, no matter what." He swallowed, watching her face. "Even in death."

She was quiet for a moment. "Do you mean that if one of us dies, the other dies, too?"

"Um, well, not always," he said weakly. "The book definitely mentioned a few cases where the survivors, um, survived."

She looked at him. "But?"

"But then they went mad."

"I see."

They kept walking. Calen was quiet. He thought Meg could probably use a few moments to digest what he had told her. He knew he had needed a few moments when he realized what the book was saying. She and Jakl were connected in a way most people would never understand. He imagined parts of it must be powerfully appealing — to be so close to someone that he or she could actually feel what you were feeling, to never, ever be alone — but there were risks as well, and Meg had taken this on without the slightest idea what she was getting into.

When they reached the cave, Meg sat down near the entrance with her back against the rocky wall. Calen sat beside her.

"You said it was a symbiotic partnership," she said. "How so?"

"Each of you can draw on the strength of the other. I'm not sure if that means physical strength, exactly — although you will be able to lend each other healing energy if one of you is sick or injured. But also emotional strength. Force of spirit."

Meg nodded. She hesitated, then asked, "Will it — will it change me? Change who I am, I mean? Will I start to think I'm a dragon?"

"Oh, no. No. I don't think it works that way. I mean, I'm sure it will change you in certain ways — obviously, someone who's linked with a dragon is going to be different from someone who is not — but you won't lose your personality. You'll still be yourself, and Jakl will be himself. You may just . . . overlap at times."

"But you don't really know that. You can't really know."

Calen sighed. "I don't know it from personal experience, no. Of course not. But nothing I read made any mention of that sort of thing happening. And there are ways to shield your emotions from your link, to a degree. I read about those. I can't see how that would be possible if you weren't still a separate person."

"And you can teach me? About shielding? And . . . and everything else you found out?"

"Of course," he said. "I'm not sure I dare remove any of the books from the mage's quarters. But I can take notes, and maybe we can find a way to sneak you into the library, if we know Serek will be away."

She took another deep breath. "Well. I'm sure we'll figure something out." Some of her usual confidence was edging back into her voice. She smiled gratefully at him. "Thank you, Calen."

He smiled back. "You're welcome."

They stood up. Meg stepped into the cave entrance, then turned back. "Does Jakl know? Did he do this on purpose?"

"I don't know. I think it's probably something dragons know how to do instinctively. Maybe when you found him, after he was alone so young, he latched onto you the only way he knew how." He hesitated, then went on. "Meg, there are some other things I need to tell you about."

"I'm sure there are. But tell me inside. He knows we're here, and he's impatient to see me." She shook her head, her expression a mixture of wonder and chagrin. Then she disappeared into the dark.

Calen hurried after her. He didn't want to navigate that passage alone.

Jakl didn't look impatient to Calen; he looked asleep. But of course Meg would know better. As Calen emerged from the darkness into the dim light, the dragon uncurled and wrapped himself around Meg, who laughed and hugged him. Calen remained a respectful distance away, not wanting to intrude on their greeting. He squinted, trying to discover if he could actually *see* anything to indicate the link, now that he knew to look for it. There was nothing — at least nothing that his inner eye could make out.

His regular eyes, however, noticed that Jakl was larger than he'd been only a few days ago. His wings were especially changed. They were larger, fuller — more like the wings of the adult dragons Calen had seen drawings of in the library.

"I think you're going to have to move him, Meg. Very soon."

She glanced at Calen and then extricated herself from the dragon's embrace, stepping back to take a good look at him. Jakl sat and looked back at her calmly.

"You're right, Calen. Gods, he's growing so fast. Is that normal?"

He shrugged. "I think so. Everything I read indicates that they grow quickly in the first year."

"Look at his wings! Do you think he'll be able to fly soon?"

"Meg, I'm not suddenly some kind of all-knowing dragon expert, you know."

She turned to look at him. "Well, you know more than I do. Can you try to find out? I want to know everything. Oh, I wish I could look through those books myself."

"All right. Give me a list of questions and I'll try to find the answers for you. I do know that he should be able to fly before he gets his fire."

Meg tapped on her chin, thinking. "Where can we put him where he won't be discovered? Especially if he does start trying out his wings. I can't have him swooping around the castle! My parents would have him killed." She didn't say what they were both thinking — that her parents would be killing her as well.

"You'll definitely want to keep him far from the castle. And far from any outlying farms, too."

"Why farms?"

"Well, think, Meg. He's probably been surviving so far on small animals in and around the cave. As he grows, he's going to start needing larger, um, meals. You don't want angry farmers complaining to the king about missing sheep. Or, um, shepherds."

Meg's mouth opened in dismay. Calen was rather pleased to see that expression on someone else's face for once. "Oh, you don't think he'd really —" She turned back to Jakl. The dragon licked his snout with a long, forked tongue.

Meg put her hands on her hips and bent toward him. "No," she said. "You are not to eat any people! Ever! Do you understand me?" She looked at Calen. "Does he understand me?"

Jakl looked at Calen, too. Calen swallowed. Those eyes were anything but tame. "I think he understands you. I don't know if he'll listen, though. He's not obligated to obey you, any more than you're obligated to obey him. But remember how you told me you didn't think he'd do anything to hurt you? I think that's probably true. I think he'll try not to upset you. But if he's starving, and he needs to eat . . ."

Meg nodded reluctantly. "He'll need a place deeper in the forest, then. Someplace with lots of wild game, and no farms. Or shepherds." She frowned. "It's going to make it harder to visit him."

A small sound came from a nearby passage. Jakl's head snapped around, and his eyes narrowed to yellow slits. He began slinking across the cave floor, stalking whatever unfortunate creature waited there.

"You'll have to find a way, Meg. If he begins to miss you too much, he might come looking for you."

"That would not go over well, would it? Certainly not right now. The guards are ready to kill anything larger than a dog on sight." She sat down near a wall. "What could that creature have been, Calen? How could such a monster even exist?"

He had no answer for that. Even Serek seemed at a loss to explain where the creature had come from. It had taken more than thirty men to kill it, and at least four of those were killed themselves in the process. Five more lay with Roeg in the infirmary, struck with the same deadly poison. Calen had assisted Serek with their treatment, enduring again the terrible screams as the reagents they applied fought the poison in the men's wounds. Serek had hoped to devise a more effective treatment by study-ing the dead monster, but the soldiers had burned the corpse in their anger and fear, and nothing was left of it but a pile of blackened bones and ashes. Serek had been furious. By the time he had finished cursing the soldiers for their stupidity, Calen guessed that half of them were more afraid of him than they'd been of the creature.

Meg turned her eyes from the entrance of the passage down which Jakl had disappeared (and in which, from the sound of it, he was now eating his recent catch) back to Calen. "Do you think the monster could have been the danger you saw in the spirit cards?"

Calen blinked at her, startled. Could it have been? The possibility had not occurred to him. But even as he considered it now, he realized he didn't believe it. "No," he told her. "I don't think so. Terrible as it was, it doesn't feel big enough to be the danger I saw." He fell silent, trying not to hear the messy crunching sounds coming from the other passage. He felt certain he was right, and yet — that would mean that something worse was going to happen. Meg met his eyes grimly, and he could tell she was thinking the same thing. After a second, he added, "I wonder, though — maybe it's related. Maybe these individual attacks are just the beginning of something larger."

"You mean, maybe someone is behind them? Maybe they're not just random terrible things?"

Calen shrugged. "It does seem possible, doesn't it? Did you ever ask your parents about their conversation

with Serek? About the spirit cards? Did they say anything about what they thought the danger might be?"

"No," Meg said bitterly. "I mean, yes, I asked, but no,
they didn't tell me anything. They won't talk about it at
all. They keep telling us not to worry, they'll take every
precaution, and so on. As though we can just stop thinking about it because they say so!"

Why did adults always seem to want to keep children
in the dark about things? Did they really think they were
better off not knowing? Or was it just too inconvenient
to bother to explain? Of course, Calen reflected, it's not
like he and Meg weren't keeping a few secrets of their
own.

He blinked as a thought suddenly occurred to him.
"You know, Meg, I have to say — you're taking this linking thing much better than I would." It was true. She
seemed to have just accepted it and moved on. "Are you
really all right?"

She gave him one of her looks. "What did you expect
me to do? Fall apart? How would that help? Besides, it's
not like anything has really changed."

He stared at her.

She threw up her hands. "Oh, all right. Of course
that's not true. Everything has changed. But I was already
concerned about Jakl's safety before. Now I've just got

more of a personal stake in it — that's all. In a way, this might actually help me ensure his safety. If I eventually have to reveal his presence to my parents, they won't be able to have him destroyed without destroying me as well. And while I'm sure they'd be quite angry with me for letting something like this happen, they probably wouldn't be angry enough to *kill* me." She thought about this for a minute. "I'll just have to make sure no one discovers him by accident and tries to hurt him before I have a chance to explain."

She turned to look at Jakl, who was now sniffing around near the passage where he had caught the whatever-it-was, apparently trying to discover whether it had brought along any friends.

"Jakl, come here," she said firmly.

The dragon glanced at her, then turned his attention back to his sniffing.

Meg chewed on her lip, thinking. "Jakl," she began again, then stopped. She closed her eyes and seemed to be concentrating. One hand reached up to rest over her heart.

Jakl looked over at her again, then turned and came across the cavern to curl up at her feet. She opened her eyes and smiled down at him. Then she looked up at Calen. "I think he can understand me if I speak to him the right way. He won't obey me — I believe you're right about that. But if I can make him understand, maybe I can keep him from straying too far or letting himself be seen."

Calen hoped she was right.

CHAPTER NINE

DAYS PASSED, AND MEG FOUND HER life settling into a kind of daily routine. A progressively strange and secretive routine, but a routine all the same.

Mornings, she woke and dressed and then had breakfast with her sisters and sometimes her parents as well. Wedding plans were discussed, and after the plates were cleared away there were always details to attend to — fabrics to examine, dresses to try on, books to peruse for appropriate readings or blessings. The ceremony would take place at the end of the month, and suddenly that was only two weeks away, and then less, and then *less* — and the amount to do seemed to be increasing as the time remaining disappeared. Only a small portion of the ceremony was standard; the rest fell upon the two families to plan and arrange.

The groom's family was responsible for the groom's court, and the bride's family was responsible for the bride's court, which was always complicated, and made more so in this case because the bride's family was hosting the wedding as well. Maerlie had her hands full, but Meg thought she was handling herself very well. She only occasionally lost her temper or seemed noticeably overwhelmed. Her sisters made some tasks easier and some harder. She had all of them to help her, plus Mother and Nan Vera, but also all of them to include in the ceremony with appropriate sisterly and motherly and nursemaidly functions. And all of their opinions to endure. Well, except Mattie, of course, who was too little to have opinions yet.

The group wedding sessions would invariably continue until luncheon was served, after which Meg would steal away to meet Calen and visit Jakl. Maerlie covered her afternoon absences with suitable excuses, never straying from her promise to respect Meg's need for secrecy. Meg knew she would never be able to express to her sister how deeply grateful she was for her help in this, so she did not try, trusting Maerlie to know how she felt.

Meg's success in escaping was bittersweet. She *had* to see Jakl — it was hard for her to be away from him for very long, and she was afraid of what he might do if he started to miss her too much — but she was all too aware of how quickly time was passing in the other half of her life. Every afternoon she spent apart from Maerlie was an opportunity lost forever; soon her sister would be far away, and Meg might have to go months, maybe even years, without seeing her at all. That hurt to think about; Maerlie had always been there. Always.

Calen would greet her daily with new information gleaned from his books. Meg was continually astounded by how much there was to know about dragons. They were so much more complex than she had ever imagined. Of course, she hadn't given much thought to the matter before finding Jakl. Everyone knew dragons existed, but they were so rarely seen that they often seemed more like imaginary creatures than real ones. Not anything people thought about in everyday life. Now she sometimes found it impossible to think of anything else. At the castle, or anywhere other than by his side, her feelings about the dragon and their connection were mixed beyond any hope of sorting out. Sometimes she loved the way she could always feel him and the way their bond seemed to get stronger and stronger with each passing day. But other times . . . she thought about the way it was a chain from which she would never be free. And she *would* never be free — it was that more than anything else that terrified her, the permanence of their link, the notion that whatever path the future held for her would necessarily have to accommodate him as well. Forever.

But once she was close enough to sense him strongly, to be immersed in the warm and gleaming *force* of him, it was hard to be anything other than exhilarated. He was so full of life. She had tried explaining it to Calen on more than one occasion but could never find the words. Jakl was alive in a way Meg had never felt before. He radiated energy like a ball of fire, experiencing sensations more fully than Meg had thought possible — and she experienced them that way, too, now, while they were together. In fact there was always a period of readjustment after she left him, during which the world felt dim and gray and pointless. And he loved her, loved her completely and unquestionably, and she could feel that, too.

All these feelings grew as the strength of their link increased. Meg couldn't help fearing that it would become harder and harder to leave his side. Would a day come when she would finally be unable to tear herself away? She tried to convince herself that that could never happen, and yet — she could see how it might be possible. What if she stopped wanting to do anything other than be with him?

They had found him a new cave farther away from the castle, one with an entrance passage that seemed large enough that he wouldn't outgrow it. It was in a small valley deep in the Hunterheart, hidden from casual view and well beyond the borders of any outlying farms. It turned out to be a good thing they didn't wait any longer; shortly after they moved him, Jakl started flying. Just little fluttering attempts at first, but Meg was thrilled to see how quickly he gained strength and confidence. Well, thrilled and anxious. She hoped he truly understood how important it was not to let himself be seen.

Calen almost always came with her to visit the dragon, and Meg was especially grateful for his company on those walks through the forest. She was grateful for him anyway — it meant so much to her to be able to talk to him about Jakl and have his help in figuring everything out — but everyone knew the woods were no longer safe for wandering around in, and she would have been very nervous making the trips to Jakl's cave alone. Calen didn't even seem to think twice about putting himself at risk for her. She hoped she got the chance to repay him someday.

They always returned by early evening, with enough time for Meg to wash and change before dinner. Sometimes she would walk to dinner with some or all of her sisters, depending on where the meal was being served that evening and who else would be in attendance. And sometimes she would walk with Wilem.

He didn't escort her every night, but often enough that people were beginning to notice. Meg worried about the comments that might reach his ear, and how he might react, but if he was bothered by anything he heard, he gave no sign. He was ever kind and courteous, and although at first he had held to a rather stiff formality of speech that made many of their conversations feel like selections from a book of approved statements and responses for respectable young men and young ladies, lately he had begun to open up to her, speaking more freely of his life and friends and experiences in Kragnir, as well as his hopes and dreams for the future.

Meg was smitten. Part of her rebelled against the idea, wanting to insist that she was not some silly girl who would let herself fall so fully under the spell of any boy, even as fine an example as this one. But she was not so thickheaded that she failed to see the truth of things. Wilem made her feel newly alive just as Jakl did, but in a completely different way. Being with him was one of the few things that did take her mind off the dragon, and when it was time to part company, she had a similar sense of forcing herself to readjust to a dull and lackluster world. Sometimes she worried about that as well. She didn't want to live her life entirely for Wilem any more than she wanted to live it solely for Jakl. She just wanted to be herself. Was that so much to ask

These thoughts always ran through her mind during the times when Wilem, too, seemed reflective and quiet. Tonight they were sitting near the fountain, keeping close to the castle (as most people did since the night of the creature in the garden) but with the tall and graceful trees to provide a measure of privacy and the soothing sound of the water to mask their words should anyone venture close enough to overhear. Not that there was anything *to* hear at the moment; they were just sitting, Wilem's hand resting mere inches from her own as he gazed off into the night, Meg staring dreamily at his profile. Her current favorite fantasy was of the day of Maerlie's swiftly approaching wedding. She pictured herself dancing with Wilem in the crowded hall, everyone's eyes upon them but their own eyes only on each other. She imagined he was a fine dancer. In real life she knew she would never astound anyone with her gracefulness, but when she danced with Wilem in her mind, she was as light on her feet as a feather, twirling with perfect timing and basking in the glow of his attention and the heated envy of every other girl in the castle.

She sighed inwardly and forced herself back to reality. Not that being in the courtyard with Wilem was such a dreadful reality to return to. Still, she hated when he caught her looking at him that way, certain that he was able to see inside her mind and know what she'd been dreaming. Better to wait until later, when she could play out the entire evening in her mind uninterrupted.

Wilem was still staring out at the surrounding darkness, his eyes focused on something only he could see. She wished she could read his mind as easily as she imagined he could read hers. Instead she had to resort to clumsy questions.

"What are you thinking about?" she asked softly.

He started slightly, and Meg let herself fancy he might have been entertaining his own romantic fantasy about the two of them. He looked at her and smiled.

"I was thinking about Ryant getting married. In less than a week, he and Princess Maerlie will be wed and everything will change."

She nodded. "They'll be starting a whole new life together, a different life."

His smile twisted slightly. "Actually, I was thinking more about myself, I'm afraid. I've grown so accustomed to spending my time at Ryant's side, but now . . ."

Meg thought she understood. "He'll need to spend that time with Maerlie. Or much of it, anyway. And then with their children, if they are so blessed." She made the sign of the Lady without thinking, touching her fist to her heart and then holding her palm out in front of her, fingers extended like the rays of the life-giving sun.

"It's selfish, I know," he said. "And I am happy for them both, of course. I will just need to — readjust — to the new order of things." He shook his head ruefully. "How the prince would mock me if he heard me talk like this. But even the little changes will be hard to get used to. I won't be able to drop by his quarters for a drink at night, once his rooms become hers as well."

"I'm sure Maerlie would never object to . . ." She trailed off. "No, you're right. Although, surely they'll have chambers large enough in Kragnir for each of them to have their own space?"

Wilem nodded. "Of course. And I know I will still see plenty of my dear friend. But I believe the evenings will belong to his new wife, especially in the beginning."

Meg opened her mouth to reassure him, and then closed it, realizing what he was referring to. *I will not blush,* she thought fiercely, even as she felt the slow fire begin creeping up from her neck. *He will think me an innocent child now.* She glanced away, unable to meet his eyes.

He cleared his throat. "I'm sorry, Meglynne. I didn't mean to embarrass you."

She forced herself to look up. "Oh, you didn't. Not really. I just — I just hadn't been thinking . . ."

"No, of course not. I think men tend to speak more frankly of these things." He was clearly uncomfortable now, which made her feel even worse. "I shouldn't have made such a comment in your presence."

She could see him folding in on himself, reaching back for the formality of their earlier conversations. *No,* she thought. *No, you don't. I don't want to lose what closeness we've gained.* She swallowed and made herself speak far more casually than she felt. "It's not as though women never speak of such things," she said quietly. "The wedding night is not just an afterthought to the wedding itself, after all."

"I'm not even certain what the custom is here, in that regard," he said.

Meg stared at him.

"No — I didn't mean — I meant where the couple will stay until they leave for Kragnir. At home, the bride would move into the groom's chambers, but here, since the groom is not the host . . ."

"They're preparing a special wedding suite," Meg said, relieved to actually have something to say to help guide the conversation to somewhat firmer ground — *where* the bride and groom would retire after the wedding, instead of what they might be doing once they got there. "It's the largest of the guest suites, at the end of the east wing near the tower, and this way it will be a new space for both of them, as seems fitting for the first night of their new lives. She's been keeping the location a secret from the prince, wanting to surprise him — you won't say anything, will you? She doesn't want him to see it before the wedding night. No one knows which room it will be except for us and the servants she trusts most." She bit her lip and added, "Well, and now you, of course."

"Your secret is safe with me, Princess." He gave her one of his small, sad smiles. Perhaps he was thinking more about missing his friend once he was wed; his smile seemed a bit smaller and sadder than usual.

He looked at her a moment more, then rose and suggested that the hour was growing late. Meg supposed it was, at that. She felt the familiar tug-of-war inside her of disappointment and excitement: disappointment that her time with him was ending for the evening, excitement at the thought that maybe, this time, he might attempt to kiss her before they said good night. It didn't seem so very inappropriate to wish for that; they'd been spending a lot of time together, and none of the parents seemed to have any objection. And wasn't that how these things worked? A boy and a girl started spending time together, they talked, they held hands, and then, eventually, he kissed her. She'd read enough romance stories to know how it was supposed to go, she thought. And if he didn't kiss her soon . . . did that mean he didn't want to? Or that the notions of appropriate behavior were just different where he came from? She wished he'd hurry up so she could stop wondering!

They walked together back into the castle. He was holding her hand, as he so often did now when they walked together, and Meg tried to communicate silently through that tenuous connection, sending him clear and explicit permission to kiss her. Sadly, it didn't seem to function as well as her link with Jakl did. At the thought of the dragon, she felt him shift his distant awareness to her, questing toward her through the link. Their bond was strong enough now that she could feel him everywhere in the castle. Sometimes that was nice, but at this moment . . . *No, not* now, *you stupid dragon.* She was with *Wilem* now; she didn't want to have to share this moment with Jakl, too. She didn't know how to make him understand that, though, so she just pushed him — gently but firmly — away and strengthened the wall between them that Calen had taught her to create.

"Meg?" Wilem was talking to her; how long had he been talking to her? Meg wrenched her focus back outward again.

"I'm sorry, Wilem — I was lost in thought for a moment. What were you saying?"

They had stopped walking, and he was looking down at her, smiling one of those heart-twisting smiles.

"Your hand, Meg. You were, um . . ."

With horror she realized she was gripping his hand tightly enough to make his flesh white. "Oh, gods, I'm sorry —" She tried to let go, but he didn't let her. She stared at their joined hands in confusion, and then he took his other hand and lifted her chin, forcing her to meet his eyes. His lovely, sad, warm, dark, impossibly deep eyes. Their color seemed to swirl and change; she couldn't tell if they were brown or hazel or black or some new shade of dark that had no name and existed only there — here — in Wilem's eyes and no place else. She felt as if she could quite literally drown in those eyes. Drown and be happily, truly, wonderfully lost forever. She knew she should look away, but she couldn't, and besides, his hand was still gently holding her chin, and those eyes, his eyes, his face, drew closer, she could see his mouth parting, and she felt her own mouth mirror his, and her eyes closed almost before she could tell them to and then suddenly, shockingly, his lips were pressed against her own and she thought she had never felt anything so soft and perfect and warm and then she didn't seem to have any thoughts at all except the one dreamy refrain, *He's kissing me, kissing me, Wilem is kissing me.* . . .

At some point he must have taken his leave, because Meg realized she was somehow standing inside the door of her room, standing even though she could feel that really she was floating and her feet couldn't possibly truly be touching the floor. Her heart was beating very fast. *So this is what it feels like,* she marveled. Did Maerlie feel like this when Ryant kissed her? Was it going to feel like this every time? She wanted to tear open the door and run back down the hall after him and kiss him again and again to find out.

She managed to resist that urge. Barely.

It took her a long while to regain some semblance of normal thought and function. She took several moments to replay the kiss in her mind a few times, then forced herself to *stop* thinking about it because otherwise she didn't believe she could move from where she was leaning against the closed door. Finally, her heartbeat as close to back to normal as it was likely to get anytime soon, she smoothed out her dress and touched her hair to make sure it was still in place and then crossed to the inner door and the short back hallway that led to the private entrances to her sisters' rooms. She poked her head in Maurel's door to say a quick good night, then continued on toward Maerlie's room, praying she'd find her sister there.

Meg knocked and stood bouncing on her toes until she heard Maerlie answering, "Come in!" She practically bounded inside. Maerlie was seated at her desk. When she saw Meg's face, she put down the letter she'd been reading and stood up. She took Meg's hand and led her to the bed, where they sat facing each other. Maerlie was still holding Meg's hand in hers.

"Tell me what happened," Maerlie said.

"He kissed me," Meg whispered. She felt herself grinning like an idiot, but she didn't care. It felt good to feel so happy. Maerlie grinned back, and that made it even better.

"And?" Maerlie asked.

"And? And what? It was . . . oh, Maer, it was wonderful." She laughed and reached up to touch her face. "Look, I can't stop smiling."

Maerlie giggled. "I noticed."

"It was like time stopped, and there was nothing else but the two of us. That must sound so silly. . . ."

"No, Meg, it doesn't. I know just what you mean."

Meg flopped back on the bed and stared up at the ceiling. "Why can't it stay like this, Maer? Why can't you and Prince Ryant stay here, and Wilem too, and it can always be like this and we can all be happy and stay together. . . ."

And then without warning, Meg burst into tears.

In an instant, Maerlie's arms were around her,

gathering her up into a fierce hug. "Shh," Maerlie murmured, holding her close. "Meg, shh, it's okay."

"Don't go," Meg whispered. "Please don't go, Maerlie. How can I get by without you here? I won't be able to stand it. Please."

"Oh, Meg." Maerlie pulled away slightly and reached up to smooth Meg's hair back from her face. "You know I have to go. But we'll see each other again before too long, you know that. And you'll be fine. You will — you'll see. And besides, I'm not leaving tomorrow. The wedding's still six days away — that's plenty of time for you to get sick of me."

Meg shook her head but couldn't help smiling a little.

Maerlie smiled back. "And plenty of time for more kisses with your Wilem," she added.

Meg was grinning again before she could help it, and Maerlie laughed.

And then Meg was laughing, too, even with the tears still leaking at the corners of her eyes. "Argh!" she said. "This is crazy. How can I be so happy and so sad at the same time?"

"That's love, my dear sister," Maerlie said softly. She took a handkerchief from her pocket and wiped gently at Meg's face. "That's love."

image

Meg's sleep was long in coming that night. She lay awake, certain she could feel the dragon reaching for her through the link, probing at her mind and emotions. He was definitely getting stronger, better able to touch her in that way. Meg kept the barrier up, blocking Jakl's presence from flooding in unchecked, but she worried that eventually he'd find a way around it. And then what? Calen seemed sure that he wouldn't actually take over her mind, but Meg didn't have the same confidence. It seemed to her that Jakl was always trying to push their connection as far as it would go, and she always had to keep holding him back.

Sleep! she thought at him, even though she knew he couldn't hear her words that way.

She wondered suddenly what Calen was doing right then. Was he sleeping? Catching up on his studies for Serek? Or sneaking into the library to steal more information for her? She wished she didn't have to ask him to risk getting in trouble on her account. He really didn't seem to mind, though. She suspected he was almost as eager to learn about dragons as she was — he always seemed so excited about the latest details he was able to discover. Plus, she knew, he was just glad to help her. That's just how he was. She smiled in the darkness. Somehow she'd been able to tell right away how nice he would be, despite the fact that their first meeting began with him almost falling out the window and then that silly argument. She'd known she could trust him. And of course she'd been right. She felt she could tell him anything.

Her smile faded. Well, almost anything. For some reason, she hadn't told him about Wilem. She didn't know why. She and Calen certainly didn't have those kinds of feelings for each other, but still she worried that he wouldn't understand. But surely it didn't matter. By necessity, her life was divided now between castle and dragon, and Wilem was part of one world and Calen the other. It had to be that way, didn't it? She tried to imagine telling Wilem about Jakl and could not. She knew he'd be leaving with the prince after the wedding, anyway; she knew her fantasies about having a future with him were only daydreams, but . . . what if they weren't? What if somehow they could end up together? Would he still want her if he knew? Would anyone *ever* want her? A girl whose mind and heart were already half spoken for . . . by a dragon?

She didn't want to think about that now. She would keep her two lives separate, as she had been, for as long as she could. And then, when Jakl got too big to stay hidden, or when she could no longer find enough excuses to steal away to visit him in secret . . . well, she would just have to find a way to make everyone accept it. Telling her parents would be awful; she knew they wouldn't understand, but eventually they would *have* to come to terms with it, wouldn't they? And then so many things would be so much better. No more secrets from her family or anyone else. No more sneaking off into the woods, where who knew what kind of monsters could still be lurking. No more dividing her life into parts, as if she were several people instead of only one. She would just be herself again, with nothing to hide and no reason to fear discovery. If her family loved her, they would accept who she was. And anyone else who loved her, really loved her, would do the same.

They would. They would have to. Wouldn't they?

She fell off to sleep imagining this singular future, which merged into a hazy, troubled dream of a fancy dinner banquet with two long tables between which everyone in the world was divided. Calen sat at one, Wilem at the other, and both were saving her a seat, but she could only sit with one of them. As she tried to decide which way to go, a great shadow filled the hall. She turned to see Jakl just outside, throwing himself against a window, struggling to get in.

CHAPTER TEN

CALEN STEPPED CAREFULLY ALONG THE HALL-way. Serek had allowed him to try working a spell that made him invisible to the casual eye — successfully cast, it would encourage others to simply not notice he was there. *Very* successfully cast — using a variant based on Calen's supplemental study and of which he was fairly certain Serek would not approve — even someone who was specifically looking for him would be unable to see him. But since Calen was not at all sure it *was* success-fully cast, to any degree, he was also trying to walk as if he had every right to be where he was. He wanted to become good enough at it to use it as a defense against Lyrimon, although he'd have to be careful trying it out anywhere in the mage quarters. Serek had made it clear that if he discovered Calen attempting to use the spell as a shield against his own instructor, there would be dire consequences, and he wasn't likely to split hairs about whether he or Lyrimon had been the intended focus.

Of course, if Calen became *really* good at the spell, Serek would never even know. But he'd have to be sure about his skill before testing it in that regard. For now he'd have to settle for the eighth-floor hallway.

Closing his eyes, he checked the invisible barrier he was trying to construct around himself. He envisioned tendrils of gray energy forming a thin layer about three hands' width from his body. The idea was that a person's gaze would encounter the barrier and slide off to either side instead of penetrating to see Calen himself. It was hard to keep the shield in place while walking, though, especially if he wanted to keep his eyes open. Still, he thought that he was getting the hang of it. And then, once he mastered the basics, he could try weaving in the other kinds of energy he thought would help to —

"What are you doing?" a voice suddenly whispered behind him.

Calen jumped about three feet in the air before he realized it was Meg. She was already laughing by the time he turned around. He really was going to have to speak with her about this sneaking-up business at some point. But right now he was too glad to see her.

"It's — never mind," he said. Obviously, he still needed some practice. "Are you going where I think you're going?"

She grinned. "Same place as you, I imagine. They

began setting up for the tourney this morning. Maerlie called off our regular wedding planning session so that she and Mother and Morgan could oversee the construction. Which means I find myself with a bit of unexpected free time." She held out her arm. "Shall we?"

Calen grinned back and threaded his arm through hers. "Yes. We shall." They walked the rest of the way together, then carefully slipped inside the still-empty set of guest rooms.

"I'm glad no one's been put in here yet," Calen said.

Meg nodded. "Someone will be soon enough, though. This will probably be our last chance for the window. I think many of the remaining guests are planning to arrive tomorrow to be in time for the tourney the day after, and then of course the wedding's just three days later."

Together they ducked behind the heavy curtains. Meg immediately hoisted herself up onto the ledge, tucking her skirts underneath her and swinging one leg to dangle out the open window. Just looking at her up there made Calen nervous. He kept both feet on the ground like a sensible person and leaned up against the wall beneath the window.

Down below, workmen were setting up for the various events. In the center of the courtyard, the long barrier intended to separate jousting contestants had already been erected. It had been painted red, as tradition dictated, the color of love and marriage and passion. And blood, of course. Smaller arenas were being cordoned off by ropes for other events. Fighting teams selected from leading warriors of each kingdom would battle with blunted weapons in the melee, and there were assorted smaller contests of strength and archery and balance and all kinds of things.

"Isn't anyone worried that the prince will get maimed or killed during all of this?" Calen wondered aloud. "Who thought up this stupid tradition, anyway?"

Meg favored him with one of her withering looks. "No one's going to kill anyone," she said. "It's just for fun, and luck. It gives the prince a chance to show off for his bride, and everyone gets to let off a little steam. It's not like the old days, when suitors would actually fight each other for the right to marry a princess and the last man standing became the groom."

Calen grimaced. No wonder Meg tended toward violence. Trelian's whole history was filled with murder and fighting and contests of blood. He still had occasional nightmares thinking about that story she'd told him about poor Queen Lysetta. He hadn't been down in the cellar since.

"I can't wait for the tourney," Meg went on, looking

eagerly down at the courtyard. "There hasn't been one here since Morgan was married. You'll see, it will be fun. I bet even Serek will turn out for the festivities."

Calen smiled at the idea of Serek cheering in the stands. *That* would certainly never happen. He turned to say so to Meg when the sound of the chamber door suddenly swinging open made them both jump. They froze, staring at each other silently.

"Mother, that's not what I'm saying." A young man's voice. Calen didn't recognize it, but Meg must have. Her eyes grew even wider, and if he hadn't known better, he thought she might have been blushing.

"Quiet!" The sound of heavy skirts rustling and the door slamming shut. The second speaker was a woman. She spoke softly, but there was an edge of iron to her voice. "Do you want our plans to come to nothing? This is not the time to lose your nerve."

A pause, filled with tension. Any chance Calen and Meg might have had to reveal themselves gracefully had passed. Whoever these people were, they were obviously in the middle of a heated argument and had ducked into what they thought was an empty room for some privacy. There was nothing to do now but keep silent and wait for them to leave.

"I am not losing my nerve," the man went on, finally.

"I would not betray Father's memory. Or Tymas's. I just want to be sure there is no other way."

The woman sighed. When she spoke again, her voice was gentler but still firm. "Wilem. I know this cannot be easy for you. The prince himself is not to blame, and I know, despite everything, you have come to care about him. But you cannot let that cloud your judgment. Is your friendship with the prince more important than revenge for your father and brother's deaths or working to bring your father's plans to fruition?"

"No, but —"

A sharp smacking sound cut off his words. She must have slapped him. Who *were* these people? She had called him Wilem. Wasn't Wilem one of Prince Ryant's companions? That didn't make any sense. Meg seemed as confused as he was.

"*But?* But what? Now that the moment of revenge is at hand, the moment we can make sure your father's wishes are carried out, that Kragnir will remain strong and not taint itself through an alliance with murderers and liars, now you will tell me that you lack the resolve to complete our task? Your father and brother were *killed* by these monsters!" Her voice broke, the strength falling from it so suddenly and completely that it was hard to believe the same woman was speaking. "Am I alone in this, Wilem? Will you truly leave me to face this final test alone?"

"No, Mother." His voice seemed to have gained in strength what hers had lost. "I am sorry. I will not fail you in this. You're right — I was weak to hesitate. Ryant is the son of a traitor to his people. My personal feelings change nothing."

Calen stared at Meg in horror. What were they *talking* about? How could Wilem be calling his own king a traitor? Meg looked lost.

The woman spoke again. "And the girl?"

"I know where they will be staying on the wedding night. I was nearly certain anyway, but Princess Meglynne confirmed it. You were correct in that as well. My time spent with her has been most — useful."

Meg's face drained of color. For a moment Calen was terrified she would faint, but she managed to take control of herself. Her eyes were enormous and dark against her face, though, and they swam with tears. He still couldn't make sense of most of the conversation, but he could guess at the last part. Something went cold and hard within his chest. He reached out and took hold of Meg's hand, and she gripped his back fiercely.

"You must remain strong, my son. The hardest part is yet to come, but always remember why we do this.

We cannot allow Ryllin to forge this alliance. It would bring Kragnir to ruin, and there is no other way to stop it. Your father tried to reason with him, and all it did was get him killed. Him and Tymas, both. Remember that these *kings* are the men who murdered your father and brother. They showed no mercy then, and neither will we. Maerlie's death will be a small and necessary evil on the path to greater good."

Meg gasped at the woman's final words, and there was a sudden terrible silence. Calen could almost feel them turning to stare toward the curtains. He looked around frantically. No way out. Just the window, but even Meg wouldn't try jumping from this height. He desperately wished he had mastered that invisibility spell. The extra-strong version.

He looked hopelessly at Meg. She was shaking her head angrily; he knew she must be furious at herself for making noise, but who could blame her? They were talking about killing her sister! Which meant, Calen realized with a sinking heart, they probably wouldn't hesitate to kill anyone else who got in their way. Or who overheard their plans.

Meg slid from the ledge to stand beside him as footsteps approached, and then the curtains were thrust aside. Wilem's cold eyes glanced at Calen, then grew wide when he looked toward Meg. He almost looked as if he would speak to her, but his mother's voice sounded from across the room.

"Who is it, Wilem?"

Wilem stared at Meg for another second and then stepped back, giving the woman a clear view of the now-exposed window. Sen Eva Lichtendor — that's who she was. He hadn't put it together before. Of course, she was Wilem's mother. Gods, this just got worse and worse. The primary advisor to the throne of Kragnir and her son, the prince's trusted companion, conspiring murder and treason!

If Sen Eva was upset to see Meg there, she gave no sign.

"Greetings, Princess," she said calmly.

Meg tore her gaze from Wilem and turned to Sen Eva. She had released Calen's hand, and now her skirts were knotted in her clenched fists. Despite the tear tracks that glistened faintly on her cheeks, she held her head high, staring back at the woman defiantly.

"Hello, traitor," Meg answered. Calen could tell she was struggling to keep her voice from shaking.

Out of the corner of his eye, Calen noticed Wilem's expression going grim and hard at her words, but this was probably no time to warn Meg to be careful. It was hard to imagine how she could possibly make things any worse, anyway.

Sen Eva merely shook her head. "Oh, Meglynne," she said. "I cannot tell you how much I regret finding you here. I assure you, however, that I am not the traitor. If you want to lay blame, look toward your own family. To further his misguided and selfish agenda, your father helped murder my husband and son."

"That is a lie," Meg said quietly.

Sen Eva smiled sadly. "I wish it were, my dear. In any case, whether or not you choose to believe me, I'm afraid you've placed me in a difficult position."

Wilem stepped forward. "Mother —"

"Quiet," she said, not taking her eyes from Meg. "No one will miss the mage's apprentice, I wager. But what am I to do with you?"

"I will not allow you to harm Calen, or to murder my sister," Meg replied. "You have to realize that you cannot succeed in this."

Calen was astounded by Meg's self-control. He could never have managed to sound so calm, or, more likely, to even speak at all. Sen Eva spoke of killing him as easily as she might talk about swatting a fly. Despite her words, she probably had every intention of killing Meg as well. Why not? She was already plotting to kill one princess.

They had to do something, but what could they do? Sen Eva stood between them and the door, with Wilem only a few steps away. If they tried to run, they'd never make it. Not both of them, anyway.

There had to be some kind of spell that would help in a case like this, but unfortunately Calen had no idea what it might be. He had learned a lot in the past weeks, more than he once would have thought possible, but Serek had never taught him anything about striking out with magic as a weapon. Mages weren't supposed to use magic in that way, except as a last resort, and it's not like either of them ever imagined he'd be faced with a situation like this one. He tried desperately to think. Was there anything he knew, anything at all that could help, that might distract Wilem and Sen Eva or incapacitate them until he and Meg could get away? He wondered if Meg was trying to stall for time in order for him to work some kind of magic in their defense. If so, he thought bitterly, she was about to be sorely disappointed. For the first time in his life, he wished Serek were there.

Something suddenly clicked in his mind. *Idiot,* he chided himself fiercely. Of course there was something he could do. Serek had been teaching him summoning. All he had to do was call to Serek, using a summoning spell. Well, that and then stall long enough for Serek to reach them. Assuming Calen managed to work the spell correctly. And assuming Serek chose to respond.

Calen brushed all that aside. No sense worrying about what might go wrong. Meg and Sen Eva were still staring each other down, trading sharp, clipped sentences about who was or wasn't going to kill whom and why. Calen closed his eyes and cleared his mind, relishing briefly how easily that came to him now, even in his current circumstances. Then that thought, too, was gone and he was ready.

Quickly, he created an image of Serek in his head. It wasn't hard — the gods knew he had stared often enough at that man's face with varying degrees of hatred and annoyance and grudging respect. He knew every line and feature. He pictured Serek's cold blue eyes; his thick black hair, kept short; the downward turn of his mouth. He saw the master tattoo spiraling down his right cheek and extending across his face, its complex tendrils and small symbols, which Serek had always refused to explain. Once the image was complete, he held it firmly in his mind, preparing to reach through the image to the flesh-and-blood man it represented.

Now — what to send, exactly? Summoning didn't allow you to communicate actual words; he wouldn't be able to give any kind of rational explanation or call for

195

help. Basically it was just a call for someone to come to you, but it was possible to shade the call with an emotion, and that's what he needed to do now. Serek would never respond to a simple, basic summons. He'd probably just ignore it and plan to make Calen sorry later for disturbing him at work. Calen needed to make Serek aware of the danger somehow, of the fact that he needed serious, immediate help. He tried to let a little of his fear back into the cleared space in his mind. Not enough to dismantle the spell, but enough, he hoped, to get through to Serek.

Taking a breath, he reached out through the image he'd created, trying to connect. To his inner eye, his sending appeared as a white cloud of energy, formless at first but then strengthening into a solid beam of communication. He focused on the beam, willing it to reach his master, to get his attention and make him aware of Calen calling to him. Almost, for a moment, he thought he might have broken through —

Someone shook him, roughly, and his eyes flew open. Wilem had his arm and shoulder in a tight grip. "None of that," Wilem said angrily. "Whatever you're up to, stop it."

Beyond Wilem, Calen saw Sen Eva smirking at him contemptuously. "I don't know what you're attempting, boy, but you might as well save yourself the trouble. Trust me. Whatever small magic you have at your disposal, it will not be enough to save you. I have suffered too much and worked too hard to allow some worthless apprentice to interfere with what I must do."

Fear and despair shot through him. Calen struggled not to show it. He didn't want to give Sen Eva the satisfaction. Or to shame himself in front of Meg, who was always so brave and sure. It was hard, though. Very hard. He really didn't want to die.

"No!" cried Meg. And then she shocked them all by launching herself at Sen Eva, shrieking and clawing like a wildcat. Sen Eva stepped back, trying to hold the girl off. Wilem dropped his hold on Calen and went after Meg instead.

Calen seized the opportunity, closed his eyes, and had his mental picture of Serek back in an instant. He gave up any semblance of control and simply sent every shred of fear and panic and need in a pure beam of white energy directly to where he felt Serek to be. Almost at once, he felt Serek stagger from the impact at the other end of the delicate, fiery bond that suddenly connected them. *Calen,* the surprised thought came back at him clearly, defying what he'd been taught about the limits of summoning. *Calen, what —*

And then the bond was ripped apart as Meg came hurling into him, thrust away from Sen Eva by her son's rough and angry hands. Wilem was glaring at Meg as if furious for making him behave in so undignified a manner. Calen regained his balance for once and reached out an arm to steady Meg. She grabbed his hand and stood by his side, waiting.

Sen Eva quickly recovered her equilibrium but no longer bothered to hide her anger. It practically shone from her like a force in itself, glowing like red fire.

Dark Lord and Bright Lady, Calen thought suddenly, numb with the shock of realization. *She's casting, the woman's a mage —*

The red fire burst forth from Sen Eva's outstretched hands. Without thinking, Calen shot out his hand, flinging up what he could only interpret as a field of blue energy, not knowing what he was doing but just wanting to shield himself and Meg from the red force of death and destruction the woman was firing at them. He could see her spell clearly, no squinting required, and there was no question in his mind that she was attempting to kill them both.

The red fire met the blue shield and exploded in a blinding flash of violet light. Calen felt himself falling, like the day he had first met Meg, falling from the treacherous ledge, but this time no strong hand would pull him back because Meg was falling, too, her hand still tightly gripped within his own, and together they fell and fell and fell and he thought, *This is it, we're dead, we're falling, I'm so sorry Meg I'm —*

And then he felt the ground beneath him and had just enough time to realize that it didn't hurt as much as he'd expected before he blacked out and thought nothing else at all.

"Calen?"

Meg's voice, calling from some strange distance but slowly growing closer.

"Calen?" He felt her hands then, touching his face. "Calen, please. Open your eyes."

He opened them. He was lying on the ground. Meg's worried face was looking down at him. She didn't look dead.

"You don't look dead," he told her.

She stared at him. Then one of her familiar scornful looks stole across her startled features and she shook her head, starting to laugh. He was glad to hear it. Dead people didn't laugh at you. They were too busy being dead. And if she wasn't dead, then probably he wasn't either. Carefully he raised his head and looked around.

They were in a forest. He was lying in the dirt and grass on the forest floor, near the base of a large, dark tree. The tree was of a species he'd never seen before. Which was very strange. He sat up.

Meg had stopped laughing and was sitting with her legs tucked underneath her, watching him. Her pale skirts were smudged with dirt. The forest was quiet, and dark for the middle of the day. The thick branches overhead blocked most of the sun.

"Are you all right, Calen?"

"I think so," he said. Nothing felt broken, anyway, or permanently damaged. It was beginning to become clear that they had not, in fact, fallen from the window ledge. Or at least, if they had, they had not landed in the courtyard. No prickly animal-shaped hedges. No castle, for that matter. Just this quiet forest of strange trees.

"Where are we?" he asked finally.

Meg's eyes widened slightly. "You don't know? I thought — I thought you brought us here, somehow. To get us away from . . ." She stopped and shook her head. "What happened, Calen? She was waving her arms around and shouting out words that didn't make any sense, and then *you* started waving *your* arms around —"

"She's a mage," he said quietly. "She was casting a spell, trying to kill us."

"But — that's not possible. She's not a mage. How could she be a mage? She's a scholar. An advisor. She doesn't even have the marks."

"I know. I don't understand it either. But trust me, that's what she was doing." He felt cold inside. All mages wore marks. It was — more than law. To have that sort of power, and walk about unknown . . . There had been a time when mages ruled lands and led countries, when they joined together into bands and small armies, long before the present standard of solitary mages pledging their crafts to individual kings and households. It had been a terrible, chaotic time, and only the formation of the Magistratum, the careful application of laws and boundaries, and the clear marking of anyone taught to use the magical arts had been able to restore order and allow non-mages to feel safe in the knowledge that mages would never again seek to use their power to rule and control and destroy.

It had been nearly three hundred and fifty years since the Magistratum was created, and since that time, mages had dedicated themselves to the proper and responsible use of their skills and talents. It was unthinkable to conceal one's ability to use magic. And it should have been impossible. Every apprentice was given his first mark immediately upon commencing his education. Sen Eva's face was untouched.

Everything about this was wrong.

Meg stood up, brushing twigs and grass from her dress. She looked very out of place in the forest. "All right. Let's — let's just figure out how to get back. We'll get back, and we'll tell my parents what happened, and what we heard, and they'll — they'll take care of it." She looked at Calen, despair fighting with hope in her expression. "Are you sure you didn't bring us here?"

"Yes. At least, I think I'm sure." He tried to remember exactly what he had done. He had been trying to protect them from whatever Sen Eva was casting, instinctively reaching for what he thought of as blue energy — the color he associated with sleep magic, water magic — maybe just somehow trying to quench the red fire of whatever deadly spell she was weaving. It sounded rather stupid now, but he hadn't had much time to consider; he had simply acted. He had never tried anything like that before. And all he had been going for was a sort of shield — certainly not a transportation spell of some kind. He didn't have the first idea of how to go about something like that. He didn't even know if it was possible.

He shook his head. "I don't know, Meg. Maybe whatever I did reacted with Sen Eva's spell in some way and sent us here as a result. Or maybe my magic didn't do anything, and this is all Sen Eva's doing." But he didn't think so — that red fire had been death, he was sure of it.

"Well, could you try? I mean, try to send us back? Not to that same room, of course, but . . ." She trailed off, watching him shake his head again.

"That sort of magic is completely beyond my ability, Meg. I'm sorry. I wouldn't even know how to attempt it."

She sighed, then planted her fists on her hips, thinking.

"All right," she said finally. "First things first. Let's try to figure out where we are. How's your geography?"

"Not very strong. I know Kragnir is northwest of Trelian, in the mountains, and Eldwinn is far to the south. I know the towns we passed through on our way from Eldwinn to the capital. I know where Haverton is, where I was born." He shrugged apologetically. "That's about it, I'm afraid."

Meg stared at him. "Well. You weren't kidding. Not very strong, indeed." After a minute she sat down next to him. "I'm sorry, Calen. That was unkind. I'm just — upset. And frightened. If we don't get back in time . . ."

"I know," Calen said softly. He looked around again. "Well, I can tell you this much. We're not anywhere near Trelian."

"How do you know?"

He pointed. "These trees. I've never seen this kind of tree before."

"What does that have to do with anything? Maybe you just never happened to see one."

Calen got to his feet and touched the bark of the nearest tree, looking up into the branches. The leaves were a very dark green, shaped like five-pointed stars. "Serek makes me study trees. And plants and flowers and herbs and anything else that grows from the ground. It's important for healing, and lots of other kinds of magic. I've painted charts for him detailing all the trees in your father's kingdom. These were not among them."

Meg digested that for a moment. "You don't just mean near the castle." It was not a question. "You mean we're not anywhere in my parents' lands."

Calen nodded.

Meg bit her lip, staring at the ground. "That's not exactly good news." She picked up a stick and poked at the dirt. "Any thoughts on what direction Trelian might be from here?"

He shook his head for what felt like the thousandth time that afternoon. "I could figure out which direction is north, but that won't tell us which direction we need to go to get home. And, Meg . . ." He thought she must already know, but he still didn't want to say it.

"Yes, Calen?" Her voice was soft. She was still poking the dirt with her stick.

"Even if we picked the right direction to travel — if we're outside Trelian, and we are, I'm sorry, but I know we are — there's no way we'd make it back before the wedding. Not on foot." And if what they had overheard was still the plan (and why shouldn't it be, now that they were out of the way?), Wilem and Sen Eva were going to kill Maerlie on her wedding night.

By the time they made it back — assuming they made it back at all — Maerlie would be dead. Meg was never going to see her sister again.

CHAPTER ELEVEN

I N THE END, THEY TOSSED MEG'S stick in the air and started walking in the direction it pointed. It seemed as good a way to decide as any. They both knew it hardly mattered whether they were headed toward Trelian or not. But walking felt better than sitting. Besides, it was cool in the forest, and moving helped them stay a little warmer.

Meg picked up the stick again before they left and was using it to strike at the tall thin plants that grew in patches between some of the trees. Calen followed silently behind her. She thought he had been about to speak several times, but so far he hadn't said anything since they made their decision to start walking. She hoped he wasn't too angry with her. She was angry enough for both of them. Of all the stupid times to lose her self-control! If she had only remained silent, they could have waited until Wilem and Sen Eva left the room and then gone and told her parents what had happened. They could have saved her sister and the prince and ensured that the traitors were stopped and punished and possibly tortured for their intended crimes. She could have seen to Wilem's torture personally.

She struck out at another of the tall plants with her stick, slicing off the wispy tendrils at the top of the stalk with the force of her blow.

Wilem's false affection for her was nothing compared to his plans to murder Maerlie, but somehow Meg couldn't stop thinking about it. It was stupid, but she couldn't help it. How could it be so easy for someone to lie that way? Was she just especially gullible? But her sisters had been fooled as well. Everyone had. But no one as — as *personally* as Meg herself. She flushed with shame at the thought of how she had enjoyed kissing him, how she had daydreamed about doing it again, and again. She had liked him so much. She had *trusted* him. And just as he'd apparently intended, she'd given him the information he needed to carry out his mother's terrible plan. He had seemed so good, so strong and honest and true and kind, and he had made her feel special and warm and all the time he was *using* her, laughing at her behind his sad, dark, beautiful eyes.

She wiped angrily at her own eyes, hoping Calen couldn't see that she was crying. Weak. She had been weak and stupid, and now Maerlie was going to pay the price for her failings.

"Meg?" Calen asked softly. He was right beside her. When had she stopped walking? She shook her head, refusing to turn and look at him. Couldn't he leave her alone? Couldn't he see that she wanted to be left alone? She opened her mouth to tell him that but instead she said, "He had been courting me. I don't know why I never told you. We went walking together that first night after dinner. He came often, after that, to walk with me or talk, and he told me that he cared about me. And then, last night, he kissed me. And I didn't know how to tell you; it just seemed hard to talk about him with you, and so I never did. And he was just a liar. A liar and a traitor and now he's going to kill my sister."

"You couldn't have known, Meg." His voice was still soft. She was facing away from him, so she couldn't read his face. "He's obviously well practiced at deceiving people. No one saw him for what he truly is."

"But I spent so much time with him! I thought I was getting to know him so well. And he was just lying! Lying and lying and lying." She shook her head, bewildered anew. Why hadn't she been able to tell? "How can I ever trust my own judgment again? How will I ever know if I can really trust someone?"

He was silent for a moment. Then: "You can trust me."

Meg's mind tried to question that; for the briefest

second she wanted to ask herself, *Can I? Can I really?* But she wouldn't allow it. Calen had risked trouble and worse for her more than once; he was helping her with Jakl and keeping her secret and hadn't ever asked for one thing in return. He had just saved her life, for gods' sake! She turned to look at him and even now she could see the difference. Wilem's eyes had been beautiful, and she thought the sadness in them had been real, but they had never been as clear and true as Calen's eyes were.

"I know I can," she said. And she did. She tried to force the truth of her words into her eyes, the way his eyes always shone with truth, so he would be able to see and believe her. "Thank you, Calen."

He didn't seem to know what to say back. He gave her a tentative, awkward smile and then made a show of looking around, studying what little of the sky they could see through the trees above. "We should probably keep walking while we have the light," he said after a moment, "but before too long we'll need to stop and think about making camp."

"Camp," she repeated, looking around at the surrounding forest. "It's hard to believe that we're really going to sleep out here in the woods and the dark, with the animals, and . . . who knows what else." *No.* She refused to consider what else there might be. *Just animals. Little ones, probably. Squirrels and things.* But then an alarming thought struck her. "Do you even know how to make a fire?" Meg had a vague idea of rubbing sticks and stones together to make a spark, but had no real sense of how one would actually go about that sort of endeavor.

He smiled at her, a real smile this time. "Fortunately, that's something I happen to be pretty good at. I'll show you when we stop." They started walking again, side by side. "Serek and I had to sleep on the road a few times when we made the trip up from Eldwinn."

"Was it just the two of you? That must have been, uh, pleasant."

He laughed at that, and she laughed, too, hearing him. "It certainly was. You know what charming company my master can be. And of course, we had Lyrimon with us, as well." He began relating stories from the trip, incidents she suspected were far from humorous at the time but that sounded quite funny now. As she listened, Meg glanced at the stick she still held in her hands, then let it fall to the ground beside her. She left it lying there as they continued on their way.

"Ready?"

"Yes," Meg said, keeping her eyes fixed on Calen's outstretched hand. He'd told her she wouldn't be able to see anything, but she wanted to try anyway. A second later the kindling burst into flame. He was right. She hadn't seen a thing.

"But you can see it?" she asked.

He nodded. "It's not exactly 'seeing,' though," he said. "At least, not the same kind of seeing as when I look at a tree, or a person, or whatever. I used to have to sort of squint and look at it out of the corner of my eye, but lately it's been getting easier to see without even trying."

"Well, that's good, isn't it? Wouldn't that mean you're getting stronger in your ability?"

Calen shrugged. "I suppose so," he said. He leaned over and fed some larger pieces of wood into the fire. "The truth is, I don't know what it means, really. Serek has never talked about this aspect of magic with me. He's never even mentioned it. I guess he doesn't want me to use it as a crutch, that he wants me to learn casting without relying on seeing the colors. But it's strange that he's never once brought it up. I don't understand it."

"You've never asked him about it?"

He shook his head and sat back. "No. He's not the easiest man to ask questions of. And I guess I was worried about how he'd react." He was quiet a moment, staring into the fire. "Seems sort of stupid now, doesn't it? I should talk to him about it. He's my teacher, after all. I'll talk to him when — when we get back."

"When we get back," she echoed quietly. They *would* get back. They had to. Calen had asked her earlier if the king and queen wouldn't postpone the ceremony once they realized Meg was missing, but she didn't think so. The wedding was too important to both kingdoms. Probably her parents would create some fiction to explain her absence and then quietly try to find her without raising suspicion. It would be difficult for them, she knew, but she also knew they would put the welfare of the kingdom before their personal feelings. The kingdom could do without her more than it could do without this union with Kragnir. Except, of course, that if she didn't get back in time, the union with Kragnir would be destroyed by Sen Eva and Wilem. And poor Maerlie. . . .

No. She couldn't think about that now. Crying again wouldn't help anything. And there was still hope, after all. Maybe her parents would find her and Calen, somehow. Or maybe they'd discover Sen Eva's plot some other way. Or maybe Sen Eva and Wilem would fail during the attempt to kill Maerlie, and Prince Ryant would kill Wilem instead. And then her parents would hang Sen Eva in the courtyard. And her limp, dead, evil body would dangle there, picked at by crows and rats, until Calen and Meg returned safely home.

"What are you smiling about?" Calen asked, startling her out of her reverie.

She shook her head. "Nothing." Back to business. "Do you think Serek might be able to help them find us?"

"I don't know," Calen answered. "I've been wondering about that myself. He might have discovered we're gone by now. I contacted him, just for a moment, before Sen Eva began casting."

She turned to stare at him. "You did? Why didn't you tell me?"

He looked at her sheepishly. "I forgot."

"Calen!" *Gods*, he could be exasperating. "So tell me now! What happened?"

"I had been trying to reach him. Magically, I mean. That's what I was doing when Wilem stopped me, but when you distracted them, I was able to get through for a second and I heard him answer me, which he always told me wasn't possible, that you can't actually really *talk* that way, but clearly you *can*, because —"

"Calen."

"Uh, yes. Sorry. Anyway, all he really said was my name, and he started to ask a question, but then everything happened and the connection was broken. I've tried reaching him again, but I can't. Maybe we're too far away now. Or maybe I'm just not strong enough."

Hope warred with disappointment within her. "Are you sure? Maybe you should try again."

"Meg, I've been trying, believe me. I can't reach him."

"Do you think he might be able to reach you?"

"That's what I've been hoping. But I can't help thinking that he would have done it by now. He knew something was wrong. I'm sure I got that much across, at least."

They both fell silent. The fire was crackling merrily, in counterpoint to their own sorrow and frustration.

"Well, look," Calen said finally. "There's nothing else we can do tonight. We might as well try to get some sleep. Maybe we'll have some new ideas by the morning."

Meg nodded. Sleep definitely sounded good. Except that she wanted her own soft bed, and some hot tea, and her sisters down the hall. She looked at the hard, cold ground and tried not to think about how unpleasant it was going to be to sleep on.

Calen seemed to guess what she was thinking. "I'm sorry, Meg. I'd conjure you a blanket if I could."

She snorted. "If you could, I'd get you to conjure me a whole bed."

"And some food, while I was at it."

"Oh, don't remind me," she said. It was hard trying

to ignore the rumblings of her stomach. She was merely uncomfortable now, but soon enough it would get much worse.

Meg tried to push all such thoughts out of her mind as she looked around for the likeliest spot to lie down. Someplace close enough to the fire to be warm but not close enough to get burned in her sleep, someplace without too many rocks. . . . She looked over to see Calen already spread out on his back, his head resting against a thick tree root. He was watching her, grinning. "You're just like a dog, turning round and round before settling in," he said. "Do you do that at home, too?"

She tried to give him a frosty stare but spoiled it by smiling back. It *was* a bit funny, she supposed. "How did you find a good spot?" she asked him. "There are rocks everywhere!"

He shrugged. "I didn't really think about it. Just lay back where I was and tried to make the best of it." He paused, then added, "Here, wait, let me try something."

He looked around, then pointed the fingers of one hand at a nearby tree that had lots of long, thick leaves. The branches shook as though being buffeted by a gust of wind, and several bunches of leaves floated free to the ground. Calen got up, gathered them together, and then laid them out like a small sort of blanket.

"How's that?" he asked. "It's no feather mattress, but it might help a little."

"I — thank you, Calen." His kindness kept surprising her; it was as if he'd been saving it up his whole life, waiting to have someone to be kind to. She wanted to believe that wasn't true, but from the little he'd told her about his time with Serek and his life as an orphaned inn worker before that, she was afraid it might be. "Did Serek teach you that?"

"No," he said. He sounded thoughtful. "I just — it just seemed like something that might work. Sometimes things just need a little push to go in a certain direction. Those leaves were going to fall eventually; I just encouraged them to let go a little sooner." He shook his head. "It's funny — I keep thinking I need to learn some specific spell for everything, but I know that's not really true. I just never think to try things on my own that I haven't at least read about. But magic isn't like that; you can play with it, try things out . . . I keep having to be reminded."

"Well," Meg said. "I'm happy to give you an excuse to experiment. If you want to try out any other magic spells that might make my stay here in the mystery forest more pleasant, please let me know."

She lay down gingerly on her bed of greenery and found that it wasn't nearly as bad as she'd feared. Maybe the leaves really were making a difference. She must have been more tired than she'd realized, because she felt herself starting to drift off as soon as she closed her eyes. *I can't even feel the rocks at all*, she thought sleepily.

"Meg?" Calen asked softly.

"Mmm?"

"Can you still feel Jakl?

Her eyes snapped open as she suddenly came back to full wakefulness. "No," she said in amazement. Then — "Wait, yes. But just barely." She sat up and turned to face Calen. "How could I not have noticed? I haven't thought of him once, since — well, since this morning."

Calen shifted up onto one elbow. "You've had a great deal on your mind since then," he pointed out. "But you *can* still feel him?"

She nodded slowly. "It's subdued. I can feel him as a presence, but I can't feel what he's feeling. Usually at night I'm very aware of him. I think he's been trying to share dreams with me or something. But now he's barely there at all." She felt the beginnings of panic stirring in her gut. "Oh, Calen, what if he tries to look for me? What if he comes out, and they find him?"

"I don't think that will happen. We haven't been gone that long. And it seems like you've made him understand that he needs to stay hidden. He can probably tell that you're farther away than usual, but that alone might not be enough to drive him out into the open." He paused, thoughtful. "Although, if he picked up on any of your emotions this morning, maybe he would suspect that something was wrong."

Meg glared at him. "Just when you're starting to make me feel better, you have to go and ruin it."

"Sorry."

She waved away his apology. "No, you're right. But it's impossible to know." A thought struck her then. It almost made her laugh, although it really wasn't funny. "But I think he must still be safe. At least so far."

"How do you know?" Calen asked.

She smirked. "Because I'm not dead."

He just stared at her, not seeing it.

"Look, if he had come out and someone had seen him, he'd have been killed. The guards would have torn him apart. They're not taking any chances these days. And if Jakl had been killed, I'd be either dead or insane, right?"

Calen swallowed and managed, "I — I suppose so."

"So for now, at least, we can assume he's still safely hidden away." She didn't add what they both knew — that that could change at any moment, and they wouldn't know until it was too late.

Well, there was nothing she could do. She tried to

send calming feelings through her link, to let Jakl know she was all right, but she knew he wouldn't be able to sense anything from her at this distance. Now that she was aware of how faint her sense of him had grown, she missed him. It was strange to realize how much she'd come to accept his constant presence at the edges of her consciousness.

She lay back down again and tried to rest. The sleepiness that had swept over her so quickly before now eluded her completely. She lay listening to the sound of the fire and Calen's soft, slow breathing for a long time before the welcome oblivion of sleep finally claimed her as well.

CHAPTER TWELVE

CALEN AWAKENED FEELING STRANGELY STIFF and cold. Had he kicked off his blankets in the night? He opened his eyes and blinked stupidly at the trees for several seconds. Then he sat up and saw Meg lying on her scattered bed of leaves, and all the unpleasant events of the day before came crashing back upon him.

He must have made some noise when he sat up; Meg was starting to stir now, too. He watched her go through the same process of sleepy confusion and sudden, shocking remembrance.

"So it wasn't just a bad dream," she said quietly.

"No," he answered. "I'm sorry."

She nodded wearily and then stretched, apparently feeling the same stiffness in her own limbs. Sleeping outside will do that to a person. At least his body had a faint memory of dealing with this during his travels with Serek. Poor Meg had probably never slept anywhere other than a soft, warm bed.

They each excused themselves to take care of personal necessities and then sat by the cold remnants of their fire and pointedly did not speak of breakfast.

Meg was frowning at the ground. Calen couldn't tell if she was deep in thought or just grumpy. Her fine dress was dirty and rumpled, and her hair had come loose from its pinnings. She looked like a strange hybrid of her real and fabricated personalities — or perhaps like Mellie the dirty errand girl playing dress-up in some wellborn lady's castoffs. He was sure he looked no better himself, save that his clothes had not been all that fine to begin with.

"So," he ventured finally, "should we just keep going?"

She nodded. "But first we need to find some water. Food would be nice, but dehydration is the greater danger at the moment." She gave him a half-smile. "Plus we could both do with a bit of a wash. I don't suppose you know how we can go about finding some water, do you?"

"Actually, I do." He couldn't believe he hadn't thought of it himself. What kind of mage was he going to be if he needed other people to suggest his spells to him? Meg was looking at him with a mixture of surprise and admiration on her face. It was a nice change from the usual ways she looked at him.

Calen stood, closing his eyes. Serek had taught him a number of wilderness survival spells. Finding north was one; locating water was another. He had memorized them some time ago, but, not expecting to need them anytime soon, had then filed them away in the back of his brain until Meg reminded him. She was dealing with enough right now; he had to start doing some of the thinking here instead of leaving it all to her. He cleared his mind and reached out with his senses, sending tendrils of invisible white energy out through the forest around them. Almost immediately he picked up a feeling of water up ahead. A small stream, but they didn't need a giant river for washing and bathing. He marked the spot carefully in his mind and then, suddenly curious, he shifted his focus slightly and looked for salt water instead. Trelian was nowhere near the ocean; Serek had had him try sensing the coast from his study, but Calen had not even been able to tell which direction it was. But now he could sense a large amount of salt water somewhere off to the east. More than a few miles away, but not far. Not far at all.

When he opened his eyes, Meg was watching him intently. Still trying to see the magical energy he was working, he guessed. He pointed toward the location of the stream. "There's some water up ahead, not too far from here," he said.

"Excellent. Let's go." She started walking.

"Wait," he told her. He knelt to examine the stone

circle he'd arranged the night before, making sure the last embers of the fire were out. He scooped dirt over the site, just to be sure. Meg watched impatiently, and then guiltily as she realized what he was doing.

"Sorry," she said when he stepped up next to her. "I didn't even think about that."

He shrugged. "It's all right. You've never had a campfire before." They started toward the stream. "What's worse is that I didn't think to check for water. You'd think Serek hadn't taught me anything!"

Meg smiled at him. "Guess it's a good thing we're here together, then," she said. "You take care of the fires and I'll make sure you put your magic to good use. Speaking of which, you're sure you don't have a spell for bringing us home, or sending a message to my father, or anything like that?"

"Meg, I told you . . ."

"Well, just checking. You did forget the water spell, after all."

Calen couldn't really argue with that. He rolled his eyes and said, "Yes, Your Highness. I'm afraid I am quite certain that none of Serek's teaching has prepared me for this particular need. I will continue to dedicate my thoughts to the subject, however, and promise to notify you of any brilliant ideas."

She gave him her best haughty royal stare. "See that you do." Then she tossed her princessness aside and was back to being just Meg. She peered at the surrounding trees as they walked. "See any trees that look familiar yet?"

"Sorry."

She nodded and they continued on their way. Calen had meant his earlier comment to be sarcastic, but all the same, he did turn his mind to sorting through his magical arsenal. Maybe there was something he already knew how to do that could be used to help them in some way. He thought back over the past two weeks of lessons. Now that Serek had really begun focusing on his education, he was aware of just how little teaching had been going on before. He felt he must have taken in a year's worth of training for every day, and there was no doubt that the magic was coming far more easily to him than it had before. He thought his spark must be trying to make up for all the lost time.

But even so, he couldn't seem to think of anything he'd learned that would be of much use here and now. There was summoning, of course, but he'd already determined that was useless at this distance, at least at his current level of ability. He could use his fire skills to set the woods ablaze, hoping to catch someone's attention, but how could they be sure who that someone would be? He still hadn't perfected his invisibility spell, and he couldn't see how that would help them even if he had. Potions, locating objects, healing, dream reading, sleep magic . . . nothing seemed the least bit useful. He kept turning over ideas, but it felt like a pointless exercise.

They came upon the stream in less than an hour. After they both drank their fill, Meg headed upstream to wash. A rocky outcrop provided her some measure of privacy, but Calen turned to face downstream just in case. A moment later he heard Meg scream.

He swung back around. "Meg? Meg! What's wrong?"

Her head appeared around the rocks. She was blushing fiercely. "Nothing. Sorry. Just a fish."

"A fish?" He couldn't quite keep the laughter out of his voice. "Was it, um, a scary fish?"

She glared at him. "It just startled me, all right? It — Oh, never mind." She disappeared again.

Smiling, he turned back to his own task of washing. The chill water would be difficult to endure for long, so he decided to wash only the upper half of his body. That would also prevent him from having to take off his pants, which he wasn't especially eager to do when Meg could easily come back downstream before he was dressed again.

He pulled his shirt over his head and placed it on

a rock to keep it dry. Then he knelt by the water's edge and splashed his chest and arms until he couldn't stand to do it anymore. Shivering, he bent forward to wash his face. Cold as he was, it did feel good to wash off some of the dirt and sweat. He dunked his head underwater and scrubbed his fingers though his hair, then swung his head up and back and shook himself like a dog.

Well, he was certainly awake now, at least. And wet, if not exactly clean. He found a spot where the sun reached down through the branches and sat, trying to dry off some before putting his shirt back on.

After a while, Meg called from upstream. "Calen? Are you, um, decent?"

"Yeah," he called back. She emerged from behind her rocks, carrying her shoes. She had taken out the remaining pins in her hair, and it hung damply around her shoulders. "I forgot about not being able to dry off," she said, sitting down beside him. "I had to put my dress back on while I was still pretty wet."

"You'll dry off as we walk," he said. "Here, I'll get my shirt and we can get moving."

"You wear the sign of the Hunter," she said suddenly.

He looked down. The charm usually lay beneath his clothing, so he guessed she'd never noticed it before. He picked it up, a half-moon carved in stone on a long silver chain. "All mages do," he told her. "It's the traditional gift from master to apprentice at the time of initiation. To remind us that all actions have consequences." Meg came closer, leaning forward to take the charm in her own hand. "We usually think of him as the Harvester, though," Calen added, "instead of the Hunter."

Most people, if they wore anything, wore the bright sun sign of the Goddess. The Hunter was a darker figure, dispensing the cold justice people sometimes deserved as a result of their actions. He was also called the Harvester, representing the idea that people reaped what they chose to sow. Serek had always emphasized that point. *Some mages become too enthralled with their own power*, he'd told Calen more than once. *They forget that directing that power appropriately is as important as being able to use it in the first place. You must never let your ability to cast a spell cloud your view of what that spell will achieve. Or destroy.*

Meg let the charm fall back against Calen's chest, smiling bitterly. "Maybe someone should have given one of these to Sen Eva," she said.

"Someone definitely should have," Calen said seriously. "She should have received her charm at the same time she received her initiate tattoo. That she has neither of those things . . ." He didn't know if Meg really understood how wrong it was for Sen Eva to be able to use magic so anonymously. "I don't know what's worse," he said. "That Sen Eva is secretly a mage or that there's someone out there who was willing to train her in secret. No mage should be willing to do such a thing."

"Much has happened that should not have," Meg said quietly. "And our only chance of setting any of it right is getting home as quickly as possible." She slipped her feet into her shoes and pushed herself up from the ground. He grabbed his shirt and followed her example.

Calen was beginning to get an idea.

He and Meg had fallen back into silence as they continued to make their way through the unfamiliar forest. At first, walking had seemed to make sense, at least made it seem like they were doing something, but it was becoming increasingly clear to both of them that they would never get home this way. And Calen knew that the only real chance they had was sorcery — magic had brought them here, somehow, and he would have to find a way to use it to send them back.

It was obvious that none of the spells he had learned would be enough in themselves. But the flicker of an answer he'd received from Serek in response to his summons suggested that the limitations he believed existed were not necessarily accurate. He was beginning to understand that there were layers of magic, and while a certain spell might not be able to help them in their current situation, perhaps the underlying principle could be applied in a different way. Serek had spoken with him directly, through the summoning connection Calen had established. It seemed clear that they were too far away for that connection to work again; even if it were just a question of Calen's skill not being strong enough, Serek would have contacted them by now if it had been possible to do so. Still, perhaps there was another way. If such communication was possible as long as a link could be established, then all he had to do was figure out another way to form that link. . . .

It was thinking of the connection as a link that gave him the idea. But there was so much he didn't know. It could be dangerous. It would almost certainly be dangerous. But there was so much at stake. Maybe it would be worth the risk. He knew that Meg would agree instantly to try his idea if he proposed it. With no regard for what might happen to her as a result. Which meant it was his responsibility to figure out if it would be safe before he said anything. Which was impossible, because Serek had never taught him anything like this, and he had no books to refer to or any other way to learn more without just going ahead and trying it out. Which meant he should keep his mouth shut and think of something else.

Meg walked slightly ahead of him, pushing through the occasional patches of taller plants that blocked their way. She was still trying to be brave, but he could see her slowly succumbing to hopelessness and despair. Sometimes she seemed to have to fight to keep her head up and her feet moving. It tore at Calen, but he knew better than to say anything. She would never forgive him for noticing.

He tried to think of something to talk about, just to break the silence and distract her from whatever dark thoughts were going through her mind. No topic seemed safe, though. Family? No. Home? No. He supposed he could say something about the weather, but surely . . .

A sudden sound from the trees up ahead made them both stop midstep.

When the sound didn't repeat, Calen edged up slowly to stand beside Meg.

"What was that?" he whispered.

"Some small animal, I think," she said. "A squirrel or . . ."

Then they heard something else — something much

larger — go crashing through the underbrush. This was followed by a squeak of terror and then a small animal cry of pain. Then some unpleasant crunching sounds.

It was too much. Calen grabbed Meg's hand and pulled her backward, stepping softly and praying to all the gods that he didn't trip on a root or stone. After several seconds of back-stepping, they quietly turned and began to run.

They ran until they couldn't hear anything behind them, and then they kept running a little farther for good measure. Calen found them another stream, so they could get some water to drink. Meg looked ashy and shaken, and Calen assumed he looked the same.

"It was probably just another animal," Meg said finally. "A bigger one, looking for dinner. Just, you know, nature taking its course."

Calen nodded. "Sure. Probably not even a dangerous animal. Probably would have run away if it had heard us coming."

They looked at each other silently.

"We're never going to get back," Meg said brokenly. Calen couldn't stand to see the pain and sadness in her eyes when she looked at him. He was failing her. She was too kind to say it, but he knew it was true.

"I have an idea," he said reluctantly.

Her face lit with sudden hope. It was almost as painful to Calen as her sadness had been.

"Wait," he said. "I don't even know if it will work."

"But it's something to try, isn't it? Come on, Calen, if you've thought of something we can try, we have to do it! You know we're not going to make it back this way."

He did know that. That had to mean trying was the right thing to do, didn't it?

Meg was watching him expectantly.

"All right," he said. "Can you still feel your link with Jakl?"

"Yes, but what does that —"

He held up a hand to stop her. Princesses were so impatient! "Do you think, if you could reach him, he'd be able to help us? Would he try to come and find you?"

"I'm certain he would. But Calen, I can't communicate with him that way. You know that. Even when I'm right beside him, I can't send him my thoughts. Just feelings."

"I know. But I think there might be a way I could use my summoning spell, the one I used to contact Serek before we, uh, left. I think I might be able to send it through you, through your link to Jakl."

She blinked. "You can do that?"

"Well, that's the thing. I don't know. I *think* so, but I've never tried anything like this before. That's why I didn't say anything right away, when . . ." He trailed off. Meg's eyes had narrowed dangerously.

"What do you mean *right away?* How long have you been keeping this to yourself?"

Oops. Calen took what he hoped was a casual step back, trying to put himself out of reach of Meg's hands, which looked like they wanted to curl into fists. "Not, um, not very long. I just didn't want to say anything until I felt more sure it would work. But then I realized that I'll never be sure unless we try it. There's no other way to know." He waited nervously to see if she was going to hit him.

Meg looked at his face and then down at her half-formed fists. Her expression softened slightly, and she clasped her hands together in front of her. Then she met his eyes squarely. "All right, then," she said. "Let's try it."

"Now, wait, Meg —"

She threw up her hands. "Calen, *what?*"

"Stop rushing me!" he shouted, suddenly furious with her. "This is important! I don't even know what this could do to you. It might hurt you. It might hurt Jakl. It might do irreparable damage to your stupid, stubborn brain, for all I know! Don't you ever think about possible consequences before you leap headfirst into action? Don't you think it might be a good idea to get all the information before plunging ahead? What if it kills you? What if

233

I screw it up and I end up killing you both? Or all three of us? What if I kill you and it drives Jakl mad and he goes on a killing spree until there's no one left alive in the whole entire kingdom?"

He stopped and they stood staring at each other.

Finally Meg shook her head. "You sure do worry a lot, don't you?" she said softly. She stepped toward him. "I'm sorry, Calen. You're right. I'm glad one of us is thinking about these things. I'm just so desperate to do something — anything — that might get us home in time to save my sister. Even if you're right about all the things that could go wrong, I still want to try." She paused, then added, "If you're willing."

Calen sighed. His anger was gone as quickly as it had come, and now he just felt weary. "I'm willing," he said. "I just wanted you to know that it could be dangerous. I don't really know what I'm doing."

"That's all right," she said, smiling. "I trust you."

He had to smile back. "You're crazy," he said. "I don't even trust me right now."

"Come on," she said. "Let's try it before one or both of us loses our nerve."

They found a large rock, and Calen had them sit down facing each other. Then, because it seemed like the right thing to do, he reached over and placed his fingertips lightly against the sides of her face. Closing his eyes, he started to clear his mind. Meg giggled.

He opened his eyes. "What?" he asked irritably.

"You look so serious."

He scowled at her, but it just made her giggle harder. "Meg!"

"I'm sorry. You're right. It's very serious." She tried to force her grin into a frown.

"You'd better close your eyes, too," he said finally. "And concentrate! I want you to focus on your connection to Jakl. Picture him in your mind as clearly as you can."

She nodded and closed her eyes. When he was reasonably sure she wasn't going to peek, he closed his own eyes again. Once his mind was clear, he reached out through his fingertips, trying to spread his awareness to include the image Meg was forming.

"Meg," he said softly, not wanting to break her concentration, "try to share the image with me, if you can. Think about opening your mind just enough to let me see the picture you've created."

"Okay," she said hesitantly.

Calen waited, trying to allow the image to come to him. And then it did. He could see Jakl clearly, and he knew it was Meg's image and not his own from the level of detail—she included things he wouldn't have even remembered. It wasn't telepathy, exactly — more like they were working together to create the spell, using a shared space that included both their minds.

"Good," he whispered. "That's good. Now hold that image in your mind and think about your link with him. Try to picture the link as a physical thing, like a long tunnel that connects the two of you." Calen reached forward with delicate tendrils of white energy, letting Meg's images guide him. When she had the tunnel firmly pictured, he began to send his spell through it, trying to reach Jakl in the same way he'd reached Serek not so very long ago.

But something was wrong. She had made the tunnel too narrow, as though she were afraid of allowing anything to go through it. And when he tried to reach through the narrow space, he found something blocking the way. Her walls were still up, he realized. She was still afraid of letting Jakl share her emotions too closely.

"Meg," he said gently, "you've got to open the link. You have to take down the barriers completely."

"They are down," she whispered back. "I took them down. It's just the distance; it makes it seem like there's a wall there. . . ."

"No, Meg. There is a wall. Maybe you didn't mean to, but you've placed it there to keep yourself separate from him. And you have to let go if this is going to work."

236

She swallowed. Calen could sense her struggling, but she managed to keep the images in her mind all the same. *Good*, he thought. *Keep focused; just open up. . . .*

For a moment the tunnel widened, the barrier thinned to near transparency, but just as Calen sought to reach through it, it closed up again. "Can't," Meg whispered miserably. "Calen, I can't. If I let him all the way in . . . he'll be everywhere. I have to hold on to some part of myself that's just me. . . ."

He hadn't realized how much she'd been keeping the dragon separate from her. That wasn't the way the link was supposed to work. He'd taught her about putting up the barriers as temporary things — the books suggested the ancient dragon-linked had sometimes put up barriers to sleep or to dim their connections while their dragons were hunting or mating. But it was never meant to be used as a permanent wall. It couldn't be good for the dragon, or for Meg. Not long-term. Once the link was established, both human and dragon needed that connection. It was part of who they were. He had thought Meg understood that.

"Meg, it's the only way. You can't go on keeping him out. Not just for the spell to work, but for both of you to survive. . . ."

"No, you're wrong; it's been fine. We're doing fine."

237

Meg was still fighting with the link, fighting with herself, trying to open the tunnel enough to let Calen through but keep it closed enough to keep Jakl out. The images were beginning to waver. Calen couldn't steady them. It didn't matter, anyway, he realized. If Meg couldn't let go of the barrier, there was no way he'd be able to reach through to summon Jakl. It wasn't going to work. This was probably their only chance, but if Meg couldn't let go . . .

"No," she whispered. "Maerlie." She must have sensed some part of his thoughts through the edges of his spell. He felt her fighting against her own fear, trying to take down the walls she'd erected. He longed to help her, but there was nothing he could do; she was the only one who could make the choice to fully open the link. The images of Jakl and the tunnel steadied, and the tunnel walls began to stretch slightly, his sense of the barrier beginning to disappear . . . Calen waited, ready to reach through to Jakl as soon as the way was open, in case Meg couldn't hold it for long. The tension inside her mind was terrible. She was the strongest-willed person he had ever met, but she was fighting against herself, and her fear and determination were equally powerful.

"Meg," he said finally. "Meg, we should stop. We have to stop. It's hurting you — I can feel it. . . ." He couldn't stand it. Gently, he started to pull away from her mind.

"No!" she cried, seizing him in a way he didn't understand but couldn't seem to resist. She held his mind in place, strengthening the connection he had sought to break and firming the images of Jakl and the link she'd created between them.

Then she let go.

The tunnel walls collapsed to reveal a shining cable of light connecting her with the dragon. Calen began to send forward the summoning energy, but it wasn't necessary; Jakl's awareness came sweeping along the link to meet him, grabbing at the edges of the spell and reaching toward Calen and through him, seeking Meg. Calen got a glimpse of what Meg was so afraid of — the dragon's presence was incredible, overwhelming — he had a moment to be astounded at the strength it must have taken for Meg to keep that wall between them standing, and then Jakl pushed through him, breaking his connection with Meg and actually forcing him physically back into himself so that he had to reach back to brace himself or be thrown from the rock to the ground below. But clearly it didn't matter — it had worked; they had reached Jakl, and if Meg was right, he'd be coming to find them.

Calen shook his head to clear it and opened his eyes. "It worked, Meg!" he said needlessly, for surely she had to be as aware of what had happened as he was, if not more so. . . .

His thoughts broke off as he watched Meg's eyes flutter and roll back into her head. He leaped from the rock and got behind her just in time to catch her as she fell limp and unconscious into his arms.

CHAPTER THIRTEEN

LYING. HER WINGS WERE FINALLY STRONG *enough and now she could soar, fast and true, piercing the sky as* she raced along the path of the link. She had taken care to get high enough that no one on the ground would recognize her for what she was, if they saw her at all, but once she reached that safe altitude, she had released all other distractions from her mind and thought only of reaching Meg . . .

Awareness shifted dizzyingly inside her. *No,* she thought. *I am Meg. That's not —*

Sensations of air and wind and cold rose up to envelop her, and she lost herself again. *Flying. Flying. Following the link.* Meg struggled and then gave herself over to darkness and was gone.

Someone was calling a name. Was it her name? "Meg," someone said. "Meg" and "please" and "I'm sorry."

Don't be sorry, she wanted to say. The voice sounded so sad. But she was too far away. It was hard to hear or speak over the rush of the wind.

The world was an explosion of color and need and physical sensations. Air was life. Water was life. Fire was forming deep and warm inside her. Flight was joy. Hunting was joy. Feeding was life. The link was everything, joy and love and life and fire and sky and earth and soul. She had been incomplete for so long, but now she knew that was ending. The walls that kept them apart were broken and they were one, as they were meant to be. She longed to be together again *now*, struggled to fly even faster. The earth was a blur of green and brown and blue.

Warmth on her face. Sun through a haze of trees. The ground beneath her was cold; why was she lying on the ground? She blinked, and the green branches above resolved into individual shapes. Energy burned inside her. She wanted to get up, to move, to fly — *to fly?* — but her body felt so weak. She couldn't understand what was wrong.

Someone was holding her hand. That was nice. She turned her head. Calen. Calen was holding her hand. She tried to smile, but even that seemed to take too much effort. He was staring away at nothing. He looked so sad. Why did he look so sad? She tried to ask him, but her voice came out as a harsh, wordless croak.

Calen was bending over her in a second. His eyes searched her face desperately. What was he looking for? "Meg?" he said softly. "Meg, are you back?"

She swallowed and tried again to speak. "Back?" she whispered. What was he talking about? "I don't —" She broke off into a cough. Her throat was so dry.

"Let me get you some water," he said. He disappeared from her view. When he returned, he held a sodden piece of cloth. She wanted to scold him — couldn't he have found a glass? — but she was so thirsty. She let him place the cloth between her lips and sucked out as much moisture as she could. The water was cold and delicious. Even sucked from a cloth. He made two more trips. Her throat felt much better. How had it gotten so dry?

He was still staring at her worriedly. "What's wrong with you?" she whispered finally. "Why are you looking at me like that?"

Calen sat down beside her. He hesitated, then asked, "What do you remember?"

Flying. The wind. The sky.

No.

Meg tried to think back. "We were watching them set up for the —" Oh. Right. Wilem. And Sen Eva. Calen waited as she worked her way back through the awful events of the day before. She remembered waking up this morning, and the stream, and the noises in the forest, and running . . .

"And then we were going to try to reach Jakl, with a spell. . . ." Thinking of her dragon brought it all suddenly back and she realized Jakl was there, taking up her mind. . . .

FLYING

"Meg!" Calen was holding her arms, shaking her. She fought back to consciousness. "He's so strong," she whispered. "I can't push him out. . . ."

"Meg, look at me."

She looked. Calen was staring into her face. She wanted to smile at how serious he looked, but it was so hard to focus. She felt disconnected from her body, as though she weren't really there. *I'm not here,* she thought. *I'm soaring, I'm flying, getting closer. . . .*

Meg struggled to keep her eyes on Calen's. Calen was here. And he was looking at her, so she must be here, too. She must be.

"Don't look away," she said softly.

"I won't," he said. He took both of her hands and held them gently. "I'm right here with you. But you have to listen to me. Don't try to push Jakl out. You can't keep the barrier up between you any longer."

244

"But it worked — we reached him," she said. "It's done." Shapes moved at the edges of her vision. Treetops. Clouds. A blur of land below.

Calen spoke carefully. "You have to fully accept the link, Meg. I'm so sorry, I didn't realize you had been keeping yourself apart all this time. It would have been much easier to adjust from the beginning, before the link had grown to its present strength. But you have to stop trying to push him away. You're part of each other now. You have to embrace that."

She was shaking her head before he finished. "You don't understand. He's everywhere. I can't hold on to who I am. I keep getting lost." She couldn't explain.

"I think that's because you're still resisting," Calen said. "Jakl instinctively reaches for you through the link. But instead of reaching back, you're pulling away. And that makes him reach further, and harder." He squeezed her hands. "Do you see? If you reach back toward him, meet him halfway, he won't need to push so hard into your mind."

There was a strange sort of sense to his words, but she didn't want to listen. She wanted her own mind back. Alone and separate and just herself.

He seemed to be able to tell what she was thinking. "Meg, you can't go back to before you found him. You know that. You can only go forward. There's no way to undo it. Ever. I think the sooner you come to terms with that, the better."

"I have come to terms with it," Meg argued. "I know that Jakl and I will be a part of each other's lives forever. But that doesn't mean I have to let him take over my mind. We can be connected but still keep far enough apart. . . ." Calen was shaking his head at her. She felt herself growing angry. And desperate. "What?" she demanded. "How can you know I'm wrong? You don't know anything about what it's really like. You don't know anything!"

His mouth thinned at that, but he didn't turn away. "I know because of everything I've read, Meg. And because of what I saw when we worked together to summon Jakl. I could see the wall you built in your mind, and I could see how it was hurting you both. Jakl was starving for your connection. That's probably another reason why he's holding on to you so tightly now that he's broken through. And I think you were starving, as well. You just hadn't realized it yet."

"No, Calen. You're wrong. It wasn't like that at all."

"Had you been getting anything positive from the link? Was it bringing you any joy? Any happiness? Or were you mostly thinking about having to share your emotions and work at keeping Jakl out of your head?"

She didn't say anything. It wasn't like that. She had experienced lots of positive things. The colors. The energy. But it was true that the stronger the link became, the more she had to work at keeping herself separate. To stop Jakl from trying to share *everything* with her. She supposed she had slipped somewhere into thinking of the link as more of a burden than a source of anything good.

"Well, so what?" she said finally. "What does that matter?"

"People used to risk everything to link with a dragon, Meg. Why would they do that unless the rewards outweighed the danger? You're supposed to be getting something from Jakl in this relationship. I think he's been trying to give it to you. But you've been working so hard at keeping him out, he hasn't been able to."

Meg didn't know what to think. What if Calen was right? Did it matter? Did she want to risk giving up what little control she still had of her own mind to find out?

But I've already lost that control, she realized. Calen's eye contact was the only thing keeping her from being swept away in the rush of emotion and sensation flooding her mind. Was she going to spend the rest of her life sitting across from him and staring into his sweet, infuriating face?

And if Calen was right, holding back was not only

futile; it was wrong. Jakl was depending on her. He needed her, and she kept trying to shut him out. She had to find a way to live with the link. To embrace it, as Calen had said. To live fully in the reality of her situation instead of clinging to a past that was already beyond her reach. She owed it to herself, and to her dragon.

Her dragon, she thought again. Jakl had claimed her as his own from the beginning. It was time for her to claim him in return.

"All right," she said softly. "Let me go."

Calen looked startled. "What?"

She laughed, and his expression swirled with resentment and confusion and relief. "You convinced me, you idiot!" she said, still laughing. "You're right. I know what I have to do. Now you have to let me do it." Meg tried to steady her breathing and ignore her racing heart. She was caught somewhere between fear and excitement; best to let Calen see only the latter. He'd have to be brave enough himself to stand back and not interfere.

"I'm probably going to pass out again," she told him. "Don't try to wake me up."

He started to object, and then visibly forced himself to stop. "All right," he said simply. "Just don't forget to come back."

She smiled at him. He managed a smile back. Small,

but still a real smile. "I won't," she promised. "You just stay here and make sure no wild animals come out of the forest to eat me." She laughed again at his startled glance at the surrounding trees and then closed her eyes, giving herself up to the rush of sensations that came streaming through the link.

Flying. Sky. Wind. Together. Joy. Joy. Joy. Joy.

For a while there was nothing other than the fierce ecstasy of flight and the unparalleled joy of connection. Then, slowly, Meg began to find the far-flung pieces of herself and bring them together. Now she was like a twig swept along a storm-ravaged river. But at least she was a whole twig and not just splinters of wood. She grinned at the metaphor. Then grinned wider at the realization that she was thinking her own thoughts again instead of the dragon's.

No, that's not quite right, she realized. *Not his thoughts. His feelings expressed through my mind. My thoughts, all along.*

Embrace the link, Calen had said. And of course he was right. There was no sense denying what had happened. She owed it to herself to make the best of this. She owed it to Jakl, too.

Carefully, she tried to reach toward him. She couldn't

say how she did it — she had no physical presence here, just her thoughts and sense of self. As soon as Jakl sensed her awareness, he reached toward her, but with such force that she pulled back before she could stop herself. *He's so strong. Too much stronger than me.*

Suddenly she realized — he didn't have to be. That was part of what Calen had been trying to tell her. She could share that strength, make it her own. Somehow.

Gathering herself, she reached forward again, and this time when he rushed to meet her, she didn't retreat. Instead she tried to open herself up to him, letting the rush of emotion and strength run through her instead of slamming against her. She still reeled with the force of it, but now that she wasn't fighting, she could focus on trying to channel it, guiding the energy he sent like the banks of a mighty river, and slowly, slowly, turning it back toward him to create a circular flow of love and power that coursed between them.

It was incredible. For a moment Meg immersed herself in the wonder of what she was feeling. Jakl's energy pulsed through her veins until she imagined she must be glowing with the sheer force of it. She felt his joy in flight, in speed, the pleasure of stretching his wings and the warm fire that was building within him. Above all she could feel his abundant love for her and his gratefulness that she was finally linked with him completely — the way she was supposed to be. That shamed her; she hoped he could sense in return how sorry she was to have kept him at arm's length for so long.

She hadn't lost herself in the dragon as she had feared. They hadn't become one being. Instead they were two that overlapped, girl and dragon, creating between them a strength and identity stronger than either of them possessed alone. Meg was still there, and herself, but she was also — more. She could live with this relationship, she realized. She thought she could learn to cherish it.

Slowly, she pulled herself back enough to become fully conscious in her own body. They were still together — they would always be together — but now the energy pulsing through her was an undercurrent to her own awareness. She opened her eyes.

Calen was watching her desperately, with that same serious expression. When she met his gaze, he flinched so slightly that Meg wasn't sure if he had even been aware of it. But if she had needed proof that she had changed, there it was. She didn't want to think about that now, though. She forced herself to smile. She was done with regret. Move forward, and seize what was good. So what if she was different? She was better. She was more. Calen was still her friend. He'd just have to learn to adjust. Meg felt her smile grow real, if somewhat predatory. It would be good for him.

"So," she said. "No wild animals?" Her next thought came unbidden: *Other than me, that is?* She fought back a giggle. He wouldn't understand.

"Ah, no," he said. He looked at her uncertainly. Then with a small effort he added, "A few mosquitoes, but I think I scared them away."

Good boy, she thought. *It's still me. You can handle it.*

Energy was still coursing through her like liquid fire. It made her think of the warmth she'd sensed growing in Jakl's belly. He'd have his fire soon, if he didn't already. She couldn't wait.

Her body felt weak, but she couldn't sit still anymore. As she pushed herself up, Calen hovered nervously, ready to catch her if she started to fall.

"Do you remember where that clearing was?" she asked. "The one we passed —" When *had* they passed it? She'd lost all sense of time, she realized. "Was it this morning? Or —"

Calen looked at her apologetically. "Yesterday morning. You were unconscious through the night, Meg."

Oh. Gods, another day lost. . . . She couldn't think about that now. It didn't matter. They were going to get back in time. "Can you find it again? Jakl's almost here. I think that would be an easier place for him to land."

"Oh," he said, blinking. "Oh! Sure. Yes. It's back this way." He waited for her to step up beside him, then started walking. Meg felt as though she was looking around with new eyes. Everything was so vibrant. The leaves were singing in the wind.

"So . . . you're okay?" he asked finally. "You're not still feeling lost?"

She shook her head, smiling. "No. Not lost. Not anymore." Suddenly she grabbed him and hugged him fiercely. "Thank you, Calen. For everything."

He stiffened for only an instant and then hugged her back, a little more gently. "You're welcome," he said softly. She could tell he wanted to say something else, but he didn't have to. She knew he understood what she was thanking him for. Without his help, she'd never have made it this far. Jakl would have swept her away forever, probably long before now. Not to mention that she'd be either completely unaware of what Wilem and Sen Eva were planning or dead at Sen Eva's traitorous hands. "I'm so glad you're my friend," she whispered against his shoulder.

He squeezed her again and then let go. "So am I," he

said. His eyes were shining as he turned and led the way back into the trees.

When they reached the clearing, Meg nodded to herself. This would definitely be easier for Jakl. Excitement bubbled up inside her as she thought about how soon he'd be here. With everything that had happened, she hadn't realized just how much she'd been missing him the last two days.

Calen was off to the side, doing his point-and-turn spell to find north. He'd said he wanted to be able to figure out where they'd been once they got back.

Something suddenly surged within her, and she looked up. There, above the clouds, a dot growing larger as she watched. He'd found them.

Calen followed her gaze, squinting. "Is that him?"

She gave him one of those stares she reserved for his stupidest questions. "No. It's Jorn and Mage Serek, racing to our rescue on the back of a flying golden unicorn," she said sarcastically. Calen looked at her and shook his head. Then he turned back to watch the sky. After a moment, she went over to stand beside him.

The dot grew slowly closer. It seemed to take forever. Meg's pride and pleasure at watching Jakl fly warred with impatience; part of her felt she could not truly believe he was here until she touched him. She wished he was on the ground already. Beside her, Calen made a small sound in his throat. "He's really high up there, isn't he?" he said quietly.

"I know," Meg said proudly. "It's amazing. I didn't realize how strong he'd become." She suspected that part of her pride was coming from the dragon himself — he was feeling quite proud and self-important. *Conceited creature,* she thought fondly. She couldn't hold it against him.

"Gods," Calen said. "Seeing him in the sky like that — he's enormous. I hadn't realized . . ."

He was right. Jakl looked even bigger than when she'd last seen him. And not just big — powerful. His wings beat steadily, his scales shining in the sun, a million shades of green. Suddenly he threw back his head and roared triumphantly into the sky. She saw Calen cringe from the corner of her eye, but Meg thought the sound was beautiful. It was everything the horrid screams of the garden monstrosity had not been — strong and true and lovely to hear, like a favorite song or a mother's lullaby remembered from childhood. As Jakl finally neared the ground, arching his back and pulsing his wings backward to slow his speed, Meg found she couldn't wait any longer. She ran forward to meet him.

"Meg, no! He'll crush you!" Calen cried out behind

her in horror. She laughed at the idea. Jakl would never harm her. She reached him just as he touched the ground, throwing her arms around his neck and hugging him fiercely. He nuzzled the edge of his jaw against her hair and then raised his long neck, pulling her up with her feet dangling above the ground. "I see you've grown big and strong while I've been away," she said. "Now put me down again, please. And say hello to Calen."

Calen had walked forward cautiously. "Hi, Jakl," he said. "Good to see you."

Jakl rammed him playfully with his head, knocking Calen from his feet. Meg laughed again. "He's glad to see you, too," she said.

"Clearly," Calen replied, scowling.

"All right, then," Meg said, turning back to the business at hand. "Jakl, do you think you're strong enough to carry both of us back home?" In response, the dragon crouched low, inviting them to climb onto his back. He did seem to understand her words, although perhaps the meaning came through the link, not her voice. She supposed it didn't matter either way.

Calen made another of those small sounds behind her. Meg turned to look. His face had gone pale, and a look of horror stole across his features.

"Well, that was the idea, wasn't it?" she asked him. "How else did you think we'd get back?"

Calen swallowed, not taking his eyes from the dragon. "I — I don't know. I guess I hadn't quite thought this all the way through." He looked up at the sky, then at Meg. "I don't know if I can do this."

"Of course you can. Here. I'll ask Jakl to take me up first, to show you. You'll see. It will be fine." She turned back to the dragon. He was so big; she guessed the hardest part was going to be getting up onto him in the first place. Jakl must have sensed her hesitation. He twisted his supple neck around, grabbed the back of her dress with his jaws, and, with a quick swinging motion, deposited her onto his broad back. "Thanks," she said once her breath returned. In a lower voice she added, "When it's Calen's turn, I think you might want to let him climb up by himself."

She settled herself at the base of his neck, where it was narrow enough that she could drop her legs down on either side. His scales lay flat and smooth beneath her. There wasn't really anything to hold on to, so she reached forward and wrapped her arms around his neck as far as they would go. As soon as she was in place, Jakl launched himself from the ground and tore straight up into the sky.

Meg forgot to breathe. Earth and sky and clouds swept by in a colorful blur as she and the dragon shot through the air. They were beyond birds, beyond clouds, beyond anything earthbound creatures could know or understand. They were a comet, hurtling through space and time. Seconds or hours might have passed before she remembered herself and their purpose. Her back was cold from the rush of wind, but beneath her the dragon was full of heat and fire, upside down and midloop, showing off for her and probably terrifying poor Calen beyond all hope. "Enough," she whispered, and he reluctantly straightened out and selected a more sedate pace, remaining upright and circling placidly like a pony in a ring. He was still magnificent, but Meg found herself longing for their former speed and power almost as much as he did. *Another time,* she promised them both. Right now they had to collect Calen, if he hadn't run away in terror, and get home as fast as they could. She smiled at that last part, and she felt Jakl's echo of anticipation through the link.

"But no acrobatics," she whispered as they made their way back down to the clearing. The dragon was noncommittal.

CHAPTER FOURTEEN

CALEN WANTED TO THROW UP. MEG and Jakl were coming back down, and once they landed, they would expect him to climb aboard so they could leap back up into the sky and fly away home. That was impossible, of course. He could never go up there in the sky like that. He did not belong in the sky. He knew where he belonged, and that was firmly on the ground. At all times. So he would just tell Meg that she should go on without him. Maybe she could let Serek know where he was, and Serek could conjure him home somehow. Or he could just walk. How far could it really be?

The earth shuddered under his feet as the dragon slammed to the ground. Calen stood where he was, frozen. He wanted to run away. He probably would be running away right now if he could just get his stupid legs to move. Meg sat looking at him for a moment, then slid to the ground. She walked over, smiling what was probably supposed to be a gentle, reassuring smile, but wasn't. It was her eyes that spoiled it; they seemed feral and unpredictable. She *had* changed, he realized. There was a wildness to her now that frightened him. He felt like a sheep standing before a lioness.

"Calen?" she said softly. "It's time to go."

Sure. Right. Time to go. She was crazy. He couldn't do it. Shame rose up inside him, coating his heart and mind like thick, black slime. He could not meet her eyes.

Meg gripped his arm. "Calen, there's no other way."

"You don't understand," he said, staring at the ground. "You're not afraid of anything. You don't know what it's like."

Her hand on his arm turned into a pinch. He jerked at the sharp pain and looked up at her in surprise.

"I think that may be the stupidest thing you have ever said to me," she said. "If we had more time, I would give you a complete list of all the things I was, am, and will ever be afraid of, the most significant of which you have been directly involved with not so very long ago but have apparently already forgotten, but for now I will simply tell you that I am afraid my sister will die if we don't get home in time to save her."

She was right, of course. He hadn't thought he could feel any more ashamed than he did already. There was nothing he could say. Meg turned and walked purposefully back toward the dragon. Calen followed. He had no choice. He was more terrified than he had ever been in his life — somehow it was even worse than the moment he'd realized Sen Eva intended to kill him — but there was no way he could look at Meg and tell her he wouldn't help her save Maerlie because he was too afraid of heights.

With each step toward Jakl, Calen's stomach inched higher into his throat. He tried to ignore it. *All you have to do is sit there and hold on,* he told himself firmly. *Sit there, hold on, don't look down. And don't get sick.* He thought Meg would probably forgive him if he threw up on her. He wasn't so sure about the dragon.

Meg said something to Jakl and then began climbing up to his back. Calen watched and tried to follow her lead. Ignoring the pounding of his cowardly heart, he placed his hands against Jakl's side. The scales were smooth and hard, but not slippery. That was slightly reassuring. He had never been much of a climber — climbing always led to someplace higher than where you were — but Jakl's foreleg provided a good starting place. He half expected the dragon to shake him off like a flea, but Jakl didn't even deign to notice him until he paused a little too long in his climbing. Then the long neck twisted slowly around, bringing the serpentine head close enough that Calen could feel the dragon's hot breath on the side of his face. He quickly found another foothold and went on.

261

Jakl was apparently eager to get underway, and Calen had no desire to start this horrifying journey by angering his mode of transportation.

When he finally reached the top of the dragon's back, he crawled forward to where Meg was straddling the base of Jakl's neck. She twisted around to look at him. He wanted to apologize for what he said earlier (especially in case he didn't have a chance later on because he fell off and died on the way), but before he could say anything she smiled at him. "Don't worry about it," she said. "I know this is hard for you. It means so much to me that you're doing this. Now sit behind me and put your arms around my waist. Pretend we're riding double on a really big horse."

Despite his ever-growing fear, he had to smile at that. "Right," he agreed. "A really big, scaly, flying horse. Not frightening at all."

She laughed, and everything was all right between them again. He reached gingerly around her with both arms and clasped his hands together. She snorted and grabbed his arms, pulling them tighter against her. "This is no time to be overly polite, Calen. Hold on tight. If you fall off, I'll never forgive myself."

She's just kidding. You know she's only kidding. But he gripped her more tightly all the same. And then the dragon lurched forward and up and into the air, and he was clutching her for dear life. Idiotically, he risked a glance down. His stomach threatened to fall out of his mouth as his heart sunk somewhere around his knees. How were they so high up already? The trees were like tiny green shrubs, the clearing the size of a paving stone. He wanted to close his eyes, but his eyelids wouldn't respond. He was grateful when the clouds cut off his view of the ground, until he realized what that meant. *We're higher than the clouds.* Blackness swam at the edges of his vision, and he fought to drive it away. He could only hope that if he fainted and fell, he'd remain unconscious the whole way down.

Meg was practically pulsing with energy and excitement in front of him. So was Jakl. He could almost feel their joy and pleasure rising in waves around him. He tried to be glad someone was enjoying this experience. It wasn't easy. He resisted the urge to ask Meg if they were almost there.

Time passed slowly. Calen grew no less terrified, but he made the surprising discovery that constant, unrelieved fear was not only exhausting but boring as well. Meg was no help. She was gone, lost in whatever place she went to in her mind to share experiences with her dragon. It

263

would have been too hard to talk anyway, with the wind rushing around them and the relentless drumming of his heart drowning out most other sounds. He needed something to distract himself from the thought of how far away from the ground they were, and how long it would take him to plummet to his death if he fell. He thought about trying to contact Serek again, but he doubted he'd be able to maintain the necessary level of concentration. Or worse, that he would be able to concentrate but in doing so would forget to hold on, and then go plummeting to his death. All lines of thought seemed to lead to plummeting and death. It was quite distressing.

One small corner of his weary, terrified mind was still able to marvel at the fact that he was riding on the back of a dragon. Maybe he'd be able to enjoy it in retrospect, once they were safely back on the ground and all danger of plummeting and death had passed. And once they had alerted the king and queen to the plot to kill Maerlie and everyone was safe. He wondered what they would do to Sen Eva and Wilem. Hopefully something painful. Maybe Jakl could carry them up high up into the air and then drop them. He bet Meg would enjoy hearing them scream as they plummeted to their deaths. He might even find it slightly pleasant himself. They deserved it for what they were trying to do.

Of course, Sen Eva might have some magical resources that would make her execution harder to guarantee. Maybe Serek would know what to do. Calen frowned. It was all so complicated. He almost wished he and Meg had never overheard Sen Eva and Wilem talking in the first place. But that was cowardly, and he knew it. Then they would have had no warning of what Sen Eva had planned, and Maerlie would almost certainly die. He could not wish for that, no matter how complicated or difficult their situation became. And besides, surely the worst was over now. All they had to do was get home and tell Serek and Meg's parents everything, and it would all be okay. Sen Eva and Wilem would be stopped and punished, Maerlie and Ryant would get married, the two kingdoms would be united, and everything else would go back to normal. He looked forward to worrying about nothing worse than avoiding Lyrimon and keeping up with his magical training.

Calen's arms were beginning to cramp. How much farther could it be? Surely Meg could get some idea from Jakl. He opened his mouth to shout the question at her, but at that moment he felt the dragon shift direction and start descending. They dropped through the clouds, and then Meg turned slightly to shout in his ear. "Jakl needs to rest! He's going to try and find a good place to stop."

"Okay!" he shouted back. He fought back his disappointment. He should have realized it was too soon for them to be approaching home.

Before he could think better of it, Calen glanced down. They were still up at a dizzying distance, but that wasn't the only thing that made him gasp sharply. He could see the tiny tops of trees, and what had to be another clearing in the woods, but there were also — shapes — moving below them. He looked at Meg; she was staring down in confusion. "What are those things?" he shouted. She only shook her head, still staring.

They were big, whatever they were. As Jakl dropped closer, Calen kept expecting the dark moving shapes to resolve themselves into something recognizable, but they did not. He was beginning to get a bad feeling.

He leaned close to Meg, putting his mouth beside her ear.

"I think we should go!" he shouted. Meg nodded slowly, her eyes still locked on the scene below. Jakl was circling now, no longer descending but not yet moving on, either.

Suddenly a terrible scream pierced the air around them. Meg sagged back against him. "Oh, gods, no," she said. She spoke softly, but her face was close enough to his that he could make out her words clearly.

"What is it?" he asked. "Meg, what is it?" The sound of the scream still lingered in his ears, in his mind, like an oily residue. He had never heard anything make a scream like that. He did not wish to hear it again.

"It's the thing from the garden," she said. "The monster. Another one. But there are so many. . . ."

Calen felt his eyes widen. If each of those lumbering dark shapes was one of those terrible creatures . . . A horrible thought occurred to him. "Meg, they can't fly, can they? That thing that attacked you. Did it have wings?"

She stared at him. "No. I don't think so." He saw her struggling to remember. "No. It didn't have wings."

They looked back down toward the ground. Now that they knew what they were seeing, they could make out heads and bodies. There were smaller shapes — people? — mixed in among the larger ones. Some of the larger heads seemed to be looking up.

Looking up at *them*.

"Time to go," Calen said. "Time to go right now."

Meg nodded again and leaned forward. She didn't say anything, but Jakl began climbing once again, moving quickly toward the layer of clouds. Another terrible scream sounded from below. Calen couldn't help it. He twisted around to look over his shoulder.

One of the shapes had separated itself from the others.

As he watched, transfixed by fear, it unfurled long, black wings from its misshapen body. They glistened slickly in the sunlight. The wings slowly pumped once, twice, and then the thing lumbered awkwardly into the air.

"Meg," Calen managed. "Oh, gods, Meg. This one has wings."

She didn't hear him, couldn't hear above the rush of wind, but then the thing screamed at them again, a challenge, and Jakl turned to meet it. "Jakl, no!" Meg started, then broke off in horror when saw what was coming for them. The dragon arched his neck and back, bringing his legs up before him. "Hold on!" Meg shouted. Calen didn't need to be told. He was already clutching her desperately, praying that she had a tight hold on the dragon, or they would both be lost. He felt the dragon's abdomen swell beneath them. Jakl inhaled deeply and then let loose a spray of steaming, clotted spittle. Meg was shaking her head. He thought she was crying. It was too early; Jakl didn't have his fire yet. They were all three going to die.

The thing from the ground was close enough now that Calen could see its awful face, a lumped-together heap of flesh and teeth and tiny red eyes. It opened its mouth to scream again, and Calen buried his head against Meg's back. The sound tore through the air, through them; he could feel the vile assault of it like a knife, like a hundred knives, and his fingers wanted to go slack in their grip from pain and terror. He forced them to hold on and screamed himself, in fear, in defiance, in prayer, spitting out the dirty strands of Meg's hair he'd inhaled to scream again. Meg was screaming too, but her screams had words to them. "Don't let it touch you!" she was screaming. "Don't let it get you with its claws!" She was thinking of the poison, he supposed. Personally he was more concerned about the teeth.

Jakl roared a warning at the approaching monstrosity, but it had seen his lack of fire and was not afraid. Calen lifted his head, compelled to watch their quickly closing doom. Even if he could clear his racing mind enough to work a spell, there was nothing useful he could cast. Lighting candles and slamming doors were one thing, but — He caught his breath suddenly. Candles. Lighting candles. Why hadn't this ever occurred to him before? He had fire of his own. Maybe not the devastating stream that Jakl would have one day, if he survived long enough, but at close range, even a little flame could cause a bit of damage.

The shock of this realization distracted him momentarily from the horror approaching, and Calen made full use of his sudden feeling of detachment. He focused inward, and in a blink his mind was clear and ready. The monster was close now, and Meg was still screaming warnings and instructions at her dragon, but everything was muted and far away as Calen studied the problem before him. *There*, he thought. Long, pointed, whiskerlike quills sprouted from several surfaces of the thing's head and face. He picked one and stared at it, blocking out everything else. *It's a wick. A long, ugly wick, and lighting wicks with flame was the first lesson I ever learned.* A glance, a thought directing the energy, and it was done. The quill ignited, bursting into flame that rose up before the creature's eyes. He hoped it could feel the pain through its tough-looking leathery skin, but even if it couldn't, the shock of suddenly being on fire was at least enough to distract it.

Jakl seized his advantage, striking out with his front talons and swiping at the thing's head. The monster dodged, reducing the strike to just a glancing blow, but it fell back, still shaking its head in an attempt to clear the flame.

"Fly!" Meg screamed. "Jakl, fly! Go now! It can't match you for speed!"

She had to be right. Calen had seen how awkwardly it flew, as if still figuring out how to use its thick, uneven wings. Jakl turned and shot into the sky like an arrow, straight and true. When the thing behind them screamed again in rage and fury, the sound was faint and lacking most of its paralyzing force. It was a long time, long after they were sure they had left the creature behind, before Jakl sought the ground once more.

CHAPTER FIFTEEN

MEG WALKED SLOWLY THROUGH THE COURT-yard, keeping to the shadows and trying to be both invisible and silent. This was not at all the triumphant return she had envisioned. Soaring through the sun-bright sky on her dragon's back, she had pictured them landing right before the main gates, in full view of everyone, then bursting into the throne room to announce Sen Eva and Wilem's villainy before her parents, the guards, and any visiting petitioners who happened to be present. She imagined all the listeners' horrified faces, her parents' expressions turning to grim determination as they sent soldiers to collect the traitors. Sen Eva would be sobbing when they dragged her in, Wilem pleading for his life, but it would be no use. She would have watched, smiling, as they were executed on the spot.

Calen had made her see that it was, perhaps, not the best plan. She smiled ruefully in the dark. For someone with no political experience whatsoever, Calen admittedly had thought things through far more carefully than she had. For one thing, it seemed best not to let Sen Eva and

Wilem know they had returned. Better to let them go on believing their secret was safe and not give them any warning that their plot was about to be revealed. If Sen Eva really was a mage, and Calen seemed certain that she was, there was no telling what she might resort to if she knew her plans were ruined.

For another thing, Calen had pointed out that now didn't seem the best time to reveal Jakl to her parents. With the murder plans and all, they would have enough to occupy them without throwing a dragon into the mix. Meg was more than happy to agree with that. She would wait until after the wedding, when things had calmed down.

Meg couldn't help chafing at the idea of letting more time go by — it had taken them through the night and most of the next day to get back as it was — but she knew that Calen was right. And so they waited until full dark, and then a few hours more for good measure. Jakl had let them off outside the castle grounds then headed back to the Hunterheart forest. Calen had set off for Mage Serek's chambers to alert his master about Sen Eva. Which left Meg to cross the shadowy courtyard alone, heading for the kitchen entrance and desperately hoping no one stopped her to ask where she was going or what errand she was returning from. In the darkness, she thought her soiled dress might pass for servant's clothing as long as no one examined her too closely. All she had to do was make it to her family's chambers without being challenged. And then she could tell her parents and sisters everything, and they would know what to do.

Despite the lateness of the hour, the kitchen was still warm and brightly lit. In her frequent excursions as Mellie, she had learned that there was some sort of cooking or washing or preparing or cleaning up going on at nearly all hours of the day and night. Tonight was no exception; the cook's assistant was supervising several scullions at their duties at the far end of the room, near the fire. Servants often stopped in to grab something to eat at odd hours, especially if their jobs kept them busy during the normal mealtimes, and no one usually batted an eye at one more serving girl passing through the room.

She had planned to walk right through without stopping, but the smell of food when she entered the kitchen assaulted her senses with an overpowering intensity. She could not clearly remember the last time she had eaten; all she knew was that the hunger pains that had faded to a dull constant ache inside her flared into full life again, and she couldn't see what harm it would do to take some bread and a bit of cheese and meat on her way through.

She had sliced off the end of a loaf of bread and was just cutting one more hunk of cheese from the table when she heard giggling. Looking up, she saw a kitchen maid and a well-dressed youth sitting in the corner, their heads bent close together. It could have been anyone — there were bound to be dozens of young men that age in the castle this close to the wedding — but she knew instantly, even before she heard his voice murmuring in the girl's ear, that it was Wilem. Fear and hatred rose up within her until she felt herself shaking with suppressed emotion. She looked at the knife in her hand. He was so close. She could walk over and plunge the knife into his back before anyone would realize what she was doing. Meg felt she had never wanted to do anything as much as she wanted to go over right now and kill him. It took her several seconds to coerce her clenched fingers to relinquish their hold on the knife. When she was finally able to let go, she clutched her bread and cheese and turned to leave, but not before her still-shaking hands knocked the cheese platter to the floor with a resounding crash.

Her heart stopped as everyone turned to look. *Don't see me,* she begged him silently as she bent to retrieve the fallen items. *Don't see me — it's not me — you don't see me, please, please, please, you traitorous bastard, please.* She tried to look sheepish and embarrassed rather than terrified, but she had no idea how well she was succeed-ing. She heard someone mutter, "Clumsy oaf," and several other people laughed. As she rose back up to return the platter to the table, she kept her head bent forward, her hair covering most of her face. Then she ran, hoping they all saw the same mortified, clumsy serving girl and that no one recognized the tatters of her fancy dress or caught a close look at her frightened, furious face. More laughter followed her out into the hallway, and she kept running until she turned the corner. Then she froze, straining to hear. No footfalls sounded on the stone floor behind her. Finally, she swallowed and moved on.

The bread was soft and delicious. Meg ripped off a huge bite with her teeth and chewed angrily as she walked. There were so many painful emotions swirling around inside her that it took her a moment to realize one of them was jealousy. *Stupid*, she told herself con-temptuously. All she should feel for him was hatred. Besides, he was probably only sweet-talking the maid for more information about the wedding night. She took a bite of the cheese next and was momentarily distracted by how good it tasted. She had never before truly appre-ciated the pure enjoyment of eating. If it weren't for all the other, far more pressing concerns, she would have gathered up a much larger collection of food items and found some quiet corner where she could sit and eat and properly focus her full attention on each tasty morsel.

Except for the kitchen, the castle seemed quiet; it was late enough that many people had retired to their chambers. On the few occasions that someone else appeared in the hallway, Meg hid her face in her hair and kept her eyes down until they had passed. Finally she reached the narrow staircase of the southwest tower and began to climb. Almost there. At least she knew she would not run into Wilem in some dark stairwell corner, since he was probably still trading gentle whispers with the kitchen maid. And surely it was too late for a noble advisor like the distinguished Sen Eva Lichtendor to be skulking about the castle. Still, Meg would be glad when she reached the safety of the royal family suites at last.

Soft footfalls suddenly sounded on the steps above her — someone headed down. Meg glanced around and then hid behind her hair again. She was too far from the next landing to get there without being seen. Better to pretend she had nothing to hide. She hugged the wall and waited respectfully for the other person to pass.

The footfalls stopped. Meg waited, trying not to fidget. The person was just standing there, looking at her. It couldn't be Sen Eva. It couldn't. She'd be able to feel the waves of evil coming off the woman if it were. Besides,

Sen Eva would have killed her by now. And it couldn't be Wilem unless he had dashed out of the kitchen without her hearing, circled around to run up another staircase, and then run down to meet her here. Why didn't the person speak? Probably he or she was wondering the same thing about Meg, she supposed. *Bloody Hunter,* she swore finally to herself, and looked up.

Maurel was staring at her, wide-eyed, her mouth open in a shocked little circle. "*Meg?* Oh, gods, it *is* you. At first I thought someone had stolen your dress and got it all dirty, and I didn't know what that meant they had done to you or whether I should say something or run and get Morgan. . . ." She trailed off, bewildered. "What happened? Where did you go? We were looking *everywhere* — poor Maerlie even made them open up the secret passage in the cellar so she could check the cell down there that they found Lysetta in that time. . . ."

Meg grabbed her sister in a rough, tight hug that made the younger girl squeak with surprise. Somehow it hadn't really seemed like she had made it home until this moment.

Maurel bore it gracefully for several seconds before she began to squirm. "Ugh, Meg, you don't really smell very good," she said, pulling away. "I think you need to take a bath."

"I'm sure you're right," Meg said, grinning like an idiot. Maurel probably thought she'd lost her mind. "But — wait a minute. What are you doing up at this hour? Oh, never mind. I'm just so glad to see you. And I don't have time to scold you; there are some important things I need to tell Mother and Father." Her grin slipped. "And Maerlie."

"But they're not here," Maurel protested. "What things? What happened?"

Meg barely stopped herself from grabbing the girl again. "What do you mean they're not here?" That couldn't be. They had to be here.

Maurel took a cautious step backward. "Mother went with Maerlie and Queen Carlinda for the bridal retreat. The wedding is in two days, remember? And Prince Ryant asked Father to come for his last hunt, so Morgan is looking after us and . . ." She peered worriedly into Meg's face. "What is it? What's wrong?"

Meg sat down heavily on the steps. They weren't here. The burden of everything she had learned fell back upon her with the weight of a thousand stones. What was she going to do? She hadn't thought any further than getting home and revealing Sen Eva's plot to her parents. She tried to force herself to be calm and think. If the wedding was in two days, that meant everyone would have to return tomorrow. There was still time. As long as

Sen Eva and Wilem didn't discover that she and Calen had returned. He hadn't recognized her in the kitchen. She was sure of it. Almost sure.

She looked up at Maurel. "Where's Morgan?"

"In her rooms. Come on, I'll take you." She reached down and pulled on Meg's hand. Meg followed numbly, grateful that her sister had stopped her endless stream of questions. It would be all right. She would tell Morgan, and Morgan would help her figure out what to do. She thought Maurel could be trusted to keep her return quiet. Her parents would be home tomorrow, and there would still be plenty of time to warn them before the wedding. It would all be fine. Meg wished she knew why she still felt such a strong sense of foreboding. She wished she was certain that Wilem hadn't recognized her. She wished she could climb back onto her dragon and fly away, leaving these problems for someone else. She tried to wrap her sense of him around her, warm and safe, like a blanket.

Maurel knocked on the door to Morgan's rooms and then pushed inside without waiting for a response. Morgan glanced up from her desk, where she sat busily writing. "Maurel, I hope you have a very good reason for being out of your bed at this —" She broke off, eyes going wide as she saw Meg. She was out of her chair and across the room in a blink, grabbing Meg's arms and staring into her face. Meg flinched; her sister looked more angry than relieved, her eyes practically throwing off sparks. A stern lecture would be forthcoming if Meg didn't start talking first, and there wasn't time for a lecture right now.

"Maurel, please close the door," Meg said. Maurel did as she asked, then sat down on the floor with her back against the heavy wood. Morgan looked at the door, then back at Meg. She backed off and sat on the edge of a chair. "Tell me," she said.

Meg told her. She realized almost immediately that she would have to tell about Jakl after all in order for the story to make any sense, so she did, ignoring Maurel's shocked gasps from behind her and trying not to notice the way Morgan's neat eyebrows kept climbing higher and higher on her forehead. Maybe she could still manage not to tell her parents that part of it right away. Maybe. She told about her time spent with Calen and how he was helping her with Jakl and finally how they had met in the east wing and gone together into the empty guest suite to watch the tourney workers from their secret window. Most of that was surprisingly easy to tell; the words seemed to flow from her almost of their own accord, casually spilling what had seemed untellable secrets such a short time before. The next part would be much harder.

Morgan went very still when Meg repeated what she and Calen had heard from behind the curtains. Stupid tears of anger and pain flooded Meg's eyes as she recounted Wilem's betrayal and Sen Eva's blunt discussion of her plans to have Maerlie killed on the night of the wedding. Maurel had gone completely silent behind her, and Morgan seemed frozen behind a wall of denial and disbelief. Meg rushed on, eager to get past this part. She gave her confused retelling of how Sen Eva and Calen had each begun *something* she couldn't understand and of then awakening in the forest, Calen unconscious beside her, with no idea of what had happened or how they had arrived there.

She skimmed over much of what had passed between her and Jakl — they didn't need to know about that, and she doubted she could explain it in any case — and only said that Calen had worked out a way to summon the dragon to take them back home. Maurel whimpered softly when Meg told about the army of monsters they'd seen and the flying one that attacked them. Meg cursed inwardly; she hadn't meant to tell that part to Maurel, but it was too late now.

"We thought it might be best not to let Sen Eva know we'd returned," she went on quickly. "Calen went to speak with Serek, and I came straight here. Well," she amended, "straight here by way of the kitchen. I was starving." Meg left it at that. She couldn't bring herself to mention seeing Wilem. She rubbed wearily at her finally cried-out eyes and wished she still had some of the cheese and bread left.

Her tale told at last, Meg collapsed into her sister's comfortable reading chair, feeling heavy with exhaustion but lighter for the sharing of her burden. "So," she said, "what do you think we should do? How should we handle it? I wish Mother and Father were here to decide, but they're not, so it must be up to us." She leaned forward. "Oh, and Calen wanted me to stress that Sen Eva is likely very dangerous. Sending the guards won't be enough. Perhaps we should consult with Serek before doing anything; with luck he will know some way to prevent her from casting any spells to attack us or escape."

Morgan was silent. She shook her head, not meeting Meg's eyes. When she finally spoke, her words were hesitant. And unexpected. "Meg, I think you're getting ahead of yourself. I want to believe what you've told me, but frankly, all together it's a bit hard to swallow."

Meg felt she must have misheard. Morgan *wanted* to believe? She opened her mouth but couldn't think of what to say. Morgan looked at her with sympathy and concern. Somehow that only made it worse.

283

"I'm not accusing you of lying, Meg. Truly, I'm not. But your behavior has been so odd of late, and this story . . . well, isn't it possible you misunderstood what Sen Eva and Wilem were arguing about? It doesn't make a lot of sense if you think about it, does it? Why would they want to kill Maerlie?"

Hadn't she even been *listening?* "I told you, to get revenge for the death of Wilem's father and brother. I mean, I know the part about our father and King Ryllin has to be a lie, but . . ."

"Meg, listen to yourself. You're saying Sen Eva and Wilem made up a lie to give them a reason to kill your sister. Does that really seem logical to you?"

"No, you're twisting it around. That's not how it was." She was getting flustered. That wouldn't help anything. But she knew what she'd heard. "Calen heard it, too! And then she tried to kill us! Did I misunderstand that as well?"

"You don't really know that's what she was doing. Calen told you that, but you said yourself that there was nothing you could actually see."

"Morgan!" She was shouting now, but she couldn't help it. "Why are you doing this?"

"Because I have to!" her sister shouted back. She struggled visibly to get her voice back under control.

"Meg, please try to understand. Even if you are right, if everything you said is true, what would you have me do? We can't just accuse Sen Eva of murder and treason without a shred of proof. At best, we'd offend King Ryllin and Queen Carlinda. At worst, they would see this as a ploy to call off the wedding and an end to the peace negotiations. They would certainly never believe this story without substantial evidence to support it. Sen Eva has been their trusted advisor for twenty years!"

Meg stared numbly at her sister. She wanted to shake her. She wanted to scream. Instead, she took a deep breath and tried to think. Throwing a tantrum was not going to help. "Morgan, please listen," she said at last. "I know this is hard to believe. I didn't want to believe it either. But I swear it is true. Maerlie's life is in danger. I fear that if we wait, you'll have the proof you seek when Maerlie is found dead the morning after the wedding."

Maurel suddenly ran to Morgan's arms. She was crying. The older girl stroked her hair gently and glared at Meg. "I don't want to hear any more about this tonight," she said quietly. "Mother and Father will be home tomorrow. We can discuss it then. For now, I want you to go to your room and get some sleep."

"I'm sorry to have upset Maurel, but that's not —"

"Meg, I mean it. Go now." She made her voice kinder.

"You've obviously been through a terrible ordeal. And I'm not discounting your story. But I have to do what I think is best, and for now, that means waiting. If you're right about Sen Eva and Wilem, then we still have time. The wedding is still two days away. There's nothing to be gained by rushing to act now. Please. I'll send for a bath to be brought up to your room, so you can wash and then rest."

Meg swallowed the rest of her objections. Morgan was not going to budge. "Fine," she said, defeated. She started toward the door. "Please send for some food as well."

"Of course," Morgan said. "And Meg . . ."

Meg paused, her hand resting on the door.

"I'm glad you're safe. We were all so worried about you. I'm sorry we argued; you know I love you, and I'm so relieved that you're all right. I just have to do what I think is best. I think if you were in my position you'd do the same."

Meg nodded. She spoke without turning around. "I know. I'm sure you're right. We'll talk more in the morning, after I've had some sleep." She opened the door and stepped into the hallway. She closed the door behind her, shutting out the sounds of Maurel's soft crying and Morgan's gentle, reassuring whispers.

When she reached her rooms, Meg opened the door and dragged herself inside. She was so tired. But there was no time to rest. The serving maid would soon arrive with her bath. Just for a moment, she closed her eyes and slipped deeper into the link, letting Jakl's comforting presence surround her. He felt tired too, and no wonder. She'd have to ask Calen if he'd figured out exactly how far Jakl had flown. Usually the dragon's energy buoyed her up without her even having to think about it, but he was clearly at the end of his reserves. Well, she'd just have to rely on her own strength for a while.

Meg sat at her desk and began to write. Once the note was ready, she folded it carefully and marked it with her seal. Then she walked over to her bed and slid the paper beneath her pillow.

She would take her bath, and she would eat whatever they brought her — it would be foolish not to eat some more now while she had the chance. After that, though, she would tell the maids she was tired and ask them to leave. And then she would go find Calen.

If something — happened, if she did not return, someone would find the note eventually. She hoped her parents and her sisters would understand her reasons for doing what she was about to do.

CHAPTER SIXTEEN

I'M NOT SURE YOU REALIZE THE seriousness of this accusation."

Serek spoke calmly, as if they were discussing a lesson or an approaching bit of bad weather. But then, Calen reflected, Serek was always calm. Often it was infuriating, but at the moment Calen was glad of his master's lack of emotion. It made the situation seem slightly less awful, as if it were only a challenging mathematics problem instead of a sickening snarl of treason and murder and giant flying monstrosities gathering in the wilderness.

"An unmarked mage is an aberration," he went on. "If informed, the Magistratum would strip her of her abilities, if they did not simply destroy her."

"They can do that? Take away her abilities?"

Serek arched an eyebrow. "The Magistratum can do a lot of things. And yes, that is one of them. The method varies, of course. A lesser criminal might only have a ward placed on him, which would alert the council if he attempted to so much as light a candle. A mage who not only hid her power but also used her magic to deceive her patron, not to mention to kill an apprentice . . ." Serek shrugged. "If she didn't die resisting judgment, she might have her ability seared out of her by a circle of more powerful mages, or maybe her mind altered, rendering her too simple to cast a spell. There are several possibilities."

Calen swallowed. He had never heard any of this before. "Of course, she didn't actually kill me."

"No," Serek agreed. "Not yet, anyway."

They were seated in Serek's dim study. Serek was at his desk, where he had been when Calen returned earlier that night. Calen was perched on the edge of a table. The chair across from the mage was occupied by Lyrimon, and Calen was too tired to fight him for it. As they talked, Calen fished black olives out of a jar and ate them. He had never cared much for olives, but he was so famished that he would have eaten almost anything at this point, and all Serek seemed to have on hand was jar after jar of olives. Perhaps, once he'd finished the current jar, he'd try some of the green ones.

He hadn't known what sort of welcome to expect when he'd first slipped through the study door. Would Serek be angry? Worried? Indifferent? Undoubtedly he'd want a full explanation of where his apprentice had been. Calen had stalled in the hallway, staring at the tapestries and trying to think of how to explain what had happened. Meg and Calen had agreed that he should tell Serek everything; it was just a question of figuring out how to begin. Finally he'd given up trying to plan it out. He was too hungry to think, anyway. He'd opened the door and walked inside.

"Ah," Serek had said, looking up from his notes. "You live, I see."

Same old Serek. Calen half expected the mage to go right back to whatever he'd been working on, dismissing him, or perhaps to direct his attention to some chores he'd missed while he was away. But Serek had placed his papers carefully to one side of the desk and sat back in his chair, looking at him expectantly. Calen had walked toward the other chair, saw that it was occupied, then made for the table instead, grabbing the olive jar on the way. And then he'd said, "Sen Eva Lichtendor is an unmarked mage and a traitor, and she and her son are planning to kill Princess Maerlie on her wedding night."

After that it had been easy to tell the rest. Serek had listened silently, only asking questions here and there for clarification. His mouth had twitched slightly when Calen confessed to sneaking into the library to read about dragons, but that was all. And now he was calmly discussing Calen's possible death at Sen Eva's hands and the possible awful things the Magistratum would do to her if and when she were caught.

"Well," Serek said finally, pushing his chair back from the desk. "First things first. How certain are you that the woman is a mage? Is there any chance you could have been mistaken?"

"I'm absolutely certain," Calen said.

"And you're sure she was trying to kill you? You did only end up transported, after all. How do you know that wasn't her intention all along — to simply send you away?"

"Well for one thing, she had just been discussing killing us. Or me, at least, although I suspect she had already decided to kill Meg also. But beyond that, I saw the spell as she was casting — it was deep red, like the spell for killing weeds, only much stronger. Or the spell you used on that soldier, that first one who was attacked, when you were trying to burn out the poison. Only this was darker, and . . . worse, somehow." Calen shuddered, remembering.

Serek had stopped and was looking at him intently. "You saw the spell?"

"Yes," Calen said, confused. Hadn't he just said that? "I didn't immediately recognize it, of course, since it never occurred to me that she could cast. But once I realized what was happening, it was unmistakable."

Serek was still staring at him. It was unnerving. Had he said something wrong? "Why?" he asked. "Isn't that what red energy does? I could have sworn —"

"And then you crafted a spell in return?"

"Yes." This was so odd. He'd never had to repeat anything for Serek before. The man remembered everything. In precise detail. "I know I'm not supposed to experiment, but under the circumstances . . ."

Serek waved that away. "How did you decide what spell to cast?"

Calen shrugged. "Well, like I said, I didn't know what I was doing. I saw that red energy coming at us, and there was no time, and I was desperate to stop it from reaching us. I didn't think; I just reacted. Blue energy just seemed right, somehow, as if it could help to block what she was casting, quench the fire — I don't know." He fell silent. Serek was frowning. Calen waited, knowing better than to interrupt his master when he was thinking. He couldn't be angry, not when Calen had just been trying to defend himself, not to mention Meg. What else could he have done?

Serek seemed to have come to some decision. He stood up. "All right. Let's try something. Watch and tell me what you see." He pointed at an unlit candle and sent a small pulse of yellow energy to the wick. It blossomed in flame.

"You lit the candle," said Calen.

"Brilliant," Serek said. "What did you *see?*"

Oh. "Yellow energy, just a tiny blob of it. You sent it to the wick, and the wick ignited."

"A blob."

"Well, yes. What would you call it? It didn't really have a shape; it was just a small amount, but it was thicker than a line." This was no time for a vocabulary lesson. Besides, it wasn't Calen's fault that Serek had never taught him the proper terms for such things. "I don't mean to question you, but do we really have time for this now? Maerlie's life is in danger, and —"

"I need to determine something. By your own words, Maerlie's life will not be in danger until after the wedding, so it seems to me that we do, in fact, have some time. Pay attention and continue." He thought for a moment and then looked at the skull on the edge of the desk. There was a faint, silent burst of purplish fog. The skull vanished and then reappeared on the table beside Calen. Calen's mouth fell open.

"You transported the skull! That's — I thought that wasn't —"

"As you have begun to discover, there are many things I have not yet taught you. Traditionally, apprentices are led to believe certain things are impossible until they are ready to learn them. It prevents them from attempting spells on their own that are beyond their abilities and potentially dangerous. Tell me what you saw."

"Violet, I think. It was very faint. Sometimes it's like that — until recently I had to sort of squint and look sideways to see anything at all. Now most of the time I can see the colors without even trying, but that one was difficult. If I hadn't been staring right at it, I might have missed it. Is that normal? Does it have something to do with how well I know the spell being cast?"

Serek didn't say anything. He was thinking again. Calen sighed and waited. This was all very interesting, but he couldn't understand why Serek was wasting time on lessons when he should be doing something about Sen Eva. She was a threat to the kingdom, and as King's Mage, that was supposed to be Serek's primary responsibility. Plus she was unmarked, which had to mean there was something Serek was supposed to do, some way to alert the Magistratum, so they could come and do whatever they were going to do to her.

Calen dug another olive from the jar and chewed it thoughtfully. He had hoped Serek would know exactly what to do, that once Calen told him what had happened, he would go to the king and queen and make some recommendation and everyone would leap into action and disaster would be averted. They would stop Sen Eva and find a way to fight the monsters in the woods, and everything would be all right again. Maybe he and Meg would even be regarded as heroes, with a big celebratory festival. After the wedding, of course. He tried to imagine what it would be like. Lots of food, to be sure, and dancing, and he and Meg would get to stand up before King Tormon and Queen Merilyn — no, not just them, but the royal family from Kragnir, too — and they'd get medals or something, and everyone would applaud. And even Serek would be proud of him, standing silently to one side, trying to maintain his usual stony expression but unable to hide the pride he felt in his young apprentice. It would be like that time Calen read the spirit cards, and Serek had been surprised and impressed....

Calen stopped chewing. The spirit cards. *This* must be the terrible danger they were predicting. It had to be. He tried to think back. Had they indicated what must be done to avoid the danger? Not everything had been clear to him, but even Meg had said that some of the readings implied there was a chance. Could they do another reading? Would it help them figure out what to do?

"Do tell me what it is that races so forcefully through your mind that your jaw has ceased to work," Serek said dryly.

Calen closed his mouth and sucked the rest of the olive from the pit, which he then added to the growing pile on the tabletop beside him. He looked at his master. "Is this what the spirit cards foretold? Sen Eva's plan?"

"I should hope so," Serek replied. "It would be unfortunate for something even worse to be brewing at the same time."

"Well, does that help us? Can the cards tell us what to do?"

Serek shook his head. "Divination is a far more subtle and complicated magic than that. We were warned, but no dealing of the cards can speak plainly about exactly what will happen or what actions we must take. Another dealing would be difficult, as our own knowledge would intrude upon any meanings the cards might suggest."

"But couldn't we —"

"Calen. Do not push me. Accept that I know more about this than you do and let us focus on what can be done."

Calen nodded reluctantly. If he had learned anything over the past few days, it was that there was a vast amount of magic lore he knew nothing about. Serek had been a full mage for years before Calen had been born, and even he was still learning. He wondered abruptly what Serek had been like as an apprentice. It was hard to imagine him ever being young or impulsive or uncertain. Perhaps he had always been as he was now. That might explain why he didn't have any friends, or any apparent desire to make any. He'd probably never had any friends in his entire life. One more reason to be grateful for Meg.

With effort, Calen forced his thoughts back to the matter at hand. His mind had such a tendency to drift off in every direction. Probably because he spent so much time waiting silently while Serek was thinking about something. His mind had to occupy itself somehow, after all.

"Well," Serek went on, "you have certainly proven yourself to be more than capable of surprising me, Calen. Not just with your news — though of course that, too — but also with your abilities and resourcefulness. You've given me a great deal to think about, not the least of which is how to proceed with your training."

Calen smiled at the implied praise. "If you're asking for suggestions, I think you should teach me some fighting and self-defense magic." *So that the next time someone tries to kill me, I'll be prepared.*

"I was not asking," Serek said. "And watch yourself.

Whatever you've been through, you are still my apprentice, not my colleague." He met Calen's indignant stare and waited until Calen lowered his eyes. "However," he went on, "I do believe some defensive magic may indeed be in order, since it appears you've developed quite a talent for placing yourself in harm's way. It is likely that Sen Eva will attempt to kill you again when she discovers that she did not succeed the first time."

"*If*, you mean."

"*When*. Unless you're planning to leave the castle grounds and remain in hiding until she returns to Kragnir or whatever she does after carrying out her plans?"

Calen shook his head. Of course he couldn't leave. He just thought he'd be able to stay out of her way for as long as it took for Serek and the proper authorities to take her into custody. Which he had expected to be immediately. But he was beginning to get the feeling that wasn't going to happen.

Serek looked at him for a moment longer before speaking again. "What I was originally referring to, if you'll allow me to continue, were the colors you describe seeing. Have you ever wondered why I haven't mentioned these colors during your training?"

Calen shrugged. "Of course. I figured you wanted me

to learn the spells without relying on the colors to help me. Is that — is there a different reason?"

"Yes." Serek was still looking at him in that strange way. "The reason is that I don't see any colors when I cast spells. Nor did the mage who taught me. No other mage has ever spoken of colors to me, and I've never come across any mention of colors in any book I've studied."

Calen felt his mouth working, but no words were coming out. Serek couldn't see the colors? *No one* could see the colors? How was that possible? "But I swear I see them," he managed. "I'm not making it up." Was he crazy? Did it mean there was something wrong with him?

"I believe you. I think you may have a talent in this that's uniquely yours, Calen."

Calen just stared at him.

"Obviously, we will have to investigate this ability further. For now, however, there is the matter of Sen Eva."

"And — and the things. In the woods." *No one else saw the colors?*

"One thing at a time. The creatures you saw were still some distance away, while Sen Eva is here." Serek pushed Lyrimon off his chair and began moving some books from his desk to the newly cleared space, glancing at titles as he stacked them and occasionally putting a particular book aside. The gyrcat watched this process indignantly for a few seconds and then glared at Calen as though it were his fault. Then he vanished.

"What will we do?" Calen asked. He wanted to pull up his legs but didn't want to give Lyrimon the satisfaction. Surely the cat wouldn't attack him with Serek sitting right there. Surely not.

"*We* will not do anything. *I* must send word to the Magistratum. That, before all. I cannot take action against Sen Eva without their consent unless she provokes it with unmistakable actions." He held up a hand to ward off Calen's protestations. "Words are not actions, Calen. She has done nothing to harm Maerlie yet."

"She tried to harm me," Calen pointed out. "Doesn't that count?"

"It would if I had witnessed it and could testify that she truly intended to kill you. I do believe what you've told me, Calen, but I cannot use that to justify taking action. Especially because your knowledge is based on your seeing the spell, which as far as the Magistratum is concerned is not possible. I do not even have proof that she is a mage, but that will not be difficult to verify now that I know to look for it."

"You can tell by looking?"

"No, but there's a way to sense her ability through

physical contact. If nothing else I can stumble into her, but I'm sure I can arrange a less obvious approach."

The thought of touching Sen Eva made Calen shudder. "But we have to do something! What if they don't respond in time? You can't just let her kill Maerlie!"

Serek sighed and fixed Calen with another of his barely tolerant gazes. "Thank you, Calen, for pointing that out. I do not intend to let her harm the princess. I will consult with King Tormon and Queen Merilyn when they return tomorrow."

"Return? Where did they go?" Serek's gaze was turning dangerous. Calen hurried to forestall a rebuke. "I'm sorry to keep asking questions, but Meg — I mean, Princess Meglynne — went to speak with them, to tell them what happened. She expected them to be home."

"Well, she will find that they are not. No doubt she will simply wait until tomorrow."

Calen laughed out loud at that. At Serek's expression, he hastened to explain. "Uh, I'm sorry. Again. It's just that you don't know Meg the way I do. I doubt very much she's simply waiting." He swallowed nervously. "Sir."

Serek opened his mouth to reply, but before he could speak, there was a hesitant knock at the door. Calen's heart leaped into his throat. *It's not Sen Eva*, he told himself firmly. *It's not. It's not.*

Serek had turned toward the door at the sound. Now he looked back at Calen. Perhaps he could tell that Calen was frozen with fear, because instead of telling him to answer the door, he went to answer it himself.

Calen tried to quiet the hammering of his heart. Even if it was Sen Eva — and it wasn't, of course it wasn't — Serek wouldn't allow her to kill him. Unless she killed Serek first. But surely if he was on his guard, she wouldn't be able to do that.

Serek pulled open the door. His body was blocking Calen's view. "Ah," said the mage. He stepped back and gestured into the study. "Do come in."

It was Meg, dressed in her serving-girl disguise. She stepped into the room and stood in the center, as though she didn't know what to do with herself. Then she saw Calen and smiled. Serek closed the door behind her and leaned back against it with his arms crossed.

Calen jumped down from the table and went to meet her. "What happened?" he asked. "Are you all right?"

"I'm fine. Just tired. And my parents aren't here."

"I know — Serek just told me."

"I told Morgan everything. She —" Meg took a breath. "She's not sure if she believes me. She won't do anything without talking to my parents, and she says even they won't do anything without proof."

"She is correct, Your Highness," Serek said from the door.

Meg turned to face him. "You don't believe us, either?" She had placed her hands on her hips.

"Actually, I do believe you. Or rather I believe Calen, which I take it means the same thing. But your sister is still correct. To act without proof in this matter would be foolish, if not dangerous. You would be wise to wait."

"Wait for what? For Maerlie to die?" Meg shook her head angrily. "I mean no disrespect, Mage Serek, but I do not see the logic in waiting. I do see the logic in needing proof, however, which is why I'm here." She turned to face Calen again and took his hands in hers. "Calen, I'm sorry to ask you this. But I need your help."

He was afraid he knew what she had in mind. "What do you want to do?"

She looked straight into his eyes. "Tomorrow, while everyone is at breakfast, I want to sneak into her rooms and find some kind of evidence that will prove to everyone what she truly is."

Calen's skin went cold, except for his hands, which were still held warmly in Meg's grip. How could she suggest such a thing without trembling in fear? If Sen Eva returned and found them there, nothing would save them. She would finish what she'd started in the guest suite, and they would both be dead. But what was the alternative? To hide, terrified and waiting, until it was too late?

It didn't matter. He didn't know why he was debating with himself. Meg needed his help, so he would help her. He met her gaze squarely, trying to reflect the same strength that shone from her eyes. He didn't even have to nod. She saw his answer in his face and grinned.

"Um," said Serek. For a moment, Calen had forgotten he was there. He and Meg turned as one to face him.

"I'm sorry, Your Highness. I can't allow this."

Meg's eyebrows went up. Calen knew that look. He almost felt sorry for Serek.

"Are you presuming to tell me what I can and cannot do?" she asked quietly.

Serek was not daunted. "No. But I can inform your sister of your plans, which would no doubt bring them to a swift end."

Meg's eyes practically threw sparks at that. "Do you truly wish to see Maerlie die at the hands of traitors? Why would you want to stop us from proving what we know is true?"

"It is not the truth I object to, Princess, but your determination to put yourself in danger. I cannot in good faith allow you to proceed without attempting to stop you. It would violate my oath to serve and protect your family." Serek spoke calmly, still standing with his back to the study door. His eyes were flat and hard. Calen knew that look, too. He thought that in a contest of wills, Meg would ultimately prevail, but it would be close.

"Could you come with us?" Calen asked abruptly. Meg and Serek both turned to stare at him. He tried to ignore their incredulous expressions. "You could help us seek proof, and be there to protect us if anything went wrong."

Meg's expression grew thoughtful. Serek, however, shook his head. "I appreciate your confidence in my ability to protect you from an unmarked mage of unknown strength and known malicious intent, but as I said, I cannot take action against Sen Eva without the consent of the Magistratum."

"But this wouldn't be taking action, exactly. You'd just be . . . observing."

"No, Calen." His voice grew even more serious. "You must understand this. A mage agrees to live by certain rules. It is sacrosanct within our order, and when you are fully inducted yourself, you will take vows to uphold them. We cannot simply bend or ignore those rules we find inconvenient. It is exactly this that we accuse Sen Eva of doing, and that makes her a criminal in the eyes of the order. I do understand your desire to act, but it cannot be. Accept this and be done with it."

Meg opened her mouth to argue, but Calen placed a hand on her arm to stop her. Serek would not budge on this. Arguing would only waste time. "Let it go, Meg," he said quietly. "He will not change his mind. We'll have to think of another way." He didn't look at her face. He didn't want to see the sense of betrayal he knew she must be feeling.

"I'll need your word, each of you, that you will not pursue this." Serek was still blocking the door.

"You have it," Calen said. "I will not."

Serek looked at Meg and waited. She glared back at him with a strange light in her eyes. "You have my word that we will not steal into her room while she is at breakfast tomorrow."

Serek hesitated. It was clear there was much that Meg's declaration did not include. But the mage only looked at her and nodded. Calen thought something passed between them. Then Serek stepped aside. "Will you escort the princess safely back, Calen?"

"Of course," Calen replied. Meg took his arm and let herself be led toward the door.

"And Princess," Serek added, "once this current crisis is sorted out, I would very much like to hear more about your dragon. I never thought I would have the opportunity to talk with one of the dragon-linked firsthand; it would be a rare honor."

After a moment, Meg nodded. "Of course," she said. "As long as Calen can join us. He's my personal dragon expert, you understand." She paused. "I suppose I'll have to think of some official title for that at some point."

Calen nearly choked at Serek's pained expression. He yanked Meg back into motion toward the door.

"Good evening, Mage Serek," she said as they passed him.

"And to you, Princess," he replied.

Then they were through and walking along the narrow hallway. Calen heard the door close firmly behind them. When Meg led him silently toward a passage that led deeper into the castle and away from her rooms, he was not entirely surprised.

CHAPTER SEVENTEEN

THE CASTLE CORRIDORS WERE DARK AND silent, save for the sound of their footsteps against the cold stone floor. Meg led Calen down passage after passage and finally down a small set of stairs. The hallway accessed by that stairway was rarely used, and surely never used at this late hour. *This early hour,* Meg corrected herself. It had to be long past midnight. She stopped and seated herself on the dusty floor, her back leaning against the wall. Calen sat against the opposite wall, facing her.

"So," he said, "do you have another plan already? Or do we need to think of one?"

"We don't need another plan," she said. "We're still going to sneak into her rooms to look for evidence. We just can't do it while she's at breakfast."

Calen gaped at her. "Meg, we just gave our word —"

"We gave our word not to look in Sen Eva's room while she's at breakfast. That's all. Really, Calen, you need to pay attention."

He shook his head. "I can't. If Serek found out . . . No. That's not even the issue. I can't go back on my word to him, Meg. It's too important."

How could someone so nice be so exasperating? Meg willed herself to patience. "Calen, think. You heard what I promised. Serek knew exactly what I was saying. Don't you think he would have insisted on less specific wording if he really wanted to stop us?"

"Well . . . but . . ."

She let him think about it. Calen was intelligent, even if he did get in his own way a lot of the time. He'd see that she was right. While she waited, she reached out toward Jakl through the link. She thought he was sleeping. Good. That had to mean he was tucked safely back inside his den. And gods knew he must need to rest. Sleep called to her as well, but she knew they couldn't spare the time. There would be time enough for sleep once this was over. If they were still alive.

"All right," Calen said finally. "I suppose, technically, that is all we promised. Are you saying that Serek wants us to find proof? Why wouldn't he just say so?"

"You heard him. He's not allowed to take any action against Sen Eva. But I'm guessing that doesn't apply to you, because you're not yet a full mage. Didn't you notice the way he made a point of mentioning the whole when-you-are-fully-inducted-you-too-will-take-the-vows business? And of course the rules certainly don't apply to me. I think Serek just needed us to make our plans out of his hearing. That way he can't feel bound to stop us by the rules of his vow to either my family or his order."

Calen looked at her. "Maybe you're right." He laughed suddenly. "I guess we're going to assume you're right in any case, aren't we?"

She grinned. "Yes. So, what we need now is some insurance that we won't get caught."

His laughter died abruptly. "Right. Oh, gods, we're really going to do this."

Meg leaned forward. "Do you have any magic that would help us remain unseen? Just in case she does return before we're done?"

He hesitated, and that was answer enough. "Show me."

"I don't know, Meg. I'm not very good at it yet."

"So you'll practice. We've got a few hours. Calen, I've seen the kind of things you can do. I don't think you give yourself enough credit. Half of achieving anything is just believing that you can do it. So tell yourself you can do it, and then show me."

He took a long, shaky breath. "All right. But it's a lot harder if you're already looking at me. It works best when

I'm not seen to begin with." He considered a moment. "Wait here. I'll turn the corner, then start the spell and come back. If you don't see me return, that means it's working." He waited for her nod, then got up and ran to where the hallway turned. He looked back and gave her a wave, then disappeared around the bend.

Meg kept her eyes on the spot he'd last occupied. She wished she could make herself invisible. How useful such a skill would be! Not just for sneaking away when she wanted to be alone but for finding things out, listening to conversations . . . She frowned, realizing where her thoughts were leading. Not exactly noble goals, those. She wondered if Serek ever used such a spell to spy for her parents. Or *on* her parents. No. Surely these vows he made to the order of mages would prevent him from using his talents against those he was sworn to serve. She began to see why it was so important for mages to be marked and bound by rules. If she couldn't even trust her own impulses with such power, how could she be sure anyone could resist such temptations?

A startling thought occurred to her. Had Calen ever —? But no, he was still just learning this spell. And she trusted him, even if he wasn't yet bound by the same rules as his master. Sen Eva, of course, was another matter. Meg went cold at the thought of that evil woman

walking unseen through the castle, possibly lurking anywhere, anytime. She swallowed nervously. She'd have to
ask Calen if there was any way to protect against something like that.

Speaking of which, where was he? "Calen," she called,
"come on. Just give it a try. You can always try again if it
doesn't work the first time."

"I guess I'm better than I thought," he said from the
empty air beside her.

She gave a little scream before she could stop herself. As she watched, Calen suddenly popped back into
visibility. There was no gradual fading; he wasn't there,
then he was. He smiled apologetically, but she could see
that he was rather proud of himself as well. She couldn't
blame him. He *was* better than he thought. She hadn't
even suspected that he'd come back around the corner,
and he had walked right past her!

"Perfect," she said. "Will you be able to extend the
spell to include me as well?"

"I think so. I don't know. I've never tried that before."
He sank back down to the floor beside her. "I think that's
the first time I've ever gotten it to work correctly. And
it's impossible for me to tell from the inside whether it's
working or not."

Meg pondered this. "Well, that means we'll have to test it someplace with other people around, to see if it's working."

Calen nodded unhappily. He looked frightened. Meg's conscience twinged, but she reminded herself firmly that they didn't have any choice. Without proof, no one would do anything to stop Sen Eva before it was too late. Technically Calen wasn't just helping her as a friend; he was acting to protect his patron family in the same way he would once he became a full mage. If you looked at it that way, it was his duty to help her. So there was no need for her to feel guilty about dragging him into danger like this. No need at all.

"The kitchen?" he suggested. "There's always someone there, and if we are seen, no one will comment on it."

"You're right, except . . . Wilem was there earlier."

Calen stared at her in alarm. "You saw him? Did he see you?"

"I don't think so. Or at least, if he saw anyone, it was Mellie, not Meg. He was — he was with someone. A girl. He seemed fairly engrossed in their . . . conversation." She looked away. Calen, bless him, didn't say anything. "It's been some time. He's likely gone by now." Back to the kitchen maid's room, probably.

"All right. The kitchen it is. We might as well get started." He hesitated. "Have you thought of another time to go to Sen Eva's rooms?"

Right. "We could try going in while she's asleep. . . ."

"No," Calen said firmly. "I think that's a bad idea, Meg. Too dangerous. I think she should be someplace else when we go. Someplace far away."

"Well, then, let me think. There are several formal events tomorrow in preparation for the wedding, but obviously we want to get in there as soon as possible. . . ."

"Obviously," Calen muttered.

"So if not during breakfast," she went on, "then perhaps . . . Oh! I've got it. The Intention Ceremony. Not as early as I'd like, but I think it's the safest choice. She'll have to be there, since she'll be part of the formal wedding procession. Wilem, as well, for that matter. And there's a banquet afterward, so that gives us a little extra time to get safely away before she returns."

"But — aren't you supposed to be there as well?"

"Yes. But when Morgan realizes I've gone, I'm sure she'll just say that I'm ill. Sen Eva thinks we're dead, or at least elsewhere, so certainly my absence won't seem strange to her. I'm sorry to have to miss the ceremony, but then of course I wouldn't be able to attend anyway. Not now." She shook her head, surprised by a sudden

314

wash of sadness. "Oh, I wish none of this had happened, Calen. I wish I could just be excited for my sister and caught up in all the fun and planning and celebration. Do you realize we missed the tourney? I know it sounds stupid — there are such bigger things at stake now — but I can't help wishing it all the same."

"I know, Meg," he said quietly. "I wish that, too." He patted her hand awkwardly, making her smile. She took a breath and pushed everything else aside. "All right," she said. "Let's go. Do you want to start the spell now, or . . . ?"

"I probably should. I need the practice casting it, and holding it, not to mention including someone else in the circle." He sighed. "I hope this works, Meg. This is a crazy plan. I really don't want to be responsible for getting us both killed." He tried to smile as he said it, to make it a jest, but didn't quite succeed.

Meg looked at him seriously. "You've already saved our lives more than once. If something happens, if we don't survive . . . well, it won't be your fault. We've only gotten this far because of you."

He blinked at her in surprise, then dropped his eyes. "No, that's not . . ."

"You know it's true, Calen. Now shut up and start working your magic." She grinned to hide her own nervousness as much as to take the sting from her words. "Will I feel anything? When you cast the spell?"

"Nope. Or at least, I don't think you will. I know I don't feel anything. That's what makes it so difficult. No way to tell whether it's working until someone sees you. Or, you know, doesn't." He got to his feet and reached down to help her up as well. "Ready?"

"Ready."

"Stay close to me. The spell works kind of like a sphere, surrounding us, but if you step too far away, I might not be able to keep you inside it." He laughed nervously. "Of course, I might not be able to keep you inside it anyway, but, uh, all right. Here we go."

She nodded, then took his hand for good measure. Calen closed his eyes. It was very quiet in the corridor.

"All right," he said. He opened his eyes slowly. Nothing seemed different.

Meg thought for a minute. "Let me try something," she said. She took a giant step to the right, stretching her arm as far as she could without releasing Calen's hand. Then she turned to look back at him.

He wasn't there. Neither was her hand, which was startling, even though she had half expected it. Her left arm stretched out into space and then disappeared at the elbow.

"It's working," she said softly. "Let go of my hand for a second."

He did, and as soon as she felt his fingers release hers, her hand popped back into view. She stared at the place where Calen must have been standing, but as hard as she tried, she couldn't see anything there. "Important bit of information," she said. "The spell only includes me if I'm touching you."

"Ah. Good to know."

"But the good news is that even though I know you're there, I can't see you."

"That's good to know, too."

Meg giggled. "It's strange, to hear you speaking from the air." She reached out, trying to find his hand again. He let her grope blindly for several seconds, and then she felt his fingers close around hers. Her forearm vanished, and she watched, fascinated, as she moved slowly closer to him and more of her body disappeared. And then she must have passed the boundary of the spell, for suddenly Calen was there, and so was she.

"Not a very big sphere, I know," he said.

"No," she said. "I'd better stay close to you." She considered a moment, then stepped behind him and wrapped her arms around his waist. "Do you think we'll be able to walk this way? I'm not sure how else to do it."

They gave it a try. It was awkward, to say the least. They could only manage several steps before tripping over each other. Finally Calen shook his head. "This is silly. It must be possible to increase the spell area." He took her hand again. "Stretch out your arm as far as it will go." She complied, and he did the same. He closed his eyes, concentrating, and then he was gone, along with her hand and wrist. And then, slowly, more of her arm began to disappear.

"It's working!" she said. "Keep going!" Soon she had to lean her head out as far as she could to keep it outside the circle of the spell.

"Do you think that's far enough?" Calen's voice asked. "It's getting hard to push it any farther."

"I think it should be okay." She stepped closer to him again, fighting the absurd urge to hold her breath as if she were going underwater. "We should still stay close together, but we should be able to at least walk side by side now."

He took a deep breath. "Ready to test it out?"

"Yes," she said. "The kitchen?"

He nodded, and they began to walk. As long as they kept their legs in step, it was easy enough to stay close together. The stairs were difficult at first, but after a few steps, they got the hang of it. As they reached the landing on the ground floor of the castle, Calen hesitated.

"Remember, we can still be heard," he said. "And touched, so we need to be sure we don't get too close to anyone. Anything important to say before we get going?"

"Just 'good luck,' I guess. And try not to sneeze or anything."

He smiled and she smiled back. "Same to you." He took another deep breath. She took one, too, and then they stepped forward through the doorway.

The first test came almost immediately. A washwoman was walking toward them, her arms stretched around a huge tub of laundry. They both froze, but her gaze remained vacant and distant, her eyes soft and unfocused, probably staring inward at some early-morning daydream. If she sensed anything in the hallway before her, she gave no sign. Meg relaxed and felt Calen do the same. Then Meg began to edge to the right, to give the woman room to pass. Unfortunately, Calen simultaneously began to edge to the left. Meg realized this as soon as she felt the tug on her hand, and jerked back to follow Calen, but she must not have been quick enough; the maid was suddenly alert and still and staring at the space where Meg had just been.

"Hello? Is someone there?" she whispered.

Meg squeezed as close to Calen as she could, and the two of them flattened themselves against the wall of the corridor.

"Hello?" the maid said again, her voice shaking. Finally she began walking forward again, staring fixedly ahead. As she passed, Meg could hear her muttering, repeated like a kind of charm: "Not a ghost, not a ghost, not a ghost." It might have been funny if the woman hadn't looked so terrified. Meg could guess what she might have been thinking. This hallway was only one floor up from the one leading to where Lysetta had been found.

They waited until the maid was through the doorway and they heard her steps on the stairs. "Okay," Meg whispered finally. "We need to avoid that happening again."

Calen nodded. "Any ideas?"

"You lead, I'll follow," Meg said. "You could try giving me a signal before you change direction . . . maybe squeeze my hand or something?"

Calen thought a moment. "I don't want to make it too complicated. How about I'll just try to move your hand in the direction I'm planning to go? One squeeze can mean stop; two can mean go."

She guessed that was probably the best they could do in short order. "All right," she said. "Lead on, then."

He lifted his foot to take a step, then gave her hand an exaggerated double squeeze before moving forward. She smiled and shook her head, stepping to keep up.

Another washwoman passed without incident, as well

as a pair of scullions who must have been late by the way they tore down the hall. When the kitchen was in sight, Calen squeezed her hand and then paused. "Should we just walk through and then back out?"

She shrugged, then nodded. "That would probably be enough of a test, wouldn't it? We don't want to spend too long wandering around and push our luck. Besides, if we're quick, we might be able to catch a little bit of sleep before going up to you-know-where."

"All right, then," Calen said. "Here we go." Meg swallowed nervously as they stepped forward. Certainly Wilem would be gone by now. She tried not to brace herself for the sight of him. A few more steps, and they were passing through the kitchen doorway.

It was crowded, more so than she'd expected. Did servants always have to start their days this early? She thought of how busy she and her sisters kept their maids each morning from the moment they rose through breakfast and often after. Probably this was their only chance to eat something before heading out to begin their daily service. She felt a twinge of guilt that she had never before wondered about it. So much happened in the castle, every day, that she was not aware of. Did her parents think about these things? Her sisters? Surely a good ruler needed to think about all that went on within the castle as well as outside of it, and yet how could there be enough time in a day to consider all these things? She shook her head, frustrated. This was not the time. But she filed the thought away for closer examination later, if later ever came and she was still around to experience it.

Right now she had to focus on staying close to Calen as he moved forward, constantly having to shift direction to avoid bumping into anyone. It was like a sort of dance, she thought as they strove to move together across the noisy room, although one in which both partners had to learn the steps as they went. She focused on Calen's hand holding hers, trusting him to tell her which way to move and when. She glanced around for Wilem — she couldn't help herself — but he didn't appear to still be there.

They reached the far wall. Turning around took a moment of negotiation; her first instinct was to release Calen's hand and simply turn about, but of course that wouldn't have been very wise. They had to circle around in place together. As they were about to set off again, Meg had a sudden idea and squeezed Calen's hand to get his attention. Slowly, she edged over toward the nearest table, pulling Calen along beside her until they were right up against it. When no one was looking — gods, she hoped no one was looking — she reached out and grasped a knife from the table, slipping it back within the fold of her sleeve and desperately hoping the spell would include things they picked up after the sphere had been created. Best to find out now, in any case; if they ended up having to remove anything from Sen Eva's rooms, she didn't want to discover too late that the object could be seen floating down the hall by anyone they happened to pass by.

Nothing happened. No one screamed, or stared, or seemed to notice anything amiss. After a glance to make sure she was ready, Calen gave her a double squeeze and set off. The kitchen entrance drew ever closer, and with every step Meg felt herself relax a little more. It was going to be all right. Calen's spell worked, and they'd be able to visit Sen Eva's rooms undetected, and they'd find something that would prove her evil intentions, and then everything would be okay again.

They had almost reached the corridor when Wilem stepped into view.

Meg froze, fear and hatred fighting for dominance within her. Calen had frozen as well but recovered almost immediately. Tightening his grip on her hand, he pulled her slowly but firmly toward the wall, out of Wilem's path. Meg let herself be led, but her eyes remained locked on Wilem's approaching face. For the second time in several hours, he was nearly within reach while she held a knife in her hand. Maybe the gods were trying to tell her something. It would be so easy to kill him as he walked past. And if she was quick, no one would know what had happened. She could plunge her knife deeply into his throat, and as he fell, clutching at the gaping wound, she and Calen could run safely and invisibly away. His mysterious death would become another castle legend to frighten children and chambermaids, and no one would ever have to know she had been the one to kill him. The knife felt so solid and friendly in her hand. Like a part of her, as if instead of useless polished nails she had razor-sharp talons with which to slice and tear and rend her enemy into bloody ribbons of tattered flesh. . . .

With an effort, she pushed Jakl's influence out of her mind. He must have awakened; she could feel him more strongly than when he'd been sleeping. Calen was crushing her fingers, trying to hold her back from what she had been almost ready to do. Wilem walked past. They stood silently in place for several seconds, letting him get farther away before they dared to move again toward the corridor. Calen gently took the knife from her hand and slipped it onto an empty table on the way out. Meg took a shuddering, quiet breath as they finally turned the corner. She felt tears on her face but did not know if they were for Wilem or her sister or only for herself.

CHAPTER EIGHTEEN

THEY WERE STANDING OUTSIDE SEN EVA'S rooms. Calen had trouble getting his mind around this astonishing fact. Sure, this had been the plan, and yes, he had agreed to it, but now that they were actually here, facing the door, about to abandon all pretense of sane and rational thought and actually *go inside* . . . He kept hoping he would suddenly wake up safe in bed, with all of this nothing more than a late-night-sweet-induced nightmare.

But of course it wasn't.

He had already checked the door for wards. At least, he had tried to. Either Sen Eva hadn't set any magical protection on the door or she had and he just couldn't see it. He was terribly afraid it was the latter. He hoped if there *were* any wards that he couldn't see, they were the alarm type, which would simply notify her that someone had opened her door, and not the death type, which would kill him and Meg instantly. He hoped that very much.

Meg was waiting for him. He knew that she knew he was terrified. It was nice of her to wait that way, giving him a chance to pull himself together on his own. She didn't seem scared at all. That couldn't be true, of course, because she wasn't an idiot and she knew how dangerous this plan was, but if she was afraid, she kept it well hidden. Perhaps it was Jakl's influence. If so, he almost wished he had a dragon of his own to fill his cowardly heart with fire and courage. Almost.

He felt Meg shift beside him and spoke before she could; he didn't want her to have to drag him through that door. He had to be able to get ahold of himself. "Ready?" he asked, for lack of anything else to say. He couldn't say what he really wanted to, of course. Something like "Run!" or "Let's get out of here!" or maybe just a mindless scream of terror as he took off down the corridor on feet made fleet by fear.

She smirked. "You asked me that already. Twice."

He made himself smile back at her. "Well, still ready?"

"Yes, Calen."

"All right, then." He took her hand. Her fingers gripped his tightly. He tried to imagine they were sending rivulets of strength and bravery up through his arm and into his heart and mind. He could almost feel it. He closed his eyes and brought the sphere of invisibility back up around them. It came easily, now that he knew he could do it. Something had definitely changed within him — the events of the past few days, the successful magical experiments, thinking he might be able to do something, and then really *doing* it . . . there was a confidence to his spellcasting that hadn't been there before. And it worked like a circle: the more confident he felt, the better his spells seemed to work, and the better his spells seemed to work, the more confident he felt.

He also felt more free to improvise, and that was important, too. The variant of the invisibility spell he'd practiced with Meg was more complicated than the original spell he'd learned — stronger, he hoped, and more resistant to discovery — and the colors involved were different. Black instead of gray, for concealment, with threads of orange to nullify attempts at perception, and just a touch of blue-white to soothe the observer into believing there was nothing to see. One he had the sphere of magic firmly fixed in his mind, he let the colors fade, trusting the energy to remain in place.

They had rested for several hours in a lower-level storage room, waiting for Sen Eva to be safely engaged in the Intention Ceremony. Meg had managed to sleep, but Calen found sleep impossible. Even so, he felt replenished by the time spent sitting quietly in the darkness,

Meg's head resting on his shoulder. He had listened to her soft, slow breathing and tried to guess what dreams played behind her closed eyelids and tried not to think about anything else.

His concentration had benefited from the break, and with a final effort he was able to push his fear aside and focus on the energy flowing from him to keep them hidden. He made himself hard and cold like a stone, at least on the outside. If somewhere deep inside his terror still boiled, what did it matter, as long as it stayed tucked away? Slowly, as if in a dream, he reached out with his free hand, lifted the latch, and pushed open the door.

Nothing happened.

Calen let out the breath he hadn't realized he'd been holding. He gave Meg's hand a double squeeze for good measure, and together they stepped into the room.

If they'd expected to find some clear sign of ultimate evil, they were disappointed. There was no arcane altar smeared with the blood of the innocent, no dark forbidden spellbooks left open on the desk with incriminating pages bookmarked, no small animals sacrificed and hanging dead from the ceiling. The bed was neatly made. A pitcher of water sat beside a clean bowl on a side table. The room was restful and decorated with soft colors and vases of lush greenery.

"So, now what?" Calen asked quietly.

Meg looked around, biting her lip. "I suppose we should start looking through her things. I mean, obviously, if she does have something here that could prove what she's been up to, it won't be sitting out in plain sight."

"Do you think it would be safe to split up? We'd be visible again, or at least you'd have to be. But maybe if we close the door . . . ?"

Meg nodded reluctantly. "That makes sense. It will go quicker that way."

Calen released the spell. Meg stepped over and pushed the door shut. Then she walked over to the desk and began opening drawers. Calen looked around for another target. *If I were undeniable evidence of evil, where I would hide?* He considered the paintings and tapestries on the walls, then approached the closest one and looked behind it. Nothing. He moved to the next.

They searched everywhere. They were both acutely aware of the time passing, and their efforts grew nearly frantic as the sun inched across the sky. Still, they tried to be careful to put things back exactly as they had found them. Calen had a moment of panic when he remade the bed after checking under the mattress. Had the pillow been positioned quite that way when they came in? He turned to ask Meg if she remembered. And suddenly they heard something in the hall. Meg's face went sick with dread. Calen felt his own do the same. *No. Oh, please, no.* They looked in horror toward the door.

The latch began to move. Calen launched himself across the room, nearly tackling Meg in his effort to grab her hand. They fetched up against a wall, and Calen thrust the protection of the magic sphere up around them. A vase toppled from its place beside them, and Calen's heart turned to ice. He braced himself for the sound of it — the vase, his heart — shattering, but then Meg's free hand shot out and caught the vase before it hit the ground. There was no time to replace it on the table, however; Meg snatched it to her breast and froze as the door swung open. Together they watched in silent terror as Sen Eva Lichtendor entered the room and closed the door behind her.

She seemed agitated. Calen's first thought was that there must have been an alarm ward on the door after all and she had returned to discover the intruder. But she didn't pause or look around to see who might be there. She tossed her small purse and an expensive-looking shawl onto the bed without breaking stride and crossed to the jewelry box atop the vanity. They had examined the jewelry box already and found nothing suspicious, but now it was clear they had missed something. Sen Eva reached around the back of the wooden case, and a hidden panel in the side snapped open. She pulled out a drawer that lay concealed within the base of the box. In the drawer Calen could see a polished blue crystal and what looked like a small book.

Sen Eva picked up the crystal in her left hand and began to speak softly under her breath — an incantation? Calen couldn't make out the words. After a moment Sen Eva turned and extended her right hand, tracing an arc before her in the air.

A glowing portal shimmered into existence in the space her hand had defined.

Meg's hand grew tighter on Calen's, and he glanced down to see her eyes wide in fear and amazement. He had a sudden mad urge to reach over and place his free hand across her mouth to prevent her from making a sound that might give them away again. He managed to resist; he had to trust her.

A figure appeared in the portal.

Calen gaped. When this was all over, he was going to make Serek tell him plainly once and for all if *any* of the things he'd said were impossible actually were.

The figure appeared to be a man, but the space within the portal was shadowy and strange, and his features were indistinct. When he spoke, his voice also seemed blurred and shifting.

"I have been waiting."

Sen Eva's face went through an extraordinary range of expressions in the space of an eyeblink, contorting to hold back whatever initial response she had been tempted to make. She took a breath, and they could see the effort with which she schooled her tone. "As I have explained to you before, I cannot simply come running whenever you happen to summon me. Do you want to make them suspicious, this close to —"

The man spoke over her. "You are a clever woman. I am sure you could have found a suitable excuse."

"I am running out of suitable excuses!" She stopped, then went on in a softer voice. "We were in the middle of the Intention Ceremony. Can you not see how strange it would have been for me to stand and walk out while the prince was stating his vows of intention?"

He waved this aside, either unaware or simply uninterested in what effect her sudden departure might have had. "What are they saying about the missing children?"

"You summoned me to ask that?" Her sharp tone seemed to injure her own ears; she placed a hand against her head and closed her eyes. "I am here now, in any case. Will you kindly remove your grasping fingers from my head?"

The man made a quick gesture, and Sen Eva's face lost some of its tension. "I summoned you because I continue to sense something moving against us. The warnings are vague, and I cannot see . . ." He trailed off, frustration plain in his voice. "Are you certain the children cannot be traced back to you?"

"Yes, as I told you. *Several* times. They are circulating a story that the princess is ill, and they will not act upon her disappearance until after the wedding. They have placed too much importance on this event and cannot risk any distractions."

"And the other?"

She shrugged. "I got the impression the boy was not the most dedicated of students. Serek probably assumes he ran off and abandoned his apprenticeship. He does not appear to be very concerned. No doubt the child was far more trouble than he was worth." She paused, then added with a smirk, "I suspect I did the man a favor."

Calen felt his eyes go hard and narrow. He could not wait to make her eat those words.

Whoever it was in the portal didn't seem to like what she had said much, either. "I hope you are not taking this too lightly, Sen Eva. I do not need to remind you what is at stake."

Sen Eva's face grew instantly grave. "No. No, of course you do not need to remind me. I only . . . I am sorry, Master, for any offense I have given. I only meant to assure you that the boy will not be missed."

"Unlike other boys," he said softly. "Or men." The words seemed to cut Sen Eva deeply.

"Please," she whispered. "Don't. Don't threaten me with that. If you harm him, if you go back on your promise, I will do nothing for you. I will tell them everything."

"Will you?" He sounded more amused than alarmed. "Even Wilem? Will you tell your son the truth after all this time?"

Her face went gray. "It wasn't my fault. He wouldn't understand that it wasn't my fault. And . . . and it's not too late. You promised. You said I could have them back. You said — both of them." She looked up at him desperately. "Show me. Just for a moment. Show me he's still alive."

The figure moved his hand again, and a smaller portal opened within the larger one. Sen Eva leaned forward, her face alight with a terrible blend of fear and hope and longing. Another man was visible in the smaller portal. This image was clear and bright, and even from across the room they could see that there was much about him that resembled Wilem. His father, Calen would have guessed, except — Wilem's father was dead. Wasn't he? Certainly the part about his death being planned by Meg's father was a lie, but Calen had thought the death itself was true. But maybe none of it was true. He shook his head, wishing he could clear it. So many lies. His brain hurt from trying to sort them out.

The smaller portal winked out of existence. Sen Eva uttered a small cry of dismay and seemed on the verge of reaching out to try to draw it back before she caught herself. Calen was shocked to see tears streaming down the woman's face. How could someone so evil be able to feel such sorrow? He glanced at Meg, but she seemed just as confused as he was.

"I won't be so cruel as to show you Tymas. He doesn't look nearly so well, I'm afraid. Years of death will do that to a person. The decay, you know. And . . . the worms."

Sen Eva was sobbing now, her face a mask of grief and pain. "Please. Please, don't . . ." She fell to her knees, her words thick and slurred with her crying. "Tymas! My poor sweet boy. . . ."

Now the figure's voice became soft and soothing, all the cruelty that had been present only a moment before gone as if it had never existed. "Shhh. Remember my promise, Sen Eva. Magic is a powerful force. You have

335

begun to see this for yourself, have you not? Once you fulfill your part of our bargain and I am free, there will be no limit to what I can do. Distances can be closed with a word. And even death can be undone, by one who knows its secrets."

"Yes," Sen Eva whispered through her tears. "Yes. Even death."

"That's right," the figure continued, still speaking softly, as to a distressed child. "I am the only one who can give you back your husband and son, Sen Eva. But you must help to bring me back. This alliance between the kingdoms must be prevented. Queen Lysetta's death was not enough, but now I can see that killing her was only the first necessary step. One death to start the war, another to ensure it doesn't end." His voice, still soft, grew thoughtful. He no longer seemed to be speaking to Sen Eva. "I have seen it. Peace will prevent my return. War and chaos will open the way. Death and destruction enough to pay the price. No united enemy to stand against me. Then I can reclaim my rightful place, and mages will no longer serve as slaves and lackeys to the lesser races of men. The Magistratum will be destroyed, and the order will serve *me*, and I will lead them all back to where we belong. . . ."

Calen struggled to maintain his concentration and

hold the spell against this torrent of confusing and alarming information. It was . . . insane. *He* was insane, whomever he was. Who *was* he? And Sen Eva had to be insane, too, to be going along with this. Meg turned to stare at Calen, her face screwed up with unspoken questions. He shook his head at her helplessly, hoping she could see that he had no idea.

Sen Eva seemed to be regaining her composure. When she spoke again, her voice was tired but steady. "Everything is prepared, Master. Whatever forces you sense moving against us will be too late. By tomorrow night Princess Maerlie will be dead, and the war will begin anew. I have done all that you have required. Your army is even now progressing toward Trelian — the slaarh and the men trained to handle them — and once they are in place, I shall create the bridge for you to return as you have foreseen."

The figure made no response. Sen Eva looked up at him, alarmed. "Master . . . ?"

For a moment there was only silence. Calen tried not to breathe. When the man next spoke, his voice was cold and black and horribly sure. "There is other magic at work in this room."

Sen Eva's head snapped around to look. Meg's nails dug painfully into Calen's wrist. Calen couldn't worry about that, however. He couldn't worry about anything other than maintaining the spell. Maybe this scary portal mage — for mage he must be — could sense the use of magic, but clearly he couldn't actually see through the spell or he would have simply told Sen Eva they were there. If Calen let his terror weaken his concentration, they would be lost. Meg waited, eyes wide with her own terror but also amazingly still and under control. Once again he tried to imagine some of her strength and surety flowing through her fingers into his flesh. And then for no reason he could understand, he suddenly thought of one of the spirit cards he had read in Serek's study — the chain, the metal links that were so much stronger when forged together. *That's us*, he thought fiercely. *Together we are stronger than either of them. We are stronger than them both.* The sphere around them felt like a wall of solid rock, impenetrable and without weakness. Calen looked up and met Meg's eyes. He jerked his chin toward the door.

She started to nod, then froze. Then she mouthed something silently at him. When he shook his head in confusion, she rolled her eyes and repeated it, more slowly. This time he got it. *The book*, she was saying. *We have to get the book.*

He turned slowly back toward where Sen Eva was

now standing, staring around the room. The portal mage was motionless. Listening, most likely, or . . . sensing, or doing whatever it was that allowed him to tell there was magic at work nearby.

The book was still inside the secret drawer of the jewelry box. The drawer was resting on the bed, easily accessible. Except that Sen Eva was standing only inches away from it. She might not be able to sense his spell, but there was nothing wrong with her other senses, and he couldn't imagine they could get that close to her without her realizing it.

He looked back at Meg. She was glaring at him impatiently. She was crazy. But she was also right. If anything was going to give them the evidence they needed, it was that book. And somehow he knew this would be their one and only chance to grab it.

Reluctantly, he nodded and squeezed her hand. She was still holding the vase in her other hand. Together, they took a single step toward the bed. Then another. Sen Eva had closed her eyes, the better to help her listen, Calen supposed. They continued to inch closer and closer to where the drawer sat waiting, the small book nestled safely within. Finally they were there. Sen Eva was standing right beside them.

Slowly, trying not to breathe, Calen reached out

toward the book. Sen Eva moved slightly and he froze, his free arm stretched awkwardly before him. After a second he swallowed and began to move again. His hand was shaking. He prayed silently to the Harvester and the Lady and any other gods that might be listening, and let his fingers touch the cover of the book. He half expected the book itself to cry out some alarm, but nothing happened. Sen Eva remained still, listening. He didn't know if he could actually lift the book from the drawer without her hearing it. But there was no help for it. He willed his fingers to steadiness and grasped the edge of the book firmly. With a final silent prayer, he lifted.

"Behind you!" the portal mage bellowed suddenly.

Sen Eva's eyes flew open. Calen snatched the book to his chest and launched himself and Meg toward the door as Sen Eva darted forward. They were going to have to stop running to open the door, and he thought that would probably be the end of them. Even if she still couldn't see them, she'd know where they were when the door began to open. Calen glanced back; her hands were already moving before her, that familiar red fire growing and glowing between them, strange guttural words sounding deep in her throat. Beside him, Meg suddenly twisted and threw the vase. It struck Sen Eva in the side of her head and she fell to one side, screaming, her spell dying unfinished as she broke off the incantation. The portal mage was shouting something, but Calen couldn't make out the words and didn't really care to try. Meg twisted back around, grabbed the latch, and pulled. Together they threw themselves through the opening. Calen's shoulder bashed into the doorframe, and he dimly felt the pain blossoming there but couldn't spare it much of his attention. They heard Sen Eva behind them, still screaming, her words mingling with the continued shouts of the other mage. Hand in hand, the sphere of invisibility still held tightly around them, Meg and Calen flew down the long hallway and around the corner and down the stairs. Sen Eva followed, but they could hear her falling slowly but surely farther behind. They ran with the speed of their fear and the power of their friendship and the exultation of what they had accomplished. Calen's heart pounded in his chest, and he felt Meg's own heartbeat pulsing in time through their tightly clasped hands.

CHAPTER NINETEEN

FOR A LONG TIME THEY WERE too terrified to do anything other than crouch huddled together in the darkness. They hadn't given much thought to where they had run — at least, Meg hadn't — and she wasn't entirely sure where they had finally stopped, some dusty nook in a seldom-used corridor, somewhere on one of the lower levels of the castle. They had run as long as they could, then collapsed against the wall and waited for Sen Eva to find them. And now that it was finally beginning to seem that perhaps they had lost her after all, Meg tried to force her mind back to rational thought. And action.

"Calen?" she whispered.

He cringed slightly at the sound of her voice, and then she cringed in response to his sudden movement. They waited. When Sen Eva didn't emerge screaming from the shadows, he said softly, "Yeah."

"What . . ." She didn't even know what she wanted to ask. What was going on? What had just happened? What was true and what was a lie and what were they supposed to do next? Then she seized upon the most immediately answerable question. "What is the book? Will it help us?"

Calen looked down as if surprised to find it still in his hand. Gently he pulled the fingers of his other hand away from her grip; she suspected he had let the spell go long before. She leaned in toward him as he opened the cover.

"I think it's a journal."

"Hers?" That seemed too good to be true. Surely she wouldn't have recorded all her crimes in a book for them to find. Oh, if only.

"No. Someone else's. A mage." He squinted. "Mage Devorlin."

Meg blinked in surprise. "But — that doesn't make any sense."

"Do you know who that is?"

She nodded. "He was King Holister's mage, during the trouble with Lysetta's disappearance. Holister had him put to death after the failed assault on Trelian."

Calen shook his head and muttered something about bloody history and violence. Meg went on. "Why would Sen Eva have his journal? Surely it should have gone to his apprentice, or . . . well, someone else."

Calen had begun flipping through the pages. "I think

this is how she learned. Without being initiated into the order. He kept very detailed notes. And I think this is only the last of several volumes." He pointed at a notation scratched inside the front cover. "But to learn and practice without any real guidance or supervision . . . It's madness. So dangerous."

"Well, it sounded like she did have supervision. That man in the — the hole in the air. . . ."

"Portal."

"In the portal. Maybe he taught her, somehow."

"Could he be Mage Devorlin?"

"No. He's dead, remember?"

He gave her an impatient look. "Not everyone who is supposed to be dead is actually dead, it seems. We're not, for instance. Neither is Wilem's father, apparently."

He had a point there. "I don't know. I suppose anything is possible at this point." She shook her head in frustration. "But if that's all it is, Mage Devorlin's journal, I don't think it's going to be enough. Even if we could prove she had it in her possession, which we probably can't now that we've taken it away, just having it doesn't prove she's actually been doing magic herself."

"Meg," Calen began.

"No!" She punched her fist into her thigh. The pain only made her angrier. "It's not fair. This was our only chance. We took a terrible risk, and we almost got caught — oh, Calen, I almost got you killed *again* — and after all of that we still only have our own word against hers!"

"Meg!"

"What?" She was shouting, but she couldn't really bring herself to care. What did it matter now?

"Look." He was holding up the book.

"What?" she said again. She looked closer. The page was covered in what she assumed was Mage Devorlin's small, cramped, precise lettering, complete with little diagrams and charts and arrows she guessed illustrated whatever magical point he was trying to make. But along the margins, underneath sketches and squeezed into the spaces between paragraphs, there was more writing. Writing that seemed far more recent, judging by the quality and freshness of the ink. Writing in long, flowing script that seemed instantly and naggingly familiar.

She looked up to meet Calen's gaze. His eyes were alight with hope and a strange, harsh humor. She imagined her own face mirrored his expression.

"She added her own notes," Meg whispered. "That's her handwriting. I've seen it. She's written countless documents since she's been here; there must be tons of them we could use to compare. . . ." She was almost too excited to go on, breathless with the sudden resurrection of their plans. She took the book from Calen's hands and turned to various pages at random. There were notes detailing failed attempts at reconstructing specific spells. Notes on variations of reagents and incantations. Notes on all manner of things that could leave little doubt that Sen Eva was fully engaged in the secret and illegal practice of magic. "Oh, Calen," Meg said. "We do have her. This has to be enough."

"We have to get it to Mage Serek."

All the fear and desperation that had drained away minutes before came rushing back, now that there was something to lose again. "How can we? Surely she'll be watching for us now."

"Maybe I can try contacting Mage Serek again. I mean, with my mind. But, um, not quite yet." He looked at her apologetically. "I'm not used to doing so much magic at once. It takes a certain kind of inner strength and energy, and I can't . . . I need to rest. Just a while longer."

"Of course," she said. "Take as much time as you need, Calen." But inside she was burning with impatience, and he probably knew it. Every moment they waited was another moment for Sen Eva to find them, or find some way to stop them, or at least find some way to escape. And they had to catch her. Catch her and stop her once and for all. Or else they'd never be able to rest, always knowing she was out there somewhere, waiting to come back. . . .

That made her think of Sen Eva's incomprehensible conversation with the mage in the portal. He had spoken of coming back. Of Sen Eva *bringing* him back, somehow, whatever that meant. He had spoken of a lot of things that didn't seem to make any sense. Like Wilem's father. And brother. It had sounded as if he had promised Sen Eva that he'd bring her dead son back to life if she helped him by doing whatever it was she was supposed to do. That couldn't really be possible, could it? Dead was dead. And Wilem . . . something about Sen Eva's fear of Wilem learning the truth. But he was in on her plans to kill Maerlie — they knew that. Meg couldn't even pretend there was a chance he was somehow innocent in all this. But clearly there was something Sen Eva was keeping from him. She tried to think back on everything the strange mage and Sen Eva had said to each other. *It wasn't my fault*, Sen Eva had said. *He wouldn't understand that it wasn't my fault.* Was she somehow responsible for whatever had really happened to Wilem's father and brother? That would explain why she would make up that lie about Meg's father having them killed.

There was a sound in the stairwell above them. Meg

felt her heart freeze in her chest. It was probably just some errand boy. But they couldn't know for sure. They had to get to Mage Serek. Now.

Silently, she took Calen's hand and pulled him farther down the dim hallway. They found another dark pocket of shadows and crouched there, waiting and listening. The sound, whatever it had been, did not come again. Meg put her mouth close to Calen's ear. "How's that resting coming along?" she whispered. "I don't mean to rush you. But, you know . . . evil unmarked mage trying to find us and kill us and everything."

Calen looked at her, his expression a painful mix of amusement and affection and regret. "I'm sorry, Meg. I'm just not strong enough. We've got to think of another way."

There was no other way. If he wasn't strong enough to cast, they certainly couldn't go wandering the hallways. They'd be visible and unprotected. She squeezed his hand tightly. "Could I . . . *help* you somehow? Like the way we worked together to summon Jakl? Could you use my strength to call Mage Serek?"

She could see him thinking about it. That had to mean it wasn't impossible. Otherwise he would have refused immediately. "Please, Calen," she said. "Let's try."

"But I've never —"

She smiled at him gently. "I know. You've never tried this before. It could be very dangerous. You don't know what effect it could have on me. You're worried about hurting me. I understand. But I want you to do it anyway. We're out of options, Calen. And we need to do whatever it takes to stop her. You know we do." She took a breath, then went on, no longer smiling. "I didn't hesitate to put you in danger when I thought it was our only chance. I have far fewer reservations about risking myself. And we cannot wait any longer."

She watched him taking in her words, watched him accept that she was right. No harm in one last little push, though. "Besides," she added, putting the journal down beside her and offering Calen that hand, too. "Don't forget I've got Jakl's strength, too. Surely between the two of us, we can lend you enough to send your little mind-message to Mage Serek."

Calen smiled at her choice of words. Then he nodded and took her other hand. "All right."

He closed his eyes. After a second, Meg closed her eyes, too. She reached out for Jakl and felt him awaken to her attention. Then they waited together.

She felt a tentative brush at the edge of her awareness. Calen, trying to find his way. She tried to make herself steady and open so he could take what he needed.

For Maerlie, she reminded herself. *And for all of us.* She didn't know if Jakl could possibly understand what they were trying to do, but she felt him behind her, supporting her, ready to lend her strength. And then, slowly, she felt a sort of . . . drawing out. It was strange, but not unpleasant. Something was flowing from her, through her hands, into Calen's. Into *Calen.* He inhaled sharply but didn't pull away. Whatever he was doing, it worked fast; she felt weaker already but made sure not to let it show. She knew Calen would stop instantly if he thought he was taking too much from her.

Softly, like the barest whisper, she felt him reaching out to Serek. The mage responded instantly, as if he'd been waiting. His sending was stronger; she could actually hear his words in her head. *Calen, where* — he seemed to stumble, and she sensed his attention directed her way. *Who* — *Idiot boy, what are you playing at? You can't* —

With an effort, Calen broke into his master's exasperated tirade. Meg's perspective was so . . . *odd.* She could feel Calen feeling his way through the spell, learning how to send the words almost as he spoke them. *Can you help us? We have proof. But she's coming. . . .*

Serek's anger and frustration cut off abruptly. *Stay there. I'll find you. Don't reach out to me again.* Then the connection was gone.

"Wow," Meg murmured, suddenly exhausted. "He's angry a lot, isn't he?"

"Meg? Meg!" He released her hands at once, nearly pushing them away. "Meg, are you all right? Did I — did I hurt you?"

She shook her head carefully. "No. No, I'm all right." She smiled thinly, wanting to reassure him. He didn't need to know she had been on the edge of losing consciousness for a moment there. Now that he'd let go and stopped the flow of — whatever it was — he had been taking from her, she thought she'd be all right. She felt Jakl gather himself protectively around her and sent him a burst of gratitude through the link. "That magic stuff really does take a lot out of you, doesn't it?"

"Yes, well . . ." He was still searching her face, trying to make sure she was really okay. "It gets easier with practice."

"So now . . . we wait?"

He nodded. Then he gave her a tired half-smile. "Care to place a wager on who finds us first?"

She thought for a minute. "My money's on Mage Serek. Seems the safest choice. Besides, if I'm wrong, we probably won't be alive long enough for you to collect."

Calen barked a short laugh and shook his head, but he didn't say anything else. He picked up the diary again, looking through the various notes and diagrams. Meg shifted so she was sitting beside him, then closed her eyes and rested her head on his shoulder. It was almost peaceful, sitting in the dark on the cold stone floor, waiting to see what would happen next. She was too tired to be terrified. She hoped Calen was too tired to be terrified, too. She hoped Sen Eva was too tired to find them. Actually, she hoped Sen Eva tripped in the dark and fell down some hole into the deepest levels of the dungeons, where no one would ever discover her. Well, no, that wouldn't work, because they wouldn't know what had happened and so they'd have to keep worrying about whether she would show up eventually. Better to hope that she fell out a window and impaled herself on a pointy fence post in front of the castle where everyone could gather around and watch her die a slow and horribly painful death. Or perhaps —

"Slaarh," Calen said suddenly.

"I beg your pardon?"

"That's what Sen Eva said to the portal mage, didn't she? Something about the army of slaarh and men trained to handle them?"

She tried to remember. "Yes, I think so. Do you know what those are?"

"I think that's what those monsters are called. Look."

She opened her eyes and looked at the pages of the diary he was holding in front of her. Along with a detailed list of instructions she didn't understand, there was a rough sketch of a creature that looked very much like the garden monster and the thing that had attacked them in the air. "So that's what we saw," she said. "An army of slaarh. Coming to kill everyone or whatever that terrible portal man intends them to do. Wonderful."

"I think Sen Eva is responsible for bringing them here. I mean, I don't think they're natural creatures. I think she summoned them from somewhere else. These instructions talk more about portals, and how to bring things through. . . ." He trailed off, reading.

Meg frowned. "So why doesn't she just bring the portal mage through as well? That's what he wants, isn't it?"

"There must be more to it than that. Maybe the monsters come from someplace that's easier to reach or something."

Suddenly she realized what he was saying. "When you say 'somewhere else,' you don't just mean another country or some distant island across the ocean, do you?"

He shook his head. "No. I mean someplace that's not part of this world."

Not part of this world. "She's very powerful, isn't she, Calen?"

"It seems she is."

"And she learned everything from a book?"

"You can learn a lot from a book," he said. "I've been discovering that myself over the past few weeks. But with that other mage teaching her as well . . . that would explain why she's able to do the things she can do."

"He doesn't seem to have been a very good influence," Meg said. "He's even more evil than she is. Those things he said. I wonder what he meant about Queen Lysetta." There had been scores of theories about what had happened to Lysetta, but she was pretty certain none of them had involved a secret portal mage with a diabolical plan to take over the world, or whatever he was planning. She wondered if he'd lured Lysetta down into that secret passage somehow, tricking her or threatening her or promising her something she wanted like he seemed to be doing with Sen Eva. Or maybe he'd had other helpers back then who carried out his orders and trapped the poor young queen alone and frightened in that dark and secret cell. . . .

A movement in the darkness caught Meg's eye and wrenched her back to the present. Her heart pounded painfully within her chest, and she realized with profound regret that she was not, in fact, too tired to be terrified, after all.

Calen had seen it too; she felt him stiffen beside her. They didn't bother to speak or move. If it was Sen Eva, they were already dead. It seemed to take forever for the dark shape to materialize into the welcome form of Mage Serek.

"How —" Calen began, but fell silent immediately at his master's sharp shake of his head. Wordlessly Calen rose to his feet, then bent to help Meg to hers. Standing was much harder than she would have liked. Calen reached an arm around her waist and supported as much of her weight as he could. As soon as they were up, Serek turned and began to walk swiftly and silently back the way he had come. Calen and Meg followed as quickly as they could.

Calen was practically carrying her, yet it took all her strength and concentration to keep moving forward. This wouldn't do; if they encountered any trouble, neither of them would be able to run or fight this way. Jakl had rested; he could probably help to strengthen her again. Closing her eyes, she tried to draw on the link. But although she could sense the dragon's energy, it didn't seem to help. Whatever Calen had taken from her had left her weak in a way that Jakl's strength could not restore.

Mage Serek led them down another dark hallway that looked just the same as all the other dark hallways, then stopped and touched the wall. A panel slid open, creating a doorway into — of course — *another* dark hallway. Serek waved them through and then stepped in, closing the panel behind them. Meg felt annoyance try to well up inside her; why didn't she know about these secret passages? She'd lived here a lot longer than Serek. But she was definitely too exhausted to deal with that now. She made a mental note to be annoyed about it later and kept moving.

Several dark hallways later, Calen suddenly stopped. Meg's eyes fluttered open — she had been relying on Calen to guide her, and besides, there wasn't really any-thing to *see* down here anyway — and she looked ahead. And up. And *up*. At the enormous spiral staircase wind-ing tightly and endlessly up into the gloom. She fought the urge to mutter something *very* unladylike and looked over at Calen. He was looking back at her, concerned. As usual. "You know," she whispered with a small smile, "if you keep that up, eventually your face is going to freeze that way."

"What?"

"Never mind." She shook her head wearily. "I can't do this."

"Can't Jakl —?"

"I already tried. It's a different sort of weakness. He can't seem to help."

Mage Serek had already begun to climb. "Serek," Calen called softly after him.

Serek turned back impatiently. He really was always in a bad mood, it seemed. Or at least at the edge of one. There was no need to explain; Meg could see him taking in the situation with a glance. He hesitated, then lifted one hand and waved it before him, palm facing out.

Meg's exhaustion abruptly vanished. She gasped with the sudden shock of it. It wasn't completely gone, not all of it — she was still tired — but it was the kind of tired you could force yourself to overcome.

Serek had already continued moving up the stairs. Meg took a breath and started up herself. Calen followed a few steps behind her. He seemed to have benefited from Serek's spell as well. She wasn't sure how long they went on that way, like ghosts drifting silently through the walls of the castle. She tried not to think about anything except putting one foot in front of the other, moving ever closer to whatever destination Serek was leading them to. Surely her and Calen's work was done now and the adults would take over, anyway. She didn't think she had ever been more ready to hand over responsibility to someone else. Maybe one day she'd be fully capable of handling this kind of thing, but not yet. She was still too young, too inexperienced, too ... *tired* — gods, when were these stairs ever going to end? She risked a glance up and almost collided with Mage Serek, who had stopped on the landing that was now directly before her. A second later, Calen bumped into her from behind. Meg turned to grab and steady him as he lost his balance on the narrow steps and nearly fell backward down into the darkness. Calen swallowed and squeezed her hand gratefully. Serek shook his head in weary disgust, then turned and opened the small door at the edge of the landing.

They emerged into the open air. Meg blinked in the sudden brightness of the day. The afternoon sky was overcast, but after the endless darkness of the lower levels of the castle, it was like walking out onto the surface of the sun.

"Where are we?" she asked Serek in amazement.

"We're above the North Tower," he answered calmly. "You can look over the edge to see for yourself, but be careful about it; we don't want to draw attention to either your own sudden return or the presence of this place."

Meg crept forward and peeked over the edge of the stone wall that ringed the flat, open tower rooftop surface. The view was amazing; she could see everything from up here. Calen made a small, horrified sound beside her and sank to the ground. His face was slightly green.

Meg turned back toward Serek and opened her mouth

to begin telling him about what they'd found, since it was apparently all right to talk out here, but he raised a hand to stop her before she got a word out. "Wait," he said. "Your parents and sisters will be here momentarily. You can tell us everything at the same time."

Her family. Suddenly she was overwhelmed with a desperate need to see them. To see them and touch them and tell them everything. No more secrets.

So they waited. Soon enough the door opened, and before she even had a moment to be terrified that it could be Sen Eva, Maerlie stepped into view, followed an instant later by Morgan, her mother, and her father. Meg didn't know if she had ever seen a more welcome sight. She rushed forward, feeling smaller and younger with each step, until by the time she reached Maerlie she was sure she had become a little child again, wishing for nothing other than to be swept into her sister's safe and welcoming arms.

Maer did indeed sweep her into a fierce hug, but a second later was pushing her away to arm's length, glaring at her with a mix of fury and relief and love and confusion and pain. And then she was pushed aside by Morgan and Mother and Father, and for a moment Meg was blissfully lost within the resulting tangle of arms and faces and bodies and group hugs in various combinations. Finally a quiet cough from Serek's general direction broke up the little reunion. Calen had gotten back to his feet and was now standing patiently beside his master. He was making a valiant effort to hide it, but she couldn't help but notice the wistful expression on his face as he watched her with her family. As the two groups converged in the center of the tower space, Meg went to stand beside Calen, taking his hand firmly in her own. He was her family too, even if he didn't realize it. She would have to make sure he *did* come to realize it and that he was duly welcomed by the others. Calen and Jakl both.

CHAPTER TWENTY

SOMEONE MUST HAVE BROUGHT THE KING and queen up to date, Calen realized, because they didn't seem at all surprised to see Meg — happy, certainly, and relieved, and concerned, but not surprised — or shocked at any of the significant words and phrases Meg was cautiously mentioning in the course of her explanation . . . words like *magic,* and *traitor,* and *murder,* and even *dragon.* He wondered who that lovely responsibility had fallen to. Morgan, probably. He did not envy her.

Serek had led them all over to a shaded area with square and circular stone structures that Calen guessed were meant to function as chairs or tables or whatever anyone wanted them to be. Currently they were chairs. He sat quietly beside Meg, nodding or adding details when she asked him to but otherwise letting her have the telling of it. The spell Serek had worked at the base of the stairs was still in effect; Meg still looked a little tired, but she was definitely more her old self than she had been before, with her inner strength practically shining from her as she told the others about what they had seen in Sen Eva's room. Serek was paging through the diary as he listened, occasionally lifting an eyebrow or shaking his head slightly in what Calen interpreted to be extreme shock or astonishment at something he read.

"So I don't know what we should do at this point," Meg said now. "Sen Eva knows she's been discovered, and she certainly must suspect Calen and me, even if she doesn't know for sure. I don't see how she can proceed with her original plan now, but I can't imagine she's just going to give up, either."

"She cannot give up," Serek said without raising his eyes from the book. "She must succeed or die. She has left all other choices far behind."

"So the choices are ours, then," Meg's father said firmly. "We must decide how to act, and quickly. She will not allow us much time to debate."

Everyone fell silent for a moment, reflecting on this. Calen wondered if Meg noticed the way her family kept stealing glances at her, almost as if they weren't entirely certain who she was. He could sympathize. He was constantly aware of the ways in which Meg was different — *more* — than before, and he'd been with her while she changed. Her sisters and parents were seeing all the changes at once. Only Serek seemed unfazed. As usual.

"What choices do we have?" asked Maerlie. She

seemed remarkably composed for someone who had recently learned she was the target of a murder plot. "Mage Serek, do you feel there's enough evidence against Sen Eva to alert the Magistratum?"

"Oh yes," said Serek, still without looking up. "There is no question that the woman's been practicing unmarked. And some very questionable practices, at that. It will take time for the council to act, however. I do not think we can wait and do nothing in the meantime."

"Agreed," said the queen. "Which brings us back to the question of what to do."

"We must detain her somehow," said the king. "Mage Serek, is there some way to prevent her from performing magic? Something you can do, perhaps?"

"If I could take her by surprise, I might be able to temporarily incapacitate her," Serek said. "But taking her by surprise at this point seems unlikely."

"What about Wilem?" Calen asked suddenly. All eyes turned to him, except Serek's, which were still locked on the book. Calen swallowed nervously and went on. "He wasn't with her; he might not know yet what's happened. What if we could get to him before she does?"

Meg got it instantly. "That's brilliant, Calen!" she said. "We can arrest him first and use him as leverage to get her to cooperate."

Maerlie looked shocked. "You're talking about using him as a hostage!"

"Well, yes!" said Meg, raising her voice ominously. Calen didn't think the others appreciated yet how strongly her anger at Wilem burned inside her. "Maerlie, he was going to *kill* you. Kill you and frame Prince Ryant and plunge our kingdoms back into war! How can you hesitate for even a second?"

"It's just, I don't —" Maerlie looked to Morgan and her parents. "We don't *do* that sort of thing, do we? Wouldn't it be wrong?"

Meg rolled her eyes. "Don't think of it as taking a hostage. Think of it as arresting him for questioning."

Meg's parents looked at each other, considering. Maerlie still looked appalled. Calen guessed that the old Meg wouldn't have been quite as enthusiastic about this idea. Surprisingly, it was Morgan who spoke next.

"I think it's the best option we have," she said. "I don't like it, either, but Sen Eva might hesitate to act against us if she knows we're holding her son."

King Tormon nodded. "I am forced to agree," he said. He turned to look at Calen. "That was good thinking, Calen, and I thank you for suggesting it." Calen nodded, a little awed to have the king speak to him directly.

"Now," the king continued, "we must —"

Calen felt it just before it happened, a subtle change in the air around them. Serek did as well; Calen saw his master's head jerk up, his attention broken away from the diary at last, but too late, too late, too late. As before, Calen acted without thought, flinging out one hand in a protective gesture before him and pushing Meg behind him with the other. He was casting before he had even looked up to see the spell, and so by instinct and blind random impulse he thrust up some kind of shield, attempting to block whatever was coming. He tried to make it big enough to cover everyone, but he was too slow, or else she was too fast. His own hand had barely finished its desperate casting arc when Morgan, Maerlie, and the king and queen fell silently to the floor. And Serek — Serek stumbled, his own protective spell half-formed and failing before him. The mage shook his head, dazed. Calen lifted his gaze to meet the cold stare of Sen Eva Lichtendor, who stood just beyond the doorway at the top of the stairs. Then Wilem stepped into view behind her, his face grim and determined. Calen felt Meg clutch his shoulder painfully, but she did not say a word.

So much for getting to Wilem first. Calen stole a glance at Serek. The mage had stopped shaking his head, which was good, but was still on the floor, which was less so. He must not have been able to fully block Sen Eva's spell. A small, bitter part of Calen swelled up with pride and a mean sort of joy at the notion that he had been able to resist Sen Eva's magic while his master had not. Calen did his best to ignore it. Despite what his selfish, secret heart might want to believe, he knew he wasn't stronger or more skilled than Serek. Quicker, perhaps. Although even that probably wouldn't be the case if not for Serek's magically granted burst of energy at the bottom of the stairs. . . .

Calen groaned inwardly at his incredible stupidity. The prideful little voice inside him fled into a shamed silence. *Of course.* Serek hadn't exactly been operating at full power. He'd certainly had to use some magic to locate them, and although Calen didn't know for certain how Serek had given him and Meg their strength back earlier, he suspected it had involved taking on some of that weakness himself. Calen felt as strong as he might have after a full night's sleep, which could mean Serek was feeling as though he'd gone *without* a night's sleep. Which hadn't left him enough strength to counteract Sen Eva's magic.

Which left Meg and Calen completely on their own.

Sen Eva stepped forward, though Calen noticed she was careful to stay far beyond arm's reach. Wilem hovered protectively behind her. Calen could practically feel Meg's hatred burning within her at Wilem's approach.

"You children have proved to be far more trouble than I ever would have imagined," Sen Eva said mildly.

"What have you done to my family?" Meg asked in a barely controlled voice.

Sen Eva looked down at where the others lay unmoving. "Relax, Princess," she said. "They merely sleep, to give me some time to decide what to do with them. And with you, of course." Her eyes narrowed thoughtfully. Calen wasn't fooled. She'd already made her decision about them, at least. But would she really dare to kill the king and queen and their two eldest daughters as well? How could she imagine she would ever get away with such a thing?

"I hope you realize," she went on, looking back at Meg, "that if you had not interfered, only one of your sisters would have had to die. Now . . . that may no longer be the case."

Before Meg could respond, Serek spoke quietly from the floor beside them. "Do you know what the Magistratum will do to you when they find you?"

Sen Eva sneered with disdain. "Your Magistratum cannot touch me. I exist outside of their pointless laws and restrictions. How can you stand to allow yourself to be bound and hobbled by their decrees? There is so much more —" She checked the rising emotion in her voice, then went on more calmly. "The one whose laws I follow knows what true power is, and how foolish it is to pretend to be less than we are. Why should we not do all that our abilities allow us to?"

"Do not dare to include yourself in our number," Serek said coldly. "You know nothing of what it means to dedicate yourself to the magical arts."

All amusement vanished from Sen Eva's face. "You are wrong, Mage Serek. I know better than anyone."

"She's right," Meg said suddenly. "Sen Eva has sacrificed many things to her magical studies, haven't you, Sen Eva? Why, you've had to live this whole secret life, and then there's the bowing and scraping before that creepy portal mage who's been teaching you —"

Sen Eva's face was white. She took a step forward before she could stop herself. Be quie —" she began, but Meg continued right over her. Calen glanced at Wilem. He was looking at his mother with confusion, and what might be the beginnings of concern.

"And there's something else, something I'm forgetting." Meg went on. "Oh, right. Your poor dead husband and son. You haven't yet told Wilem the truth of that, have you?"

"I know your father helped kill them," Wilem said, but his eyes shifted between Meg and his mother with something less than certainty.

"How do you know?" Meg asked him. "Because *she* told you? She never told you about her secret mentor, did she? Why not ask her what else she might be holding back?"

"Be quiet!" Sen Eva screamed, raising her hands before her. Calen braced himself, hoping he could hold his shield against whatever she sent next. But before she could release her spell, Wilem put his hand on her arm, and all the strength and fury seemed to suddenly drain from her.

"Mother," he said softly, "is — is there more you have not told me?"

An expression of such heartbreak passed over Sen Eva's features then that for one moment Calen almost felt sorry for her. She turned and grasped Wilem's hands between her own. "You were too young to understand at first," she said earnestly. "That's the only reason I didn't tell you everything right away. But you're right, you're old enough now — I can see that. When we're finished here, I will tell you the rest of it, every last thing — I promise. . . ."

Wilem was shaking his head, slowly and with apparent regret. "Tell me now."

Sen Eva struggled with obvious effort to put some of her former authority back into her voice. "Don't be foolish, Wilem. We must deal with our enemies before anything else."

Wilem said nothing. He looked desperately unhappy as he stood there, watching his mother's face.

Finally, she dropped her eyes and whispered, "It wasn't my fault. I was still learning, you see. From the books. And I had been so careful. And Tymas knew, he *knew* he was not to disturb me while I was working. He ran in, burst through the door, and before I could even shout at him to stop, he had crossed the circle and — and —" She glanced up at Wilem's frozen features, then quickly away again. "I was learning to open portals. But the books were vague, you see. I had to discover much by trying things out. And this particular day, the portal had opened on someplace I hadn't seen before. When — when Tymas crossed the circle, he broke the protective spell and there was something — something alive. It took him. Before I could even scream, it grabbed him. Snapped — snapped his neck. Right there, while I watched."

Wilem swallowed, then asked with difficulty, "And Father?"

"He came chasing after Tymas. When he entered the room and saw what was happening . . . he threw himself after Tymas, trying to save him. It was already too late, but he just . . ." She paused but did not risk looking up again. "The portal closed after he went through. I spent years trying to find him. I searched relentlessly, opening doorway after doorway, certain that if I could just find the right one, I could get your father back. But then I found — someone else, instead. And he knew so much. So much more than even Devorlin had known. He was a true mage, not one of the spineless pack animals that call themselves mages today. They had exiled him, you see, because he refused to let them place limits on his power. And he promised to help me. He found your father; he showed me. He promised to return him to us."

And now she did look up, reaching out one hand toward Wilem's shocked and horrified face. "He told me that with magic, all things are possible. He said he could bring back your brother as well."

Wilem jerked away from his mother's touch as if burned. "My brother — my brother is dead."

Sen Eva shook her head, so eager to convince him that she could not see his revulsion. "But don't you see? He doesn't have to be. We can have him back, Wilem. Your brother. And your father. We can be a family again. That's what all of this is for. A trade, of sorts. There were things my master needed me to do, and then, he promised —"

Wilem backed away, his eyes bright with pain. "You lied to me."

371

"Only because I didn't want you to share the burden of the truth, my love. And is a lie such a great crime compared to what we would have achieved?" Sen Eva's voice was growing hard again, her pain slowly thickening into anger. "What harm in a lie, if it could bring your brother back?"

"What harm?" Wilem whispered. "I was going to kill —" He looked over at Maerlie, still unconscious alongside her sister and parents. He shook his head again, as if trying to clear it of this new information. "Everything I've ever believed has been a lie. You said we were carrying out Father's wishes. You said we were doing what he and the old king had wanted. Your secret magic, all the plans, you told me it was for the greater good. For Kragnir, and for Father's memory, and for revenge ... but there is nothing to take revenge for, is there?"

He looked sick. "They didn't kill Tymas. *You* did. But you made me hate them. You made me —" He shot an anguished look at Meg, then back at his mother. "You were going to make me a *murderer*...."

"Yes!" Sen Eva screamed at him. "Yes! And why not? What life is worth more than that of your own father? Your own brother?"

Wilem seemed to have nothing left to say. He only stared at her, his grief and horror plain and undeniable.

Sen Eva took one more faltering step toward her son. He recoiled with loathing, as if she were a poisonous snake about to strike.

The motion seemed to wrench something out of her. She threw back her head and screamed, a wordless outpouring of rage and pain and loss.

And from someplace far away — but oh, not far enough — something answered.

Calen shuddered. He knew that sound. It called again, and this time it was closer.

Sen Eva whirled, turning her back on her son and staring at Meg with eyes that seemed to glow with pure and powerful hatred. "You," she said, advancing slowly toward them. "You have taken my second son from me."

"Mother, no —" Wilem began.

Without even a glance in his direction, she reached back one hand and sent a burst of deep blue light at him. Wilem fell bonelessly to the floor.

Calen watched, ready — oh, gods, he prayed he was ready — as the familiar red glow once more formed between Sen Eva's slowly moving hands. She sent forth the spell, and it shattered against the shield he still held up firmly before him. Then she sent another. And another. He didn't recognize most of them, and couldn't spare the attention required to try; every shred of his concentration was channeled into maintaining the shield. Dark, swirling missiles of color came quickly, one after another, and slowly, very slowly, Calen felt his strength beginning to wane. His stupid little voice didn't even try to convince him that he had the strength to outlast Sen Eva.

He felt Meg press against his back, as if to help support him. Sen Eva smirked contemptuously at this and increased her barrage, continuing to mutter incantations with barely a pause for breath. And then, against his ear, he heard the slightest whisper of Meg's voice. "Hold on," she said. "Jakl is coming."

Sudden hope flared within him, swiftly tempered by fear and doubt as another of those soul-wrenching screams pierced the air. Jakl wasn't the only one who was coming.

"Sen Eva," Meg called from behind him, her voice already stronger and deeper with the approach of her dragon. "Give over. What can you hope to accomplish? Even if you kill us all, no one will believe that Kragnir had anything to do with it. You will not get your war."

"Stupid child," Sen Eva spat, still casting. "There is more than one way to keep countries at war. There are a hundred ways. A thousand!"

"But will those other ways still please your master? Surely all this secret treachery was for a reason. Will open war through some other means still be enough to win you your rewards? You have enough blood on your hands. Let this go!"

"No!" Sen Eva screamed, throwing renewed force into her spells. Calen staggered, and now Meg really was supporting him. "I will have my son returned to me! I will —" She broke off, words and magic both, staring at the sky behind them.

Calen didn't dare turn, but then the dragon's shadow passed over them and Jakl circled around, drawing Sen Eva's full attention. Calen couldn't blame her.

The dragon was magnificent. Terrible and terrifying and astoundingly beautiful. Surely he couldn't be any bigger than he'd been the day before, but he seemed to fill the entire sky, his wings stretched out to full size, his long neck reared back as if to strike, his powerful jaws held wide to show his many, long, sharp teeth.

Sen Eva turned slowly, keeping the dragon before her. She was recovering from her shock already and raised her hands to cast anew. With dismay, Calen noticed that she didn't seem to be tiring in the least. He himself was nearly out of strength. He didn't dare try to cast anything at her, even while her back was to him; he was afraid that if he let go of the shield, he wouldn't be able to re-create it. Meg, on the other hand, was fairly glowing with power and energy. She stepped past him, no longer concerned about staying within his protective field, staring raptly up at Jakl with pride and love and joy plain upon her face. The dragon screamed in triumphant fury, and Meg screamed with him. Then her scream changed to one of horror as Sen Eva thrust her hands forward. Meg couldn't see the poisonous red glow that came shooting forth, but she knew what Sen Eva was doing all the same.

But the spell parted around Jakl without touching him. Calen exhaled in relief. Apparently what he had read about dragons being resistant to magic was not an exaggeration. Meg must have felt the resistance; she was laughing now, and Calen managed a shaky smile. Perhaps it was going to be all right after all.

Sen Eva seemed temporarily at a loss. Then she looked at Meg, and back at the dragon. A terrible under-standing came into her eyes, and she turned away from Jakl and raised her hands toward Meg once more.

Meg froze. Calen lunged toward her, desperately will-ing his shield to grow large enough to enclose her. He knew Meg was only a few feet away from him, but the distance seemed so much greater than that, and he was moving so *slowly* — he felt as if he were trying to push his way through day-old pudding. Jakl screamed again, stretching his mouth open wide and sending forth a blast of hot air. Meg gasped in anticipation, and Sen Eva stumbled with the force of the dragon's breath. So did Calen, falling back with a grunt beside Mage Serek on the cold stone. Serek seemed barely conscious, still fighting the effects of Sen Eva's sleep spell. Sen Eva, no match for Calen in clumsiness, turned even as she caught herself, her own shield half forming before she realized what Calen had already seen, what Meg could feel too, judging from her fallen expression: it was only air. Jakl still didn't have his fire.

Sen Eva dropped her shield, laughing. "Children," she said, almost fondly. "Even your dragon is only a child." She was still smiling as she raised her hands toward Meg once more. Meg didn't try to run. She stood and faced her enemy, tears of anger and frustration shining in her furious eyes. Calen knew he couldn't get to her in time, but he tried anyway, pushing himself up and forward in an awkward, lumbering half-run, half-crouch. Jakl was turning in the sky, perhaps planning to launch himself at Sen Eva to kill with claws what he could not burn with fire, but there was no way he'd be in time, either. Sen Eva's fingertips began to glow as the red power grew again between her hands.

And then Wilem's hand reached forward and grabbed his mother's ankle, pulling her off balance. Her spell flew wide, passing harmlessly above Meg's head.

This time she did fall, and in her surprise she did not manage to thrust her hands out before her in time; one forearm slammed against the stone with a crack that made Calen wince. Her face whitened, but she did not cry out. Calen doubted she was even truly aware of the pain. She twisted around to stare at her son, whose fingers still gripped her left ankle. Most of his body lay motionless, not yet recovered from whatever Sen Eva had cast at him before.

"No," Wilem said, forcing the words with obvious physical effort. "Mother, I cannot allow it."

She opened her mouth but seemed unable to speak. Her eyes were wide with shock and grief and madness.

Calen reached Meg at last. He grabbed her wrist, probably too hard, but he didn't care; he wasn't letting her out of range again. Sen Eva would remember them in a moment, he was sure.

For now, however, she was still staring helplessly at Wilem. She began to raise her hands toward him, then winced and allowed her right arm to hang limply at her side. With her left she slowly pointed her shaking fingers at her son's face.

"Will you kill me, too?" he asked calmly.

She appeared to be thinking about it. For one instant, Calen thought he saw the merest tinge of red energy dance around her fingertips, but he could not be sure. Then she turned her hand palm upward, her threatening gesture becoming one of supplication instead.

"If you stop me, it will all have been for nothing," she whispered.

Wilem looked back at her sadly. "I'm sorry," he said.

For a moment everything was silent. And then a black, misshapen creature rose screaming above the short stone wall on the far side of the tower rooftop.

CHAPTER
TWENTY-ONE

M EG AND CALEN BOTH FELL TO their knees, pummeled by the horrible noise. Even then, Calen did not release Meg's wrist. His grip was making painful indentations in her flesh, but she didn't want him to let go. Not when that thing was there — gods, right *there* — screaming its awful, heartrending scream. Wilem had cringed as soon as it appeared. He seemed as frightened as they were. This must be another secret that Sen Eva hadn't shared with her son. Serek was staring at the monster with an unreadable expression, still apparently unable to move from where he lay.

The sound seemed to reawaken something in Sen Eva; she kicked her leg free of her son's grasp and got awkwardly to her feet, cradling her injured arm against her chest. "It will *not* be for nothing," she spat, looking down at him. Then she turned her face to the monster and seemed to take comfort in its terrible presence. It was twin to the one they'd encountered with Jakl earlier. She pointed her good arm at Meg and Calen. "Kill them!" she shouted. "Kill them now!"

The creature — the *slaarh*, Meg thought distantly — shrieked again and started toward them. Calen's grip grew even tighter, and Meg opened her mouth to scream, and then Jakl came hurtling at it from the side, smashing against its oily-looking hide and pushing it off course. The dragon barely avoided a deadly slash as he tore away, preparing to circle for another attack. It was a hopeless tactic, Meg knew; without his fire, Jakl would only tire himself out against the larger creature, if he didn't get too close to the poisonous talons first.

"Jakl, no!" she cried, although she knew it wouldn't do any good. He would fight to protect her until he died. And then they would all die after him — she and Calen and Maerlie and Morgan and Maurel and Mattie and her parents and Nan Vera and probably Lammy the stupid kitchen boy and gods knew who else. Herself and everyone she'd ever known or loved. She couldn't let that happen.

She pulled Calen closer so he'd hear her over all the screaming. "He can't stop it," she said. She was crying; she felt the hot tears spilling down her face, burning. She thought they must be scoring her flesh by the heat and pain, but she didn't try to brush them away. "It's going to kill him. Calen, please, you have to help him!"

His expression filled with anguish at her words. He

looked back at her, his eyes begging her to understand. "I can't," he said, shaking his head. "I'm so sorry, Meg. I don't have the strength. And even if I did —"

She ripped her wrist free of his grip at last and grabbed both of his hands in hers. "Take mine," she said desperately. "Take my strength — take all of it — only save him! Please!" She closed her eyes and *pushed* at him, trying to force her energy across to him through their clasped hands. He was resisting, fighting her, but she would not let him refuse. He had to do this. It was the only way. "Take it!" she screamed at him. "Calen, please, you have to!"

Above them, Jakl and the slaarh clashed and separated again. Calen tried to pull away from her, but she clamped her hands tighter around his. She was stronger than he was; she would make him listen and do as she said. She was right; he had to see that!

"Meg, no!" he shouted. "Even if I let you, what could I do? I don't know how to kill it. I don't know that kind of magic! Not yet!"

She opened her eyes and gazed at him with the full force of the confidence she felt shining in her heart, willing him to see how much she believed in him. "You can do it, Calen. I know you can. I'll help you. We'll do it together." She watched him watching her, indecision and doubt warring on his face with the clear desire to do what she was asking him to do. She tried to make her own expression as open as his always was, tried to let him see the pain and hope and sorrow and hatred she felt swirling and twining like flames inside her.

And then suddenly his eyes widened and all the doubt fell away.

"Meg, no!" he shouted at her again, but this time something in his voice was different. "The other way," he said. "The other way! *You* take *my* strength. Take mine, all I've got left, and combine it with yours, and give it to Jakl. Use your anger. Use everything! Give him fuel for his fire."

She had only a moment to stare at him as understanding slammed into her, and then she quickly closed her eyes again as she felt him reverse what she'd been trying to do. She stopped pushing and *pulled* instead, feeling the energy begin to flow from Calen's hands into her own. *This* was what he'd felt down in the dark corridor of the castle, this sudden strength and power . . . she shuddered with the intensity of it and then, quickly, before it could overwhelm her completely, she made herself a conduit, sending everything through the link and into her dragon.

She opened her eyes. Jakl was circling for another

strike. This time, when he screamed in challenge, the sound was fiercer; there was a heat to his call that hadn't been present before. *Please let it be enough,* Meg prayed silently. She thought it was. She could feel how strong he was now. *She* was that strong, too. Even though she was sending her strength through to him, the link made it circle back, looping between them, feeding into itself and making them both even stronger. She felt she must be radiating light and heat, blinding with intensity. It was impossible that this much power could remain contained within her flesh without spilling out into the air around her.

This time, instead of ramming himself into the monster's side, Jakl reared back as he drew near and opened his mouth. Meg watched raptly and at the edge of her vision saw Calen turning his head to watch as well; as one, they took a long, deep breath to coincide with Jakl's inhalation. For a moment everything seemed to hold still. And then a brilliant tongue of flame lashed out from the dragon's powerful open jaws.

The slaarh jerked back in pain and fear. Sen Eva shouted something to it that Meg couldn't hear over the lovely deep roar of the fire, but she saw the thing shift its dull gaze to where she and Calen were sitting. Jakl saw it too, and as before, the great awkward abomination could not match him for suppleness and speed. He darted forward and let loose another burst of flame, even greater than before, forcing the creature back and away. Then the dragon landed lightly on the tower top and placed himself firmly before Meg and Calen, daring the other creature to try to approach.

Meg needed to stand; she couldn't bear sitting still with all the energy coursing through her. She released Calen's hands and turned to share a triumphant look with him as she rose, but instead she saw him fall back against the stones, eyelids fluttering.

"Calen? Calen!" She dropped back to her knees and shook him, trying to stop him from losing consciousness completely. She looked to where Serek was lying nearby, but he only shook his head apologetically; no help there.

Frantically Meg peered around Jakl's legs to make sure Sen Eva was still standing where she'd last seen her. They were at a standoff of sorts, she guessed. Sen Eva couldn't hurt them with magic while the dragon protected them, and her creature couldn't — or wouldn't — attack again now that Jakl had burned it. Sen Eva seemed almost paralyzed by frustrated indecision, standing halfway between Jakl and Wilem.

Faintly, she thought he heard shouts from far below. Well, it made sense. Surely someone had noticed the two

385

giant creatures fighting and screaming above the tower. Meg hoped the captain of the guard knew about the secret stairway to this place. It would be very convenient for lots of armed soldiers to arrive right about now.

Calen still appeared to be teetering on the edge of passing out entirely. Shaking didn't seem to be accomplishing anything. Meg let go with one hand and then slapped him, hard, across the face.

"Ow," he muttered weakly. She slapped him again, and again, and was rewarded with his eyes opening to tiny slits and finally seeming to focus on her. He tried to fend her off, flapping his hands at her feebly. She slid her hands under his arms and tried to lift him up.

"Meg?" he said. "Let me go. I'm tired."

"No," she said. "Come on, you have to get up. Stay with me. This isn't over yet." She tried again to lift him, but he was surprisingly heavy. They didn't have time for this. "Calen, come *on!*" She lifted her hand to slap him one more time but his eyes fluttered open again, and he managed to raise one flimsy arm to fend off her swing. This time he really seemed to see her.

"Stop hitting me," he said to her. "You're so violent."

She grinned and hugged him until he pushed her away. "Ow," he said again. "Don't forget, you're very strong right now, okay? No squeezing, either."

"Sorry," she said, still smiling.

Calen struggled the rest of the way upright, and together they peered around the dragon. Noises came drifting up from below; those were definitely shouts, and getting closer.

"Is that the guards?" Calen asked. "Please let it be the guards. Lots and lots and lots of guards."

Sen Eva looked toward the stairs, then threw one last, hateful look at Meg and Calen and abruptly turned and ran to where her monster was waiting. Surprisingly agile for someone using only one arm, she climbed up onto its disgusting back. Wilem watched her; he was still on the ground.

Slowly, she reached out toward him one more time. "Wilem, please. Come with me."

He said nothing. He just looked back at her and shook his head sadly.

"Do you think they'll have mercy on you?" she asked. "If you stay, I have no doubt they will have their vengeance. They'll kill you for what we've done. Don't you understand?"

This time he did speak. "They have every right," he said softly.

Sen Eva gave a final cry of anguish, and then the thing beneath her lumbered awkwardly into the air. Jakl tensed as if he might launch himself to follow, but Meg placed her hand against him and he stayed where he was. As much as she hated the idea of Sen Eva escaping, Jakl was the only one among them with any real power, and if he left them, they'd be totally defenseless. Of course, all the evil villains and monsters who wanted to kill them seemed to be flying away. But still.

Her gaze drifted back to Wilem. Still, indeed. She didn't have the will to sort out how she was supposed to feel about Wilem now.

Finally, and too late, the guards came pouring through the doorway entrance — and stopped, staring at the scene before them in a strange tableau of confused horror. Nothing they were seeing could possibly make any sense to them at the moment, Meg guessed. A few more guards came running out onto the roof, and one actually plowed into the man in front of him, not expecting his comrades to be standing there in shock. It wasn't really funny, but beside her, Calen started laughing anyway. Meg began laughing with him. Mostly it was relief, she supposed. Surely now, finally, things really were going to be okay.

The sound of their laughter roused some of the guards from their paralysis. The captain's mouth dropped open as he took in the sight of Jakl standing protectively before them. Then he snapped it shut and raised his crossbow.

"Princess!" he shouted once, and let fly. The shaft flew straight and true, right toward the dragon's exposed neck.

"No!" Meg screamed. Everything, except the crossbow bolt, seemed to stop, frozen. *Oh, come on,* she thought miserably. *This really, really isn't fair.* She watched numbly as the bolt came flying toward them, somehow impossibly fast and agonizingly slow at the same time. They hadn't been ready; they had all of them been starting to relax and let down their guard, even Jakl, and no one could react in time. The danger was supposed to be over, gods curse them! And now, after surviving Sen Eva and that awful shrieking monstrosity she rode away on, her dragon was going to be killed by a stupid iron shaft through the throat. And then Meg would die with him. And she would never get to see her sisters again and tell them how much she loved them and never get to run or laugh or fly again or explore the full mystery of her link with Jakl and never get to grow up and fall in love for real and find out who she was and what she would turn out to be and never get to tell Calen how much he meant to her and how very, very glad she was to have him as her friend.

The bolt stopped a handsbreadth from its target. It hovered in the air a moment, then clattered harmlessly to the stone floor. All of them — Calen, Meg, Jakl, the guards, even Wilem — stared stupidly at it lying there.

"Please," Mage Serek said quietly from the ground. "Let's all just wait a moment, shall we?"

Several pairs of eyes turned in unison to look at him. One of his hands was still stretched out toward the fallen crossbow bolt. No one moved. Serek cleared his throat weakly. Then he continued, "Captain, I commend your eagerness to protect your princess, but I promise you she's in no immediate danger. The dragon is, ah, on our side."

Flooded with relief yet again, Meg let her head fall forward against her dragon's smooth, scaly side, warm with the fire that lived inside him now. Then she heard a sound beside her and turned just in time to catch Calen as, apparently overwhelmed by one close call too many, he succumbed to unconsciousness at last.

Grinning fondly, she eased him to the ground and wished him pleasant dreams.

CHAPTER TWENTY-TWO

ALEN HAD NEVER BEEN TO A wedding before. Of course, he guessed that even if he had, it wouldn't have been anything like this one. At first it had all seemed rather boring. There was a lot of watching the members of the different families standing around repeating things back and forth to each other, and about a hundred different people got up to read long passages from various books, and then there were songs, and then possibly some other part he missed because he dozed off, but then finally people were shouting and cheering and he woke in time to watch Prince Ryant lean forward to kiss Princess Maerlie in full view of every living person that had been crowded into the enormous grand hall. Calen wondered if the prince was nervous. *He'd* certainly be nervous if he had to kiss a girl in front of an audience! Well, he'd probably be nervous about kissing a girl in any event, he supposed. But the audience would make it even worse.

Calen had woken up late yesterday afternoon in the royal infirmary to find Meg sitting by his bedside. After teasing him about his supposed fainting (deliberately failing to see that passing out from legitimate exhaustion was not the same as *fainting*), she filled him in on what he'd missed while he was unconscious. Mage Serek had managed to prevent anyone from doing anything else hasty or stupid while they waited for him to recover enough to wake up the sleeping members of Meg's family. Wilem had been half escorted, half carried to the dungeons under heavy guard, and then there had been a rushed conference at one end of the rooftop to decide what, exactly, to tell the guards (the remaining number of whom had been sent to wait at the *other* end of the rooftop) and everyone else. Calen suffered an embarrassing vision of everyone standing around his splayed-out body talking over him while he lay senseless at their feet, but Meg assured him that a pair of guards had immediately been assigned to carry him down to the infirmary.

It had been decided that Jakl would officially be announced as the Royal Dragon, employed to help protect the castle and surrounding lands, with Meg assigned to be his keeper and trainer. The link would be kept secret from everyone outside her immediate family. And Serek and Calen, of course, who already knew. Wilem probably suspected, and Sen Eva had seemed to understand there was a connection between Meg and her dragon, but there wasn't much they could do about that now.

They had also had to inform King Ryllin, Queen Carlinda, and Prince Ryant what had happened to their trusted senior advisor. *That* had to have been a difficult conversation, to say the least. Ryant had immediately demanded to see Wilem, refusing to believe he'd been betrayed until he heard Wilem's solemn and regretful confession for himself. Wilem's testimony went a long way toward convincing the Kragnirians the truth of what was, Calen knew, a rather extraordinary explanation of events. That, together with the diary, had finally been sufficient proof for the Kragnir king and queen and, eventually, Ryant. Calen guessed it had been hardest of all on him, since Wilem had been his closest friend for years.

So the wedding had been allowed to proceed as planned, with Richton standing as Ryant's second in Wilem's place. And now everyone was rising and talking and beginning to move toward the banquet hall, which Calen assumed meant the wedding part was over and now they could eat. He slipped into the stream of people heading for the doors and saw Meg waving at him from the front of the room. He made his way over to where she waited.

"Look at you," she said, smiling. "All dressed up and everything."

"You're one to talk," he said. "Can you even walk in

that dress? I've never seen so much fabric in one place before."

She stuck her tongue out at him in a most unprincess-like fashion and then took his arm, leading him past the elaborately arranged bunches of white and red ladylace blossoms hanging from nearly every available surface.

"So," he said, "Maerlie's married now."

"Yes, thank the gods," she said, making the sign of the Lady. "And now the marriage is more important than ever, of course. I'm so glad everything — well, you know. It's silly to keep saying it, I guess."

He squeezed her hand through her long white glove. "It's not silly."

"Do you think —?" She looked over at him, not needing to finish the question.

"Serek had me help him with another divination reading last night. I don't know why he bothers, since no matter what the cards say, he just goes on about how divination is vague and unreliable and so on. . . ." He glanced at Meg's face and changed tactics, quickly. "But of course I myself have developed a good amount of faith in spirit cards, and as we know I'm apparently some sort of divination genius. . . ."

"Calen."

"Anyway, the cards look good. I mean, for the near

future, anyway." They both knew that Sen Eva would be back eventually, of course. But right now even a short time without immediate danger would be a welcome change.

They turned the corner, and the banquet hall opened before them, a landscape of black and white and red linens and flowers and fabrics. Calen noted all of that only in passing, however; he was too busy staring at the enormous banquet table piled with just about every kind of food he had ever seen or heard of or imagined. He leaned toward Meg and whispered, "This is the part of a wedding that people really get excited about, isn't it?"

Meg laughed at him gently, releasing his arm. "Go forth and fill yourself a plate," she said. "I'll meet you at our table. You and Serek are both sitting with us on the dais."

Calen nodded absently, already planning his plate-loading strategy. It was only after he'd piled as much as he could on two plates and turned toward where Meg had pointed that he realized the dais was like a big stage on a raised platform where the entire rest of the hall could see them. Well, at least it was easy to find. He climbed the steps, found the empty seat beside Meg, and sat down.

Meg was looking toward the end of the table, where Maerlie and Ryant were sitting, their heads bent close together in conversation. Calen watched her watching them, happy to see Meg so happy. They all knew, of course, that nothing here was really finished and that there was trouble waiting not so far ahead. But tonight, he suspected, every one of them was choosing not to think about any of that. Meg certainly seemed determined to spend one evening just being safe and happy, and he couldn't think of anyone who deserved it more. He thought back to the day they'd met, trying to remember how it had felt to have so little he truly cared about. It was hard, now that he had so much.

He turned away and found Serek watching him across the platters of bread and cheeses. Serek quiet and aloof and seemingly unaffected by recent events, other than having finally and grudgingly admitted last night that, yes, perhaps some magical weapon training was in order. He had sent a lengthy missive to the Magistratum, detailing the crimes Sen Eva had committed and recommending that the order take steps to locate her and strip her of her magical abilities. He also reported everything he'd been able to discover so far about the slaarh, which apparently hadn't been very much other than the fact that they were definitely not natural to this world. He still hadn't been able to cure the effects of the poison that ran in the blood of the wounded guardsmen, but he had managed to keep any of them from dying so far, which was something, at least. Not enough for Serek, of course, but then he wouldn't be Serek if he were ever satisfied with anything.

The mage was still looking at Calen with that unreadable expression. Calen waited, unable to look away or eat or think of anything to say. Surely Serek could let one evening, at least this evening, go by without a reprimand or rebuke or reminder of something left unfinished or not done well enough, but a long look like this one was rarely followed by anything good. Maybe if Calen ever developed the stone-hard exterior that Serek carried everywhere, he'd finally be able to shrug off his master's criticism without feeling it the way he prepared himself to feel it now. It shouldn't surprise him that even after everything that had happened, Serek would find something to complain about. But just once, he'd love to hear a simple positive statement with no modifiers. Something like, *You did well, Calen;* or maybe *I am unable, no matter how I try, to find any fault with your recent performance;* or maybe even possibly, someday, *I'm proud of you, Apprentice.*

"Try the olives," Serek said finally. "They're quite good."

He took in Calen's fishlike stare for a moment, twitched his lips very slightly, then pushed back his chair and rose from the table.

And then he shocked everyone by asking Meg's mother if she'd care to dance.

CHAPTER TWENTY-THREE

EG LAY ON HER BACK ON the lawn, staring up at the sky. Nan Vera would be furious about the grass stains she was creating on her dress, but Meg couldn't bring herself to care. Beside her, Jakl snorted in his sleep and clenched and unclenched one long-taloned claw. Meg smiled. He was *here*, with her, in the garden, in plain sight, and it was wonderful. No more secrets. She felt so free and unburdened, she thought she could fly right up into the clouds.

Jakl twitched again when she thought of flying. Meg reached out and patted his scaly hide. *Not now, silly,* she thought at him. She was still pretty certain he couldn't actually hear her exact thoughts, but the meaning always seemed clear enough to him. She thought that in time their ability to communicate through the link would grow stronger along with their bond. Calen was looking into that. She smiled again. He was done with secrets, too. No more sneaking into the library; Mage Serek had grudgingly agreed to let him use whatever books he wanted. It helped that Meg had made it a royal command.

The only thing marring her pleasant mood — well, there were two things. She hated that Sen Eva had gotten away, flying off who knew where to plot some horrible revenge. Meg had always assumed that there were only two possible outcomes to their recent altercation. Either Sen Eva won — killed some or all of them and got her war and whatever reward her portal mage was really prepared to give her — or they won and Sen Eva rotted in a cell or was executed in some hideously painful way. But as usual, everything was turning out to be so much more complicated. They'd won, at least Meg thought they had, but Sen Eva was still out there somewhere, now with even more reason to want to kill her and Calen and her family and maybe everyone in Trelian and Kragnir combined. And while Sen Eva was alive and free, it would never be over. Not for any of them.

Worst of all, Sen Eva still had her army — or maybe it was the portal mage's army — that great horde of creatures and men they'd seen from Jakl's back as they flew above. Meg tried not to think too much about that. At least now both Trelian and Kragnir knew they were out there. And surely Sen Eva would take some time to regroup before she attacked, and maybe by then Mage Serek would have worked out a medicine for the creatures' poison. And Jakl would be strong enough to burn them all to a crisp from a safe distance.

The other thing was Wilem. She wanted to hate him. She *did* hate him. There was no excusing what he'd done, what he'd been about to do, no matter what reasons he'd thought he had. And yet — her hate had lost its fire and was left a painful, infected thing, aching and festering inside her. She understood him far better than she'd like.

Her parents had left it to her to decide his fate. It was funny, really. There had been a time when she would have given anything to be seen as mature and responsible enough to make important decisions like this, but now she wished she didn't have to. How could she possibly know what the right choice was? He deserved to be punished, and yet . . . and yet . . .

Calen appeared — literally — out of the air a few feet away.

"You're really very good at that, you know," she told him. "I didn't even hear you coming."

He shrugged, but she could tell he was pleased. "Maybe," he said. "Or maybe you just had other things on your mind." He sat beside her on the grass. "Still deciding?" he asked.

"Yes, if you can call it that."

Calen gave her a sympathetic look, then plucked a blade of grass and wound it around his finger. "Maybe you should go talk to him."

"No," she said. She heard how harsh her voice was and tried to soften it. "It won't help anything."

"Maybe not," he said quietly. "But it probably can't hurt anything, either."

Meg hadn't been down to the dungeons in a long time. When she'd been much younger, around Maurel's age, she supposed, she used to sneak down to peek at the prisoners, to try to see what a criminal looked like. Mostly they looked like other men. Or occasionally a woman, though that was rare. Mostly they'd just looked sad or angry and alone, and eventually she'd stopped going. Villains in stories were evil and exciting and dangerous, until they were caught and vanquished by the forces of good. But in real life — she supposed it had been one of her first realizations about the differences between fact and fiction — more than anything else, she'd felt sorry for them, the way she felt for creatures chained in a menagerie. And if she knew the crimes for which they'd been imprisoned, she'd had trouble connecting the beaten, broken men in the dank cells with the monsters who'd stolen and beaten and sometimes killed to earn themselves a spot in the

401

dark under the castle. She didn't like that it wasn't easier to tell they were bad just by looking at them.

She should have learned that lesson better, she thought bitterly as she walked down the stone corridor between the empty cells. A guard trailed at a respectful distance. She'd wanted to come alone, but the most she could convince the watchman to do was to stay in sight but out of earshot.

She walked to the end and then stopped, bracing herself, before she turned to face him. He sat in the center of the cell, on the floor, his arms draped over his bent knees. They looked at each other in silence for what seemed a long time. This was stupid. She didn't know what she hoped to accomplish here.

"You should have left," she said finally. "You've only made things harder."

"I know," he said softly.

"I mean for me," she said.

"I know."

They looked at each other again. Even tired and dirty and marked with sadness and shock — and shame? — as he was, he was still beautiful. It made her angry. He didn't deserve to look that way. Maybe that should be his punishment. To be scarred and maimed and made to look as ugly on the outside as she knew he was within.

"Did they tell you they've left it to me to decide what happens to you?" she asked.

He blinked. "No. I didn't know that." He was quiet for a moment, then nodded to himself. "It makes sense, I suppose."

Meg felt rage boil inexplicably within her. She clutched at it. She had earned that rage. She would *not* let him take that from her, too. "Why are you so calm?" she demanded. "I could have you whipped and beaten and tortured a thousand different ways! I could have you killed, slowly and painfully, right this very instant if I wanted to. Why don't you beg for mercy? For forgiveness?"

"Because," he said quietly, "I don't deserve them. I know that. I want to pay for what I've done. For what I almost —" He shook his head, not looking at her. "I'm so sorry."

"No," she said. "Oh, no. You don't get to do that. You don't get to do the right thing now. It's too late. You *lied* to me. You used me! You were going to —" She couldn't speak. She was so angry she was choking on it.

"I know."

"No!" she screamed. The guard started forward in alarm, but she waved him back impatiently. On some level she knew she was angrier than she should be — he was caught, he'd been stopped, she could make him pay, and she didn't *have* to be angry anymore — but she was still burning with fury. She hated him; she wanted to hurt him, make him bleed, burn him —

She took a shaky breath, trying to calm herself. Jakl was amplifying her emotions, of course, but that didn't make them any less real. It wasn't fair. She'd won, they'd *won*, they should get the righteous pleasure of giving him what he deserved, but it didn't work if he *wanted* to be punished. He was robbing her of even this last satisfaction. But he would *not*. She would not let him.

She let Jakl's hatred merge with her own and felt the rage burning with red hot flames inside her. This was her chance to make Wilem pay for everything, to make him suffer in the way that he deserved — she was angry enough to kill him right now with her bare hands, and she believed her dragon could give her the strength to do it. She felt on fire with fury. And when he looked up at her again, and paled, she felt a cold smile touch her lips. He could see it; she could tell. For the first time he looked truly afraid, and she reveled in it. He *should* be afraid. He deserved to be afraid and he was right to be, because she had all the power here, and he had none. But even as she watched, she saw his fear replaced with resolve. She admired him for it — she couldn't help it — and that made her hate him all the more. *He lied to me*, she thought at herself furiously. He helped his mother try to kill her and Calen, and he would have killed Maerlie, and he lied, he *lied*, he *lied*, and he hurt her and now there was nothing to stop her from hurting him, nothing except . . .

Except . . .

With effort, she fought back against the strength Jakl had lent her, the heat he had poured into her heart and soul and mind to feed her fire. This was not a decision she would allow her anger to make for her. She took another breath and forced herself to look at Wilem objectively. Not with the eyes of a victim, or a sister, or even a young woman — certainly not of a dragon. As a princess, charged with delivering justice tempered with mercy. Punishment but also reprieve. He was a boy still. Older than she was, true, but still quite young. He had done some terrible things, but only because of what he'd been led to believe. His own mother had lied to him, fed him the tales to turn him into a killer at her side. And once he'd discovered the truth of things, he turned away from the only family he had left to do what was right. And now he was alone, alone in a way she could only imagine, without parents or siblings or even friends. Alone with his conscience, which now told him he deserved to be punished. It occurred to Meg that perhaps — perhaps — sometimes justice and mercy could be one and the same. Forgiveness might be the kindest and the cruelest thing she could do to him.

Without a word she turned and strode back up the corridor. The guard waited for her to pass, then followed along silently behind her. There were practical matters still to consider, of course. If they weren't going to execute him, then some provision would have to be made for keeping him alive. And if they weren't going to leave him to rot in his cell, then . . . She would talk to Maerlie and Calen and then present her parents and the king and queen of Kragnir with some viable options. Meg smiled and felt some last piece of doubt and darkness fall away from where it had clung around her heart. She could do this. She could think without ceasing to feel, feel without ceasing to think, choose without losing herself among the choices. Jakl sensed her sudden lightness of spirit and rejoiced in response. She doubted he had any concept of the details of the situation; he'd just known she was angry and in pain, and now no one was hurting her anymore. *Because I won't let them,* she thought fiercely. *I can stop them, and my choices are all my own. Despite everything, I am still myself. And I can do this. If I choose.*

The guard stepped forward to push open the heavy door to the outer exit. Meg was still smiling as she walked past him, her delicate and proper princess steps lengthening stride by stride until she was bounding, laughing, up the stairs and emerging into the light.

ACKNOWLEDGMENTS

THIS BOOK IS THE RESULT OF MANY YEARS OF DREAMING and doubting and working and writing, and would not have come to be without the help of several important people. Initial thanks must go to my parents: my mom, Flo Knudsen, for telling me about the stories and characters of the fantasy novels she was reading when I was little and sparking my own love of fantasy literature; and my dad, Paul Knudsen, for leaving his copies of *Analog* lying around and helping to inspire both my interest in speculative fiction and my early attempts at writing short stories. Thanks also to Mrs. Blumenrich of I.S. 75 for making me start to love English class in eighth grade, and to Mr. and Mrs. Rivlin who kept that love of English class going strong in high school.

Special thanks to my very nice friends who read drafts and gave me excellent and useful comments and suggestions: Kristin Cartee, Bridey Flynn, Michael McGandy, Michael Mellin, Rebecca Stead, Jenny Weiss, and Matthew Winberg. Also to Jennifer Rosenkrantz and Stephanie Santoriello for their enthusiasm and belief and for countless years of friendship. And to everyone (all of the above and more) who contributed thoughts and opinions in response to my frantic late-night e-mails about name pronunciation and flap copy and other random but important things.

Extra special thanks to my agent, Jodi Reamer, who read the incomplete draft and said I had to finish, and to my editor, Sarah Ketchersid, for caring about Meg and Calen as much as I do and for helping me to make the story as strong as I could. I feel incredibly lucky to have both of you in my corner, and appreciate your encouragement and occasional tough love and seemingly infinite patience more than I have probably ever expressed to you.

And above all, I owe a debt of gratitude to Matt Winberg, who read the first chapter and told me to keep going. Your support and encouragement, then and now, mean so much to me.

Thank you.